Acknowledgments

In the South, we love football. In writing this book, I'm not trying to make a statement for or against the sport. My husband and son loved playing the game. After my son suffered a torn ACL, torn shoulder labrum, and four surgeries, he could no longer participate in the game he loved. He mourned the loss of the brotherhood of his team. I saw the popular pastime differently from his eyes. For young men, I believe it is a bond between friends for a common goal. Though the character in this book is totally fictional, I'm dedicating this book to my son, Luke.

The other sensitive topics in this story seemed particularly sad, but relevant in our society. Trust me, I didn't prefer to research acquaintance/date rape or human trafficking, but both are going on all too often in communities both small and large. There are a number of organizations set up to assist victims of these crimes if you feel a calling to help.

My thanks go out to:

God for loving and searching out prodigals like me

Dr. P. Ben Kerr who answered questions on brain injuries

My cousin, Brian Hudspeth, who recruits for Tampa Bay

Sandy Rawlings whose son plays for Ole Miss. She answered many logistical questions

My amazing ACFW critique partners

Volunteer proofreaders, Melissa Thompson, Kimberly Berry, Betty Lister, Marilyn Poole, Kathy McKinsey, Karla Patterson, Kalea Derrick

My husband, Bruce, for supporting me

My daughter, Mary Kristen, for reading my manuscripts

Mentor author Misty Beller, Editor Robin Patchen, Cover artist Paper and Sage

My dog and cats who sit on or beside me while I write, the reason pets end up in all my stories.

Tackling the Fields

Southern Hearts Series

Book 3

Janet W. Ferguson

Copyright © 2016 Janet Ferguson

Southern Sun Press LLC

Publisher's Note: This book is a work of fiction. Names, characters, any resemblance to persons, living or dead, or events is purely coincidental. The characters and incidents are the product of the author's imagination and used fictitiously. Locales and public names are sometimes used for atmospheric purposes.

Scripture quotations marked (NIV) are taken from the Holy Bible, New International Version®, NIV®. Copyright © 1973, 1978, 1984, 2011 by Biblica, Inc.™ Used by permission of Zondervan. All rights reserved worldwide. www.zondervan.com The "NIV" and "New International Version" are trademarks registered in the United States Patent and Trademark Office by Biblica, Inc.™

ISBN-10: 0-9974822-8-1
ISBN-13: 978-0-9974822-8-7

...to proclaim freedom for the captives...

Chapter 1

Huge hands ripped at Cole Sanders' shirt and yanked him away from Audrey Vaughn's embrace. Adrenaline raged through Cole's veins as he balled his fists and spun on the hot blacktop of the University's Christian Student Union parking lot. Ole Miss lineman, Grant Vaughn, stood four inches taller and seventy pounds heavier, but the guy wouldn't intimidate him. As a quarterback, Cole knew better.

"Back off, Grant."

With three hundred pounds of muscle held by a six-foot-seven frame, Grant growled at Cole and tugged harder at his shirt. "I told you to stay away from my sister."

Cole's vision tunneled, and his palm connected with Grant's chest. "Let. Go."

Grant's punch came from the left, and Cole's reflexes took over. They exchanged more shoves and blows, but numbness sheltered Cole's body, like in a football game. Fury thundered through him while his brain shut out everything else.

Until strong cage-like arms clamped around him, heaving him away. "Cole." Coach McCoy's voice broke through the haze. "You hear me, Cole? Get in my truck. Now."

Other players pinned Grant against a car.

Still dazed, Cole trudged across the parking lot with Coach's fingers digging into his bicep. Coach flung open the back door of his truck, and Cole slid onto the hot leather seat. The door slammed, and Coach moved to the front one and cranked the truck before stomping back to where Grant stood. Coach was ticked. No doubt he and Grant would pay for the fight with extra drills all next week. Maybe even all month.

Wavy lines of heat rose from the asphalt as the Mississippi summer raged full force outside the windows. Cole reached over the console and bumped the air up to high, then leaned back and closed his eyes. Why couldn't Grant chill? The mission trip in Honduras had already been an emotional roller coaster.

Though he'd only gone to please Coach McCoy, once Cole's feet touched the soil of the mountainous village, something shifted inside. And losing one of the children from the Vacation Bible School to dengue fever had left his heart in pieces. Audrey had helped put those pieces back together—to make sense of it all.

He'd felt something he'd never experienced before, both for her and for God.

Minutes passed before Coach McCoy and his wife, Sarah Beth, finally tossed their bags in the bed of the pickup and took their seats up front. The travel bus that had delivered them all from the Memphis airport to Oxford pulled away, along with the rest of the vehicles.

"Benjamin's taking his mom's van to the house." Sarah Beth took Coach's chin in her fingers and turned his face toward her. "Oh, we're going to need to get ice on that eye."

A bitter taste coated Cole's tongue, and his stomach lurched. Had they hit Coach?

Had he hit Coach?

With a shrug, Coach McCoy waved off her concern. "Just a shiner."

She released his chin. "I know you're trying to make me feel better, but I was scared to death out there. Are you sure you're okay?"

One side of Coach's mouth cocked up. "Don't worry. I'm still your trophy husband."

A small snicker colored Sarah Beth's words. "You better be, mister." Her head rotated back to study Cole. "Are you hurt?"

"No, ma'am. Sorry about losing my temper." But Grant had started the whole thing.

Though the truck's engine still rumbled, Coach McCoy left the gear in park and gave Cole a hard look. The look that unsettled even the biggest college lineman. "Are you sure you're okay? No injuries?"

Cole nodded. "Yes, sir."

"I don't understand." Coach's volume increased. "Our plane hit the ground one hour ago, here you are after a mission trip to Honduras, and you're already punching a teammate?"

Cole's throat thickened as he tried to come up with an answer. "I just hugged Audrey goodbye, and Grant went ballistic. I've seen overprotective brothers, but Grant borders on psycho. I mean, Audrey's a nice girl. I like her. But I wasn't about to attack her." Cole huffed out an extended breath.

Coach's glare still pinned Cole to his seat. "Trust me, I'll have another powwow with Grant. But, y'all are college seniors—both of you are likely first or second round draft choices, and I expect my seniors to lead the team, not tear it apart. Especially my quarterback." He swung one hand around to point at Cole. "You and Grant will learn to work together on and off the field. I'm not sure how that's gonna go down yet, but know that you will lead together. Comprende?"

"Yes, sir." On the field, he could agree to that. But off the field? No way. He'd have to find a way to be with Audrey without her brother finding out.

~~~

A shiver ran across Audrey Vaughn's shoulders. And the cause wasn't the air conditioner blasting in her brother's truck. The fight shook her. Unleashed locked-away memories. Thank the Lord that Coach McCoy and the others stopped them before someone was seriously hurt. Why couldn't Grant move past his guilt and anger? She gave him a minute to settle down and get on the road, and then she faced him. His jaw was still clenched, but too bad. Enough was enough.

"Cole isn't Harrison. You've got to stop this."

Grant shook his head. "They're more alike than you think. And I knew Harrison all my life. I thought that warped jerk was my best friend, and what he did… I won't make that mistake again. You shouldn't either."

Audrey's muscles twitched as an image of Harrison came to mind. Dirty fingers grabbed at her, ripped at her soul, left her empty inside. The images that threatened to steal her peace. Again. And she was sick of fighting. Growing closer to Cole was like sinking a shovel into a yellow jackets' nest for both her and her brother. It unearthed buried pain. But Cole had done nothing wrong.

"Cole's different now. Honduras changed him. I saw it. God is changing him." She shook her head and shrugged. "It's like God's been throwing me and Cole together for a year now, first with the academic tutoring the last two semesters and then again with the kids last week in Honduras. There has to be a reason. Maybe Cole needs to know the Lord, or maybe I have more healing that needs to happen. Maybe both."

Grant answered with heavy silence as they drove through town until they hit the old highway toward their condos.

She'd give him time to chew on her words. Fresh rows of cotton lined the fields outside the truck window, reminding her that almost exactly three years had passed since that nightmarish graduation bonfire. The brutal mistake that left her with a damaged and leaking soul. Deep green cotton plants emerged from the muddy, dark soil. And she, too, was emerging, however slowly, from a muddy, dark place thanks to God's continuing care.

After wheeling into the condo's parking lot, Grant jerked the truck to a stop and turned to face her. "You don't know Cole like I do. I've been in the locker room with the guy for three years, heard the way he talks about girls, and I won't believe he's changed until I see it with my own two eyes." He flung open his door, but halted, glancing back. "You need to steer clear of that guy, Audrey. Before you get hurt." He stomped toward his condo, which adjoined hers.

"Oh, Grant." He wasn't letting go any time soon. And she understood to a certain extent. Tutoring Cole last year, she'd only found arrogance in his brown eyes. But on the mission trip, sparks of kindness filled his gaze as he'd played with the children. Then when a sweet little boy died from dengue fever… She swallowed back the lump in her throat. After the death, Cole's being seemed to shift. Almost like a child himself, he reached out to her for comfort. For answers about life in Christ.

But would he really change? Especially back in the small world where he reigned as king of the field?

Chapter 2

Cool air blasted from the vents of Cole's BMW, whipping his hair away from his face as he zipped down Highway Six. He glanced in the visor mirror and pushed a few strands back in place. A haircut would help, but summer break gave him time away from anything remotely reminding him of school. Appointments included. At least he only had one more year of college, and then he could forget school. Forever.

If Coach McCoy hadn't asked him to speak about the mission trip, he'd skip this Christian Student Union gathering. But so far, there'd been no word of punishment for the fight with Grant. A whole week without even a mention of the incident. He'd prefer to run the stadium stairs every day for a year. Speculating wreaked havoc with his nerves. That and thinking of Honduras. And Audrey.

An overflow of vehicles lined the Christian Student Union parking lot and adjoining street. Unusual for a summer Saturday night. Interesting and unnerving. Plenty of times, he'd spoken in front of cameras and reporters. It was part of the game in college football. Talking about the team or an opponent came as naturally as wrapping his hand around the leather ball. Speaking about matters of the heart or faith...that had never happened before. In fact, before this trip, he'd had no faith to speak of, other than in himself on the field.

Shifting the vehicle into park, he held the wheel for a minute longer. *God, if You're really here, help me not screw this up.*

He released a pent-up breath, cut the engine, and headed toward the side door of the old converted warehouse. Across the lot, local news vans pulled near the curb. Another unexpected twist. Maybe he could catch Audrey before things got rolling. Run through his words at least once with someone else. If her brother wasn't stalking too closely.

Inside the crowded room, a gentle hand tapped his shoulder. "Hey. You look worried." Audrey's freckled cheeks spread with a smile. Her brown hair cascaded in soft waves just past her shoulders.

Every muscle in his body screamed to reach out to her, but he filled his chest with air and locked his arms at his sides. Even in Honduras after the loss of one of the children, the girl had seemed shy about hugging him. "Hey, yourself. I've missed you."

Her gaze roamed the floor. "You, too." She raised her shoulder toward her ear as if working out a kink in her neck, then brought her eyes back to his. "Are you okay?"

Cole lifted one side of his mouth in a nervous smirk. "Coach asked me to"—he made air quotes with his fingers—"share about my experience." A small whistle pushed through his lips. "Out of my comfort zone. Way out."

Compassion softened her face. "Me, too. We could do it together. Give each other courage." She arched her brows, waiting for his answer.

Her willingness to stand with him sent warmth through his chest. His arms no longer obeyed, and he wrapped her in a gentle embrace. "Thank you, Audrey. You give me courage. I love how you're always here for me when I need you." He glanced around the room, searching for any sign of Grant.

~ ~ ~

Oh, mercy. Audrey inched away from Cole, the tingle from his breath still warm on her cheek. She faced him, studied his strong jaw notched with a small dimple in the middle, studied his straight honey-colored hair. Despite the turmoil Cole's touch provoked, Audrey allowed the quarterback to hold her. But his gentle contact moved her in places she'd sealed off three years ago. Broken places.

Clashing urges warred inside her head. The inclination to struggle against his arms persisted, though the yearning to melt into his firm chest and rock-solid shoulder seemed to be winning. When would she be able to relax with a guy?

"Audrey. Cole." A deep voice yanked through Audrey's thoughts.

Her arms fell away, and Cole gave her a tender smile before turning to face Coach McCoy, one hand still lingered on the small of her back.

Coach McCoy stood close. When had he walked up? "Tonight, I'm announcing a new initiative that I'm calling Summer of Service." His voice quieted, and he gave Cole a hard look. "You and Grant will head it up. Together."

Cole's jaw ticked, but he held his same expression. "Okay." He glanced at Audrey. "We decided to partner to share our story since we both worked with the kids. Right, Audrey?"

Audrey nodded, heat swirling around her head. Did she look as goofy as she imagined?

Why'd she offer to make a speech beside him? Anxiety clutched at her stomach. She'd carried out dozens of presentations in her marketing classes over the past three years. Why did this talk make her so tense? Was it Cole or the topic? Probably both, but the mission trip had affected her deeply. All the more reason to share. *Lord, help me shine a light…for You and for Honduras. Please give me the words.*

She took a deep breath. Now where was Grant lurking?

~~~

When Coach McCoy moved to speak to another student nearby, Cole let out a sigh, dropping his head back for a second. "Finally. At least now I know what I'm dealing with. A summer of service. With Grant." He peered across the large open room for any sign of the enormous lug. "Um, I'd rather do most anything than spend even more time with your lunatic brother." He checked Audrey's reaction. "No offense."

Brows knitted, Audrey's freckled cheeks shaded a light pink. "I'm sorry he started all this mess." Her fingers touched his for the briefest second.

That one little act opened a well of emotions inside him. Unfamiliar emotions. As an SEC quarterback, plenty of girls had been available to him in the past, but the heat of their touch hadn't sunk beneath his skin. How could this girl penetrate his heart with that small gesture? He studied her profile and smiled.

"What? Do I have something on my face?" Her hand rubbed across her cheek.

"Some really cute freckles."

"Oh. Thanks." She took in a large gulp of air.

Her shyness crashed through every idea he'd ever owned about himself. Ego and his position on the team seemed irrelevant when he was with Audrey. "Don't worry. Things will probably settle down and get back to normal soon."

Her head shook, chocolate-colored bangs falling over her eyelashes. "No. I don't want to go back to normal. I want to remember the people, the feeling of Honduras…" Her brown eyes met his for a fleeting moment, and what looked like pain wrinkled her forehead. "Everything. Do you want to forget?"

He leaned close to her ear to whisper. "Never."

No matter what. He wouldn't forget. But how could he be around Audrey and keep peace with her brother—for Coach McCoy and the sake of the team?

Chapter 3

It was time. Audrey followed Cole through the crowd toward the front of the large room. The going was slow. Between Cole and Coach McCoy, it seemed every person in the place felt the need to connect with one of them. A room full of fans. At least they'd present to a friendly crowd.

Most of them friendly, anyway.

Near the stage, Grant threw an angry scowl their way, his lips drawn into a grim line. Her brother loved her—wanted to protect her—but it was time for him to back off. If only he could quit blaming himself for the past. Over and over, she'd assured him and tried to free him from his self-loathing and guilt. Audrey shook her head and sent him a pleading look.

His big torso rose and fell, along with his massive shoulders. Could they make it through the evening without another fight?

A television anchorman and camera crew hovered to the left of the platform as the student minister, Chris, addressed the crowd. "Welcome. As you've heard, student volunteers, including a number of our football players, arrived back in the States last week after a mission trip to Honduras. Tonight, they'll share a bit about our journey."

He motioned for Audrey and Cole to join him. "You recognize this guy coming to the stage—our starting quarterback for the past couple of years. He made us proud during our adventure in Central America, and I've asked him to offer a few words about his experience." He pointed Audrey's way. "Also, Audrey Vaughn, a regular at the CSU and sister to offensive linebacker, Grant Vaughn, partnered with Cole to serve the children of the community."

Holding her elbow, Cole escorted Audrey to the microphone. Butterflies, more like giant bats, circulated in her midsection as he nodded for her to speak first. She cleared her throat. "Traveling out of the country for the first time was a bit intimidating. Especially to a place so far away and so different. But once I looked into the faces of the children of Honduras, once I ran and played soccer with them, once we sang songs of praise that first day, all fear disappeared. The country and the people were stunning.

"Cole and I were assigned to a sort of Vacation Bible School, where we led group games, mostly soccer, and got to know the kids. One adorable boy stole our hearts from day one. Sadly, by the end of the week, he succumbed to dengue fever, the very disease the clinic has committed to fight." Audrey's breath hitched. This was so difficult.

Cole took the mic. "That's right. That kid grabbed onto my heart and didn't let go. I'll never forget him. In my mind, he represents the battle to help the kids in Honduras and other places like it—places where mosquitoes transmit deadly diseases, and communities need help securing clean water and sturdy housing. Places where food is limited. In one meal at home, I down more calories than these kids get in three days.

"The country and the people were worth getting to know. Worth helping. I'd go again in a heartbeat. I hope next year, more students will join a mission that will change their lives. I know my life changed for the good—more than winning a championship bowl game ever could." Cole nodded to Coach McCoy and made eye contact with the camera and anchorman as he finished.

Audrey studied the way his lips lifted higher on one side when he smiled for the camera, his confident brows raised above soulful, light brown eyes. Cole had a gift with media many quarterbacks lacked. The press loved him, especially the female sportscasters. An attractive aura surrounded him. His Southern accent didn't hurt either. Not too drawn out, but enough to render his voice sultry to his listeners. So the chatter went, anyway. Audrey chuckled to herself. And the chatter couldn't be more right. She should tear her eyes off him.

One by one, more students shared their experiences. Then

Grant and another lineman took the stage, flanking a hooded man donning sunglasses. In a quick movement, the man dropped the hood and removed the glasses.

Dylan Conner. The world famous actor grinned, sending a collective gasp through the crowd. "Weren't expecting me, right?" The cameramen pushed closer. "Beside me are a couple of brawny guys I worked alongside on this trip." He elbowed Grant. "My large, new friends and I shoveled mud, mixed cement, and did all sorts of dirty, smelly jobs Coach McCoy assigned us. But I want to tell you, as Cole mentioned, no award compares to serving others. If you can go on a mission trip, do it. If you can't, find out how to help in other ways." Dylan directed his gaze toward the camera. "You'll never be the same."

Motioning to the petite redhead in the first row, he waved his hand. "Come up here, Cassie. We may as well tell the world." Turning a deep shade of red, Cassie moved to his side. "I'll treasure Honduras for another reason now, as well. She said 'yes.' This is my fiancée, Cassie Brooks." The actor planted a lingering kiss on her lips in front of the crowd.

Amid the applause and cheers, Audrey's cheeks burned. Dylan and Cassie's relationship had certainly progressed. Had Honduras changed the relationship between her and Cole, too? At that exact moment, his fingers squeezed hers, and he winked. What did that mean?

~~~

As the last student left the stage, a human squeal, as loud as the ref's whistle on game day, reverberated against Cole's eardrum. He glanced around the platform. Where had it come from, and why was it screeching his name?

A blonde in a low-cut, purple tank bounced toward him. She looked vaguely familiar. Had he hung out with her?

When she reached him, long manicured nails ran across his chest. "Cole Sanders. Remember me?" She leaned closer, her body pressing into his, the scent of sweet perfume drifting to his nose. "Cassie's sister. Emma. I'm moving in and starting summer school at the university. Isn't that great?"

Audrey dropped his hand and edged away. Cool air replaced the warmth of her presence. Cole turned to catch her. "Audrey, wait. Don't leave." He snagged her arm, gave her puppy dog eyes, and gently tugged her closer to the blonde. "Remember Cassie's sister? She just moved here."

A look of recognition ran across Audrey's face as her lips pressed upward into an awkward smile. "I remember meeting you a few weeks ago. Where are you living?"

"Daddy bought me one of those new townhouses on College Hill Road." Emma's blue eyes never left Cole. "Where do you live?"

A lump formed in Cole's throat. Would Emma notice if he ignored the question?

Audrey raised her palm. "The light blue townhouses? With a front porch?"

"That's the place. The new ones are so cute. I kinda wish they'd demolish the old condos across the lawn. They ruin the view of the golf course. Where do y'all live?"

Though Audrey's smile didn't falter, it didn't reach her eyes, either. "The older rentals across the lawn."

Emma's gaze slid to Audrey, her mouth slowing and gaping for a second. "I'm sure they're nice inside."

Audrey shrugged. "They're okay."

Emma turned back to Cole, shaped eyebrows raised. "And you never answered my question."

Shoot. She noticed. Dueling emotions warred inside him. Happiness that Audrey would live nearby and slight annoyance about the other reality. "I'm moving into one of the new townhouses next week."

Another shriek. "You might be next door."

A summer of service with Grant and an overly perky new neighbor. At least Audrey would be close, too. Life's little surprises.

But wait, where did Grant live?

~~~

Not being intimidated by the girl with perfectly styled blond hair and manicured nails, not to mention the curves busting from her tank top, proved impossible. Audrey's lungs emptied, jagged discomfort replacing the air. Was this what jealousy felt like? She forced herself to keep smiling. Maybe her new neighbor possessed more substance than it appeared. Even if Emma was all fluff, God called Christians to love everyone. Right? But did the girl have to keep staring at Cole like he was the last cake on a cakewalk?

Audrey sighed inwardly. Being considered plain had worked for her—especially after grad night. And jealousy wasn't something she'd been troubled with. Until this moment. Good gracious. Cole had to notice how pretty this girl was, despite the screeching voice. But what Cole did was his business.

Across the stage, frantic waving caught Audrey's eye. Bryan Freeman held up his guitar and mouthed, "Let's sing."

Though this evening had been a little different with the press and testimonies, most nights at the CSU, students worshipped in song. Audrey swallowed back a bit of nerves and nodded. If she didn't know the songs he'd chosen, she'd fake it. That would give her space to think about the neighborhood developments—Cole and Emma somewhere across the sidewalk and Grant next door. Sounded like the makings of a catastrophe.

Pulling herself away from Cole's light touch, she stepped up on the platform and took her place beside Bryan.

He plugged in the amp, set out the music, and inclined his head near hers. "I matched more of your poetry with my tunes. Let me know what you think, and join in with your harmony whenever." His warm smile shook away her worry. "You got this, Audrey. After all, the words are yours."

The guitar chords alerted the crowd to their presence. Then Bryan's voice filled the room. The sound left one believing in all that is good and beautiful and lovely. Now her poems left his lips and became something altogether new.

Skies too far, oceans apart,
I know Your Spirit's with me
The problem is my heart.
Too dark, too deep,

I think You can't reach it.
My flesh pulls away,
And begs just to quit.
Thoughts ugly and unwanted,
A past messy and haunted,
Sprinklings of fear, insecurity, lust,
Misguided places given my trust.
No person, family, or friend
Can heal the place
Needing to mend.
You alone can cleanse
My desolate heart.
No realm too far
To keep us apart.

Somehow, Audrey's voice melded with Bryan's as though they'd written the song together. Because in a way they had.

And the crowd stood mesmerized.

If only the song didn't unearth emotions she'd worked so hard to bury.

~~~

Even the squealing girl quieted at the blend of Audrey and Bryan's voices. Something in Cole's chest pinched at the sound. Sure, Audrey's voice melted his heart, but the words she'd written and read in Honduras moved something deeper.

As if God called them into his mind, Cole's sins paraded before him. Images he'd watched on his computer, wild nights with different girls... Filth washed over him and clung to his skin. The way he'd lived his life for pure pleasure had never bothered him until a couple of weeks ago. Not much anyway. Rationalizing that he wasn't hurting anyone hardened him against the criticisms and warnings from guys like Grant who claimed to be Christians.

Was it true? Had sin damaged him? Damaged others? Even if the actions were no one's business. And if it were true, would God forgive him? Could the Lord bridge that distance and cleanse his desolate heart?

Chapter 4

"Thanks for driving. After three days at Mom and Dad's, I should feel refreshed not exhausted." Twisting to her side, Audrey rested her head against the passenger seat. Thin pines bordered the hilly landscape outside the windows as her brother's truck rumbled down Highway Seventy-eight.

With a satisfied sigh, Grant took one hand off the wheel and rubbed his midsection. "Yeah, but we had some good food."

"Is food all you ever think about?"

"High on a short list."

The truth in his answer made her laugh. "But the chaos of four extra voices and bodies crowded in our living room wears me down. Our cousins could've given us a little quiet time with Mom and Dad. They have a house across the field." They seemed to prefer the Vaughn household, though.

"You know, since Uncle Phillip's accident, they like to hang out at our house."

"I guess." The chaos at home might be nothing compared to what they'd find back at their condos. Questions nibbled at her. Was Cole's condo as close as she suspected? What about this Emma? Not only that, Bryan had mentioned her going with him to Nashville to record a demo. Was the music industry part of her future? The questions strained her tired mind. Better to shut it all out and focus on the present. Or nothing.

Lost in thought, the two-hour drive from the outskirts of Jasper, Alabama, passed quicker than expected. Turning into the asphalt lot beside her condo, the present kicked her in the gut. Cole carried boxes toward the new condo directly across the sidewalk from her own. She took a deep gulp of air.

Grant uttered a low growl. "Can't be. Tell me he's helping someone else move in. This is too much."

The sound and the irony almost brought a giggle. Almost. "Be nice. He's not that bad."

Her brother rolled the truck into a vacant spot, shifted to park, and then pointed his gaze her way. "You don't see the same Cole I see."

"You're right, I don't. And when I was tutoring him last year, I would've agreed with you that he didn't have much...substance. But I'm telling you, he changed in Honduras."

The driver's side door flew open, and Grant stepped out. "For his sake, I hope so."

Audrey made a quick exit from the passenger side. Maybe she could stay between her brother and Cole.

The slamming truck door turned Cole's head. His gaze met hers. The sight of him warmed her cheeks. She offered him a small wave and smile, trying not to look too excited. Neither of the guys needed to know the way she felt at the moment.

Cole grinned and pointed his chin toward the condo door. "This one's mine."

After removing her keys from her purse, she motioned toward her place. "I'm here on the poor side of the sidewalk. Need help? I could—"

"He's strong enough to carry his own boxes." Her brother's voice interrupted. "I'm right next door to Audrey." Grant jabbed a finger at Cole. "If you can't lift something, knock on my door."

Only an idiot would think Grant was being neighborly. His furrowed brow and blistering stare coupled with his size could've intimidated a herd of wild hogs.

Cole offered a somewhat flat smile. "Great."

Audrey shot Grant a hard look. "I can unpack boxes. Hang pictures if he needs it."

Taking her elbow, Grant's voice rose. "Good grief. Don't go in his condo."

"Let go." Audrey shook her arm loose.

Cole dropped his box and strode toward them. "You don't need to yank her around."

Cold waves coursed through Audrey's extremities. Not another fight. Grant could kill Cole. He'd almost killed Harrison. If the sheriff's department hadn't gotten there when they did, he would've.

From around the corner, a shrill voice called, "Hey, y'all." A bikini-clad Emma came into view, blond hair flowing under the red designer sunglasses that topped her head. "I was catching some rays at the pool. I thought I saw you guys."

The black material of the swimsuit barely covered Emma's body, and the fringe that hung from the top bounced as she jogged over. Audrey's eyes widened. She glanced at Grant. Mercy. His eyes might just fall out of his head and land in his gaping mouth. At least Emma had distracted him.

But what about Cole? *Don't look at him. You don't want to know.* Audrey's eyes disobeyed and cast a glance his way.

Cole pulled his hat down lower on his forehead and took quick steps to his open door. He lifted the box and backed into the condo. "Will I see you at Chris's house tonight, Audrey?"

She nodded, and Cole slipped inside.

A flash of disappointment crossed Emma's face. She cocked her head and continued over. "It's Grant, right?"

Her brother's Adam's apple rose and fell as he swallowed hard, his eyes never leaving the perky blonde. "Yeah. You're Emma. Cassie's sister."

"Yay, you remembered. I'm still learning my way around, and it looks like you've got room in your big red truck." A moment later, she'd closed in and caressed Grant's bicep. "Could I catch a ride tonight?"

His Adam's apple bobbed as he swallowed. "Sure. Ride with us."

"Us?" Emma's brows rose.

"My sister." He shoved a thumb at Audrey.

At last, Emma glanced her way. "Right. Your sister."

Like the girl didn't remember. A definite player. Audrey glued on a smile. If she had to stand here much longer, she'd need super glue to keep it up. "I'm taking my own car. I have to stay late to practice with Bryan." And she didn't want to watch this girl break Grant's heart. She'd warn him, but the choice was his.

~~~

With a long sigh, Cole closed the door and brushed at the streams of perspiration running down his temples. The rest of the junk could wait until the sidewalk cleared. He'd gotten almost everything, anyway. He flopped onto the old leather recliner he'd claimed from his father's man cave and pulled the lever to stretch out his legs. Once he closed his eyes, the vision of Emma and Audrey outside his door unsettled him.

A few weeks ago, he would've been happy to see the blonde strolling around like that. In front of Audrey, though, shame washed over him for the urges Emma's barely-dressed body dredged up.

Even if there were no Audrey, he should probably steer clear of that one. A little voice he'd ignored for many years warned him Emma was trouble. He wouldn't ignore it this time. With Grant breathing down his neck, the less hassles the better.

Restless, he let down the footrest and pushed to his feet. Near the kitchen, he scanned the open living area. The place looked good enough. He'd gotten the furniture set up, and his clothes hung in the closet. The last boxes held plates and cooking equipment his mother insisted he might need. Doubtful he'd use most of the stuff.

Unpacking the remainder of the items breezed by. He flipped on the TV, the first thing he'd set up. As far as he was concerned, the most important. Maybe he'd check out the predictions and updates for the fall season. Where was his computer?

Spotting the laptop on the side table, he grabbed it and returned to the recliner. Once he'd typed in the password, he waited and flipped through the sports channels with the TV remote.

The screen on his computer popped up. His fingers

hovered over the keys. By habit, he opened his social media tabs, ESPN, and The Bleacher Report. But a few other sites crossed his mind. Sites he'd told himself were harmless fun. A sour taste inched into his mouth. He closed the laptop and moved from the chair to the couch. A nap might be a better choice.

Four hours later, Cole woke, the sports channel still playing on the tube. He bolted upright. How had he slept so long? Coach McCoy would be ticked if he was late. After a quick shower, he threw on shorts and a polo. When he glanced in the mirror, he ran fingers through his hair, then pulled his designer sunglasses around his neck with the strap that bore the red and blue emblem of his team.

He cracked the front door an inch and looked both ways. The summer sun still hung in the western sky. No one was outside, so he sprinted to his car.

The drive to the student minister's house only gave him five to seven minutes to think more about a strategy for getting through the Grant issue. He had to figure out a way to get along with the guy for the good of the team. Would Audrey understand if they only talked when her brother wasn't around? At least until after the season? He didn't want her to think he was scared of Grant, but this was his final year in college football. The possibility of being drafted for the pros waited right around the corner. Drama was the last thing he needed. Okay, injuries wouldn't be good either.

Once he reached the corner near the house, he pulled over. Parking down the street gave him the option of leaving early. He hesitated as he exited. Did he actually have to be here? Religion hadn't really been his thing and still made him a bit tense. But Coach said he and Grant had to plan for the service hours together.

Up the street, the singing guy, Bryan, stepped onto the sidewalk, carrying his guitar case. Bryan raised his free hand. "What's up, dude?"

"Got a deal in Nashville yet?"

Patting his case, he smiled. "Recording a demo there soon.

If I can get Audrey to sing along, my chances at a contract would improve. She's a natural."

His jaw clamped shut, and he swallowed back what felt like a football stuck in his throat. What was going on?

So far, Audrey had only been a friend. They hadn't kissed or anything, and Bryan was a nice guy, but... Cole tempered his anger and squeezed out words. "Good luck with that."

Leading the way, Bryan opened the side door of the pale yellow cottage. "This is your first time over on Tuesdays, right?" He waved him through the door. "They don't expect us to knock. Come in and make yourself at home."

Cole nodded. "Chris and Kim seem cool."

"And they serve food. Always a plus."

Coach McCoy rose from the red and white plaid sofa, his gaze locking on Cole. "Thought you were trying to back out."

"Fell asleep." Cole shrugged. "Can I back out?"

"I never asked you to go the CSU or Honduras. That was your call. But..." With a look that left no room for error, Coach moved to Cole's side and squeezed his shoulder. "After that fight, you *will* put in service hours around the community."

~~~

From her perch near the deck, Audrey spotted Cole making his way out the back door to the grill with Coach McCoy. Her heart bounced against her ribs. Why couldn't she control her own body? Was Grant right about Cole being another Harrison? She shuddered. Caution wasn't a bad idea. The feelings she and Cole shared could've been situational—the emotions that stemmed from a shared experience.

Bryan exited next, his edgy dark hair intersecting above his kind blue eyes. He cast a smile her way and crossed the wooden flooring to an open lawn chair on the grass nearby. "I've been looking forward to seeing you. Practicing the songs I sent you?"

Beside her, Grant broke from Emma's steady chatter and offered his hand to Bryan. "Recovered from the trip?"

Bryan nodded and returned the handshake. "I'm good. But I'm trying to get your sister to record a demo with me in

Nashville. Um, with chaperones and the blessing of her beefy older brother."

The unexpected chuckle from Grant turned her head. The corners of her brother's lips rose in a smile. "Sounds cool."

Something about Bryan set her at ease. Even set Grant at ease. He had that effect on people. Bryan seemed…safe.

~ ~ ~

Cole stayed close to Coach McCoy near the grill but slipped a side-glance toward Audrey. The smoke and scent of roasted meat hovered in the dense humidity. Already Bryan monopolized Audrey's attention. She laughed easily at something he'd said. Gone was the tension she normally carried in her expression. Even Grant grinned at the guy.

Though he'd not eaten in hours, Cole's appetite faded.

Coach McCoy motioned to the group. "Huddle up. But before we eat, Sarah Beth will throw out a couple of opportunities to begin our local missions."

Sarah Beth hustled to her husband's side. Her eyes lit up when Coach McCoy spoke her name. Cole chuckled. The two of them practically glowed when they looked at each other. Maybe there was something to monogamy—a word he used to laugh and change to monotony.

A small crinkle furrowed Sarah Beth's brows, and a serious look covered her face as she began. "I have some news from Honduras today. Three teen girls were kidnapped from a village twenty miles from the clinic. The authorities suspect this is part of a human trafficking ring. Most likely one that uses young girls for prostitution or pornography."

Cole's stomach sunk like a bad pass in the playoffs. A few of the others gasped and mumbled.

Once the group settled, Sarah Beth continued, "These aren't the only abductions, and the acts are becoming more and more brazen. It just so happens that next week the university is holding a summit on international sex trafficking, and I was contacted months ago to assist. In light of the Honduras connection and the focus on service that we're kicking off, I thought some of you could volunteer your time at the conference. For those of you not comfortable with this subject matter, another option is the Sunnyside Nursing Home. They need bingo partners for the patients in the Alzheimer's unit every Sunday afternoon." Sarah Beth smiled and gazed back at her husband. "That's all I have for now."

Coach McCoy returned her smile then made eye contact with the students. "So what do y'all think?"

Cole groaned inside. He'd rather a three-hundred-pound tackle land on him. Neither opportunity fit into his comfort zone. Old people and bingo? Prostitution rings? Both awkward. He bit at the inside of his cheek.

No one spoke. Coach McCoy's eyes flashed from him to Grant and back again. "Well?"

"I…" A small squeak came from Audrey. Her lips opened and shut and then opened again. "I'd like to help with the summit. On trafficking."

Why'd she have to choose that one?

Grant nodded. "Yeah. We should care what happens to those people. Hits close to home after our trip."

Coach McCoy cocked his head Cole's direction. "Your thoughts?"

This was hard. "I don't know. I was hoping we'd be playing sports with school kids or something."

A menacing huff came from Grant. "He probably watched the kidnapped girls online already."

Fury blasted through Cole's midsection as he fisted his hands. In an instant, Coach McCoy caught Cole by the shoulder and waved at Grant. "Inside. Now."

"Oh, wait, Coach." Emma stepped out and grabbed Grant, clasping his arm in hers. Her full, red lips spread into a grin more fitting a beauty pageant. "You forgot to tell the guys the good news. Something y'all can really get pumped about." Her shoulders lifted as she batted her eyelashes. "Daddy sent Jet Skis up here for the summer." She paused as if waiting for a drum roll. "CSU will be rocking Sardis Lake."

The fire in Cole's muscles doused, he shook his head and released a heavy breath. Jet Skis? Was the girl totally oblivious to the conversation around her?

But Grant seemed to hang on her every word. Maybe Emma was the perfect distraction.

~~~

Why did Grant have to say things like that? Audrey longed to run to Cole and tell him to ignore her brother's obnoxious comments. He was snuffing out the light she'd seen in Cole's eyes. But Cole had yet to speak to her the entire evening.

Maybe he was avoiding Grant. Or her. Or was he going back to the way things had been before Honduras, when he barely noticed her? A hollow ache filling her chest, she wrapped her arms around herself and returned to her chair without a plate. A vision of Cole in Honduras replayed for at least the hundredth time. His laughter with the children. His tears over the loss of a child. His warmth as she slept beside him on the plane, waking to find herself leaning on his solid shoulder.

The thought of going back to the way he'd been the last two semesters when she'd tutored him crushed her throat. How he'd seemed to look through her and fidgeted, like a wild animal waiting to escape a trap. She'd have to let Coach McCoy know she couldn't tutor him anymore.

A voice broke into her gloomy thoughts. "I brought you a plate of food."

Bryan's smile greeted her and boosted her spirits. "You always know what to say." She took the plate and nibbled at a chip.

"That's why we should be partners."

More kind words.

Like most summer nights in Mississippi, dusk quadrupled the number of mosquitoes already buzzing around her legs. She swatted at one that persisted at landing on her ankle.

On the deck, Grant and Coach McCoy huddled in a corner before slipping inside the back door. Once they disappeared, Cole's intense gaze found her, and he took brisk steps across the yard.

At the same time, Bryan set his plate aside and rose to his

feet. "You need insect repellent. You're so sweet, the varmints won't leave you alone." He smiled. "So sweet, I've been waiting for someone like you all my life."

Cole's feet planted a step away from her chair. His lashes lowered, and creases formed across his forehead. Was it pain that pressed his lips tight? Or anger?

The smile on Bryan's tan face faltered. "Cole. Didn't see you. Take my chair. I'll bring back another along with the bug spray. Pests are attacking our Audrey." Bryan took off toward the deck.

Not moving any closer, Cole's eyes searched her face. "*Our* Audrey? Am I interrupting?"

Her cheeks heated at his implication. "Of course not." His brown eyes captivated her. "Sit down."

"I'm leaving, but can we talk later? Away from Grant? Things are too complicated with him around. Too volatile. I can't risk—"

"Got it. We're safe." Chair and spray in hand, Bryan neared.

Cole held up his phone and keys. "I've gotta finish unpacking at my new place. I'll catch y'all later." With one last glance at Audrey, he mouthed, "I'll call you."

Her eyes followed him until he disappeared on the street. The risk had to be fighting with Grant. Would he call?

Bryan held out the can of repellent. "Is there something between you and Mr. Football? I didn't mean to cause a problem."

She shook her head and shrugged. "Don't worry about it."

If only she knew what was between her and Cole.

~~~

Through the open sunroof of the BMW, heavy bass sounded from the door of Cole's favorite bar near the Square. It had been a couple of weeks since he'd even had a beer, and so many questions raged through his mind. Not the least of which was Audrey. The thought of a cold brew pulled him to a parking place. Why not? A drink might clear his head.

He entered the glass-and-wooden double doors of the dimly lit room and plunked down on a stool near one of the large TV screens. He glanced at the tall blond guy one chair over nursing a beer. "Sam Conrad. What's an old man like you doing out here?"

With a smirk, the former quarterback lifted the sleeve of his shirt and flexed his bicep. "I could show you a move or two." He returned his focus to the screen. "Does my buddy, Coach McCoy, know you're out? It's past your bedtime."

"He's not my momma."

"No, he's your daddy for one more year."

The bartender lifted a frosty mug toward Cole. "The usual?"

Cole nodded as the smell of the draft drifted to his nose. A familiar sweet smell. But was this the right choice for the evening? He wouldn't drive his car when he left. "You taking a taxi home?"

Sam smirked again. "Ten bucks is a whole lot cheaper than a DUI."

"I can share the cost of the ride. I've got a lot on my mind."

With an eye roll, Sam laughed. "Besides football?"

"Maybe."

"What's caused the shift in the universe?"

"The trip to Honduras. God. A little kid who died." Cole shrugged. "A girl."

"Stop." Sam held a palm out. "Women are a wicked lot—not to be trusted." A hiccup followed his statement.

Cole chuckled. Sam had obviously been at the bar a while. "I see you're keeping it classy, dude."

"Keeping it real. You have to be careful. Guard your heart."

"Who tore you up? I haven't heard that story."

A bitter glint radiated from Sam's eyes. "And you won't."

Cole waved for the bartender to refill Sam's mug. "Chill. Have another beer." Slugging back a big gulp of his own draft, he shook his head. "This girl's different." He could trust Audrey.

Chapter 5

Had two hours already passed? Audrey punched the button on her phone to double check. Singing with Bryan offered her an outlet for her worries and an opportunity to praise the Lord. The way the music blended with the summer sounds of tree frogs and cicadas in Chris's backyard restored her soul. Could this be what David felt as he wrote songs in the fields with his sheep? Psalms and verses sprang to mind as they sang beneath the tall pines.

She looped her purse over her arm and folded the lawn chair. "Bryan, I like the songs you wrote."

"We wrote." His light touch to her shoulder sent none of the alarms that plagued her the way affection from other guys did. "Can we get together again soon? I'm serious about Nashville. I told the agent about you and the songs."

"I don't know. I've never given any serious thought to a singing career."

"What kind of career are you looking for? You're a business major, right?" He reached over and took the chair from her as they moved toward the deck. "I got this."

Good question. "I picked marketing because I had no clue what I wanted to do when I started college, and eventually I had to pick something." She shrugged. "Seemed as good as anything else." And at the time, nothing had mattered to her. She'd barely been able to function.

"Audrey?" Eyes as blue as an April day shimmered, even in the low light.

"Yeah?" She cocked her head to study Bryan's serious expression.

"Pray about going to Nashville. I won't pressure you, but I'll need to know in ten days."

"Fair enough."

He stacked the chairs against Chris's house and inched closer as if he was going to offer a hug, but stopped. "Goodnight, Audrey."

~~~

A thumping noise shook Audrey from a light sleep. She sat up then checked her phone. Midnight. What was that sound? Her heart thudded. Maybe she should call Grant.

And live in fear the rest of her life? No.

After tossing the blanket aside, she pushed to her feet and padded down the hall to the front window beside the door. One look through the crack of the blinds sent a different kind of fear through her. Cole. Thank goodness she'd fallen asleep in her shorts and T-shirt. What was he doing here this late? The deadbolt turned with a clack beneath her shaky fingers. She cracked the door. "Everything okay?"

His eyes found hers as he leaned against the door frame. "Can we talk?" His face inched nearer, and the smell of beer drifted to her nose.

No, Lord. Please don't let him be like Harrison.

A tremble passed through her. What should she do? "Can we talk tomorrow? It's late."

His gaze fell to the ground, and he shrugged. "Sure. Sorry I woke you." He turned and stepped down the sidewalk toward his door.

Audrey's heart sank. Hadn't she wanted to talk to him all evening? Maybe they could sit outside for a minute. "Wait, Cole." She jogged across the grass to catch him. "I'm awake now. Want to sit on the curb?" She pointed toward the parking lot close by.

Glancing at Grant's condo door, Cole shook his head. "Is there someplace we won't incur the wrath of the Titan?"

Uneasiness settled over her like a load of rocks. A place that was safe for her and safe for Cole? Two very different orders.

The lights in Emma's condo still shone, bringing to mind the bathing suit. Or lack of. "We could sit by the pool or tennis courts." Though closed, streetlights illuminated both areas, plus chairs and benches dotted the grounds.

"That's cool." His hand slipped in hers, his thumb caressing her index finger. Chills more like zings of electricity shot up her arm. Despite the intense heat of the Mississippi summer night, she shivered. He halted and lifted her fingers to his lips. "Are you okay?"

The feel of his soft lips surrounded by stiff five-o'clock shadow dried her mouth. "Fine."

A few more steps and they reached the gate to the fence circling the pool. A lock blocked their entrance. Cole pointed toward the tennis courts. "Gate's open."

They crossed the sidewalk and continued through to the flat asphalt pad. Wooden benches lined the chain link slats. Night sounds crowded her ears while lightning bugs hovered and flashed their tails. A memory from her childhood flitted through her mind. Was she brave enough to ask? Was she safe enough?

At the bench, she stopped and turned to Cole. "Weird idea for you."

A smile lifted his lips. "Love weird ideas."

He was so close now, and his chest rising and falling captured her attention. Was he as nervous as she was? No way.

"My dad used to take us out to look at the stars." She pointed toward the center of the court. "We'd lay on the ground and find constellations and watch for meteors. I mean, we could do that. Me and you. And talk. That's all. Not... Unless you think it's too silly."

His hand dropped hers. Was he angry? Such a stupid, naive idea.

A second later, he jogged to the center of the court, squatted and swept pine straw away with his hands, then sprawled out on the pavement. "It's all good. Come on."

His willingness to play along reignited the emotions from Honduras. Feelings overwhelming and intense. She traced his steps and dropped beside him on the hard concrete. Her gaze fastened to the sky, and the sweet scent of honeysuckle floated through the fence. "So, you wanted to talk?"

~~~

Stars blinked in the darkness. The thrill of Audrey lying at his side enveloped Cole. And they weren't even touching. Was the beer muddying his thinking? Or this girl? "I heard one of my tutors say this to a kid when I was in school, and I never understood it until I got to know you."

"What?" Her soft voice joined the chorus of crickets.

"A face without freckles is like a sky without stars."

No answer.

The beer had loosened his tongue. Not a good idea. Why'd he gone to the bar anyway? He'd planned to straighten up after the trip. Giving his heart to the Lord weighed heavy on him. He'd wanted what Coach had. What Audrey had. Not to mention Bryan and Sarah Beth.

A sniffle came from beside him. Man, now he'd hurt her feelings. Why was he so stupid? "I'm sorry. I meant that as a compliment. I love your freckles. And your face. I mean—"

"No. That was such a sweet thing to say." She sniffed again. "My grandfather used to tell me that when I was a little girl. He passed last year, so when you said those words, you caught me off guard."

"I'm an idiot as usual."

In an instant, Audrey sat up and stared into his eyes. "You are not an idiot. Don't you dare say that."

A cloud passed over the moon, deepening the darkness of the night and Cole's mood. "It's true. You're not my first tutor. I've had them since kindergarten. Learning disability."

Her fingers found his and took a gentle hold. "You learn, and you pass your tests. It takes more effort and time, but you've done it. You're going to be a senior. In the home stretch. Besides that, to be a quarterback, you had to memorize all the possible plays and be able to spot defensive patterns. That's a lot. It's a specific type of intelligence."

Her words flooded his soul with light despite the darkness. If only he could be the kind of man a good girl deserved.

"Cole, why'd you drink tonight? Was it what Grant said?"

How'd she know? Either someone saw him, or she could

smell the alcohol. Wouldn't he love to blame it all on Grant? But no. "Partly Grant's comment. I don't want to get in a fight with your brother at every turn. I have to be able to get along with him on the field. The other part is, I don't think I can be a good Christian like you. Or Bryan. I'm not like y'all. Grant's right about the way I've lived." His stomach twisted and soured. "I've done too many bad things. I'm too far gone."

"No." Audrey lifted his hand, tightening her grip. "That's the point. No one's good enough. Not me or Grant or Coach McCoy. Only Jesus is perfect. His love and His blood and His sacrifice are strong enough to cover the worst of sins. When you say you're too far gone, you're insulting His strength and His death. You're saying it wasn't enough, that He wasn't good enough."

Moonlight illuminated the courts and danced in the tops of the nearby pines as the clouds parted overhead. The glow surrounded Audrey's face and arms, blurring the edges where light ended and she began. In that moment, her words made sense, even in his buzzed thinking. God's grace was strong enough to cover his sins. Even the deepest, darkest ones.

~~~

Moon shadows danced across Cole's golden brown hair, wreaking havoc with Audrey's heart. But she'd said what had come to mind in the moment. Never having thought hard about God's grace herself, it seemed the Lord had provided the words. Now would Cole listen?

Cole brought her hand to his lips, and then released it. Pushing to his feet, he smiled. "Let's hit the sack."

Her muscles retracted. What did that mean? She stood and made quick steps from the court out to the sidewalk.

Cole matched her steps with little effort and without speaking. A pleasant look covered his face. How drunk was he? What was he thinking? Would he remember any of this tomorrow?

At the entrance to her condo, she trembled when he caught her arm before she could open the door. "Audrey."

She couldn't look at him, but she stopped.

"I get it. God's strong enough—even for a bad boy like me."

His words released a dam in her heart. Hot tears filled her eyes. Why was she freaking out? His intentions weren't... She pulled her gaze to his face. Cole glowed, not just from the moonlight. He did get it. And it showed. "Even for a damaged girl like me."

"Why are you crying?" Both of his hands cupped her face. "I see no damage. But if you'd let me, I'd kiss away your pain and tears."

"I'm happy you understand about God's love and grace. You're smart like that, you know."

Honey-brown eyes searched her face and moved to stare at her lips. "Could I?" He swallowed. "Would it be okay if I kissed you?"

Her arms felt like hundred pound weights, but she lifted them to rest around his waist. "Okay." Shaking inside, she closed her eyes. His breath warmed her cheeks, but instead of her lips, he placed a gentle kiss on her cheekbone where the tears had dampened her skin, then moved to the other cheek. His thumbs brushed away the remaining moisture. Her eyelids fluttered open to find him waiting. "What?"

He blinked. "You're afraid of me. You're trembling."

"No. Not of you." How could she explain without explaining? "I do want to kiss you. But there's stuff... I don't know how to start."

Their foreheads touched, his nose nuzzling against hers. "Then you kiss me. When you're ready. I'll wait."

Chapter 6

No sleep came. All night, the thought of Cole's lips on her cheek nudged at Audrey's thoughts. And his sweet words. Why couldn't she kiss him? He said he'd wait, but how long? She could slap herself for being such a wimp. Maybe next time. If there was a next time.

Now that the darkness was fading, she threw on her khaki pants and tucked in her black uniform shirt. She hoped she wouldn't mess up anyone's orders due to sleep deprivation. Although most of them were polite, members of the country club preferred getting their food right the first time.

She grabbed her keys and purse and hurried out the door. Before turning to lock the deadbolt, she spotted Grant. Lip-locked with Emma. He lingered in the threshold of Emma's doorway, his hair poking up at the back like the tail feathers of the chickens that ran around their Uncle Phillip's backyard.

"Grant?"

His head spun, but his words were slow to come. "Oh, hey." He held the look of their black lab when she'd gotten caught dumping over the garbage cans. Turning back to Emma, he spoke in a lower tone. "I better go. See you in a little while."

Was this a walk of shame? Had he spent the night with the girl? Good grief. Emma had been here a few days, and her brother had already thrown out all his values?

Emma's blond hair hung down in fuzzy tangles around her shoulders. Not seeming to care what anyone thought, she called after him. "Bye, Grant. Go pump your iron. I can't wait to see you at the pool after your workout."

A stupid smile covered her brother's face as he paraded toward his door. Audrey beat him there and blocked his entrance. Punching him in the arm probably wouldn't change his behavior—probably wouldn't hurt him…much—but she might feel better.

Audrey rounded her fist, protruding her middle knuckle farther than the rest, and let it fly.

"Ouch. Doggone, girl. You frogged me." Grant massaged his forearm.

"Yeah. I'd like to knock some sense into you, but I doubt it'll help. It's obvious you're falling about as hard as Goliath."

His eyebrows and lips pulled into a tight pout. The same pout he'd formed when teased by kids for extreme height in elementary school, until he wised up and used the size to his advantage. "This is different. I've never felt this way about anyone. You think she's playing me?"

Audrey groaned. The truth would hurt, and she hated upsetting him. Deep down, Grant was a tender soul. "Of course, I think she's a player. But even if I didn't, jumping into bed with her goes against everything you've stood for all your life."

"She cares for me, too. You don't know her the way I do." He ran his fingers through his hair, smashing down the chicken tail. "It's not what you think anyway." Keys jangled as he pulled them from his pocket, while his brows knitted so tight, they might switch sides. "Mostly."

A bitter chuckle escaped her mouth. "Mostly." She wagged her finger at him. "So, you're walking on the coals around flames but haven't plunged into the fire yet. It won't be long before you get burned."

One look told her she'd gone too far. Anger clouded Grant's hazel eyes. "How about this? You do you. And I'll do me." The door flung open, and he stepped inside. A second later the windows rattled as he slammed it shut.

Her phone chirped an alarm. Ten minutes to get to work. At least the Country Club was close. She sprinted to her car. No time to let the air cool.

Backing out, she expelled a pent up breath. *You do you.* Hadn't she been telling Grant that same thing? About her and

Cole? At least she'd said her piece. Now she'd keep out of it. But not without praying for her brother's heart and soul. And maybe her own, as well.

~~~

An hour before his workout, Cole knocked on Coach McCoy's open office door. "Hey, you busy?"

"Always. But come in and have a seat. It's not often you get up before your alarm. I'm curious." He shut his laptop then reached into his desk drawer. A squishy stress ball in the shape of a globe rolled into his palm. "You took off pretty quick last night and missed the singing. Audrey and Bryan tore it up."

Cole rested his elbows on his knees, then propped his chin in his hands. "Bryan's good." His flat tone betrayed him.

A smirk twitched on Coach McCoy's lips. He tossed the little world replica up and down. "Sounds like that bothers you."

"Why should I care?"

"Audrey sings with him. And I'm thinking you've figured out that Audrey's a nice girl. And sometimes nice girls get a hold of your heart in a way you didn't know was possible." He nodded toward a picture of Sarah Beth on his desk, then flung the ball at Cole. "Catch my drift?"

With a quick movement, Cole snatched the flying globe. "You're a regular joke machine, Coach."

"I'm trying to be serious. But if you don't want to talk, that's cool. You came in for some other reason?"

"No. But I have a hard time being serious about this stuff." Cole ran his running shoe across the dark blue area rug and studied the indentions in the weave. "I guess you speak from experience, though." He pointed to Sarah Beth's picture. "About love."

"Yeah, and I highly recommend being the kind of man a nice girl, like Audrey, deserves. You know what I mean?"

Cole nodded. Last night he'd done his best to be a gentleman.

The coach's forehead wrinkled the way it did when Cole threw an interception. No frown or harsh words, but a sure sign Coach McCoy had more to say. "I saw your BMW near the Square this morning when I went for a run."

Guilt gnawed at Cole's stomach. No use denying the truth. The town was way too small for that. "Had a couple of beers and caught a cab. Didn't want to take any chances on getting pulled over."

No words from his coach, only the famous stare that mutilated the composure of the toughest guys on the field. How did the man do that with his eyes? "I hadn't planned to get wasted. And I didn't. Just a little buzzed. I wanna get right, you know. With God."

Still nothing. Coach McCoy touched his fingertips together below his chin, as if listening and thinking intensely, but didn't speak.

"It's hard, Coach. I thought once I made the decision things would come easier. I did treat Audrey with respect last night, though."

A thud shook the desk as Coach McCoy's hands dropped. "You didn't take her out drinking, did you? If you thought Grant was mad when you hugged her, he might kill you if—"

"I didn't take her with me." Cole's palms flew up. "I stopped by after."

"After? You stopped by her place drunk?"

The more Cole talked, the worse it sounded. Maybe he should leave. Quick-like. "I wasn't drunk, and we just talked." He rose.

"Wait. How'd you get home after that?"

Cole shrugged. "Walked."

"Walked?"

"She lives right across a sidewalk and a grassy patch of lawn."

Head flopping back, Coach McCoy moaned. "Couldn't you have moved somewhere else? Anywhere else? As my wife would say, 'What a hot mess.'"

"When I paid a deposit six months ago, I didn't know they lived there. Or that I'd fall for Audrey."

"I know. You were blindsided by all this, too." His brows

questioning, he glanced around. "Where's that stress ball?"

Cole held it up. "Do you have another? I think I'm gonna need to keep this one."

Chapter 7

Three more tables to clear out from the lunch crowd, and she could go home. Audrey glanced across the country club grill. If the guys in the corner would ever wrap it up. At least they tipped well. Most of them were regulars, but a new addition to the group of golfers caused her to steer clear of chatting with them today. Something about the bearded man gave her an eerie feeling, especially when he'd touched her arm and said she looked identical to someone he used to know.

Paranoid. That was all she was. When would she quit thinking evil lurked behind every corner?

Through the swinging door that led to the kitchen, Ivy Patterson bopped out, one of the few other girls who'd also gone on the mission trip. The sophomore with flawless skin and flowing hair the color of chocolate milk pocketed a wad of bills and smiled. "Racked up today. You?"

"Pretty good." Probably not as much as Ivy. The girl's grin radiated sunshine. And the men tipped well for bright smiles. Audrey released a quiet sigh. Maybe someday laughter and subtle charm would flow as freely from her as it did from her coworker. But a black emptiness nibbled at her soul. A battle she still fought every day.

The clinking of forks and the scrape of chairs signaled the departure of her last few diners. Finally. Audrey wiped down the counter while she waited for the men to leave. "Are you going to the coliseum to help set up for the summit?"

"Yeah." Ivy's keys jingled in her fingers. "I brought a change of clothes in my car. Are you going?"

"As soon as I finish here. My condo's not far. If you don't mind waiting for me to dump the uniform, we can go together."

"Sounds great. I'll help you clear out."

Thirty minutes later, they'd both changed and scooted out of Audrey's. Grant jogged from his door a second after they passed his window.

"Hey, Ivy." He smiled for a second then turned toward Audrey. The smile disappeared. "I bought this for you. Here." His large hand held a gray bottle on a key ring.

"What is it?"

"Pepper spray. You attach it to your keys." He extended his arm further toward her, and his lips twitched as he pressed them together. "Take it. Just in case."

A sinking feeling scrambled her insides. Was Grant backing off at last? And why did getting what she asked for terrify her? "Thanks."

His gaze travelled to Emma's door. "We'll see you on campus. Emma's not quite ready."

"Oh. Right. See ya." Her feet took her toward the parking lot, but it seemed her heart trailed behind. She and her big brother had always been close, until the last couple of weeks.

Born only ten months apart, they'd been playmates as long as she could remember. In kindergarten, Grant had been held back like most boys in their town whose families hoped they'd play college football. That extra year to mature and gain size made a huge difference in high school. Everyone said they held them back because of the spring birthdays, and being boys and all. Of course, if her parents had known how large Grant would end up, they might've made another choice. But having classes with her brother saved her parents' time helping with the homework, plus she and Grant studied together. Still did.

Praise music filled the short ride to campus. Thank goodness she had a few minutes to collect herself. Would Cole be working at the symposium already? Though he'd balked at the project, Coach McCoy was clear. Grant and Cole would both be expected to volunteer.

Once they reached the coliseum and found a place to park, Ivy led the way down the long, brick sidewalk toward the entrance. "Did Sarah Beth tell you what we'd be doing?"

Audrey shook her head. "I heard her say the guys will be doing some heavy lifting at first." Glancing around, she spotted Cole's BMW. Her stomach pitched into her chest. Her heart responded and seemed to sprint in two opposite directions, one toward Cole and the other away from him as fast and far as possible.

A colossal smile spread across Ivy's face. "Look who's here." She must've noticed his car, too. "You and Cole seemed cozy on the trip. How's that going?"

"We're friends, I guess." The memory of Cole's eyes under the moonlight struck her full force. The vision lured her heart out of the dark closet she'd closed and locked three years ago.

A second later, Cole emerged in the flesh through the glass double doors, flanked by three other football players. His eyes brightened, and his lips lifted as he changed course and headed toward her. "I hoped you'd get here before I had to go." Once he reached them, he pulled Audrey into a close hug. "Coach gave me permission to leave. My dad's passing through on the way to a seminar in Memphis. We're playing nine holes at the University course and then having dinner downtown."

She melted into Cole's embrace, his warmth surrounding her like her favorite quilt. The other three guys stood gawking as he held her and explained his exit. Heat rushed to her face and ears then traveled through the rest of her. A public display of affection wasn't what she'd expected. She'd imagined their relationship would remain a secret. At some level, she figured he'd be embarrassed about hanging out with her.

Pulling away an inch or two, she avoided his eyes by staring at his chest. A decision that didn't help douse the flames at all. "Have a nice time with your father."

Not seeming to notice her efforts to allow him to leave, his fingers slid up and down her arms. "It's hard for us to talk sometimes. My dad's a genius." A bitter sigh followed. "Like my brother."

No wonder Cole's reading disability ate away at him. Poor thing. Her gaze traveled back to his face. If only his friends weren't staring, she'd kiss him right then and there. "Don't do that to yourself. We've already established the fact that you're smart."

His head inclined toward hers, lips brushing her cheek. "You always know the right thing to say." He released her and smiled. "I'll call you later."

At that moment, the realization slapped her—she was falling in love with Cole. Along with that came the realization that Cole would likely shatter her heart.

~~~

An elbow slammed into Cole's ribs as he continued down the walk. "What was that for?" He turned to stare at the running back on his left.

"Why are you talking to *that* girl? She's not your usual style, and you're grinning and stuff. Like you got something serious for this one."

The question set off defensive alarms throughout his whole body. "You got a problem with her?"

"She's plain vanilla, you know. That's all."

Anger detonated in Cole's chest. His eyes narrowed, and he drew in a deep breath. Busting his teammate's face wouldn't be the wisest choice. The fight with Grant had landed him in enough trouble already. Words squeezed through his clenched teeth. "Maybe I like vanilla."

The guys snickered as they reached the end of the sidewalk and stepped into the parking lot. "We'll see how long you stick with one flavor."

Turn away and walk to the car. He forced his arms to his side and his feet forward. Why did the insinuations irk him so much? And could they be right? Would he be satisfied with one girl?

The question clawed at his brain as he yanked on the car door and slid onto the searing hot seat. The last thing he wanted to do was hurt Audrey. But would he?

Chapter 8

All the way back to the condo, Audrey relived the moments with Cole that afternoon. His arms around her. His lips on her cheek. The fear and unease that plagued her about his touch lessened. A lot. After three years of shutting herself off, she needed to move on.

Only the laughter of his teammates as he left spoiled the moment. Were they giving him a hard time about her?

Who was she kidding? A guy like Cole with a girl like her...

Night crept up outside her window, the setting sun splashing red and orange through the clouds in the western sky. She'd opened and shut the blinds at least ten times. Although she preferred to leave them open, if she stood in a certain spot, she could catch a glimpse of Cole's doorway. And she wouldn't look there. Again.

The site beckoned her eyes over and over, but she fought the urge. *Don't be a stalker.* So far, she'd only peeked a few times, and no lights were on in his place.

Her keys lay on the bar that separated her living room from the tiny kitchen. The small gray spray bottle attached to the ring reminded her of Grant. He'd barely spoken to her all afternoon. Emma had buzzed around the convention area, flirting, her shrill voice slicing through the hum of activity, while he lifted partitions and set up the stage. Why couldn't he see past her long legs and fake smile?

A sad chuckle escaped from her chest. Who was she to judge? Wasn't she doing the same thing, pining after Cole?

Back to him again—and the urge to peek out the window.

She needed a distraction. Maybe a good book. She pushed her hair behind her ears and perused the bookshelf by the TV. Her fingers ran across the spines of her used book collection.

So many stories she'd looked forward to reading over the summer. She pulled out a few and flipped through the pages, scanning the first lines of each. The words met her vision, but stalled, never reaching her brain. No concentration at all tonight. After slipping the books back to the shelves, she crossed to the other side of the room and flopped onto the couch.

Minutes later, her phone buzzed, signaling a text. A skip of hope bounced through her chest. Could it be Cole? She grabbed the phone and checked.

Saw your light on. I'm all about some stargazing if you are.

Joy and fear rippled through her arms to her hands. What should she type?

Me too. Delete. Not right. *Can't wait.* Delete.

Oh, mercy.

Sure.

Send.

She held her breath. Maybe she shouldn't have answered so fast.

See you in five at the tennis courts?

Five minutes and she'd be alone with Cole again? Her breathing shallowed. Could she trust him? Her fingers trembled as she touched the letters on her phone.

Sure.

What kind of idiot couldn't think of something else to say? Her kind.

She stumbled off the couch and ran to the mirror in the hall. Should she change? Into what? It'd look stupid to wear anything other than a T-shirt and shorts. She ran her fingers through her hair and pushed out a deep exhale. Brush her teeth. That's what she should do. And mouthwash. Just in case.

Seven minutes after his text, she rushed out the door, her heart fluttering. A little late, but she'd brushed her teeth really well. She forced herself to keep a slow pace, though her legs longed to run.

Her breath caught as she swung open the gate to the tennis courts. Moonlight etched Cole's profile, highlighting his strong chin and full lips. His light brown hair paled in the glow. As she neared, he turned his face toward her, his smile capturing the last of the oxygen in her lungs.

The last few steps, her legs betrayed her, shaking like pine needles in a thunderstorm. At last, she reached him and dropped down beside where he lay. With no clouds to mask their glow, tiny pricks of light filled the southern sky. As her eyes adjusted, the enormity filled her vision. The steady drone of cicadas kept beat with a nearby cricket.

Cole still hadn't spoken. What was he thinking?

"Hey." Her voice squeaked the word in her twangy accent. Which she hated. They were both from the South, but Cole was clearly a city boy.

He rolled onto his side and stared at her. "Hey, yourself. Thanks for coming." His eyes roamed to her lips. "Sorry we didn't get to hang out today."

"How were things with your dad?"

One shoulder lifted. "Okay. Like I said, he and my brother are more alike. They get each other." He lay back flat on the ground.

"What does your father do?"

"Biomedical researcher. He's got a PhD, and my brother's working on one at MIT. So you can imagine we don't have much to talk about. At least Dad plays golf. We have that."

This time Audrey rolled to her side. Her hand reached toward his face. "That's something." Despite the heaviness in her arm, she touched his cheek. "Lots of people don't have much to talk about with their parents, especially at our age."

He leaned his cheek into her palm and pressed his lips against her fingers. Small, tender kisses covered her hand and drew her toward him. His hands and arms stayed planted to the ground. No grabbing or pulling. He was waiting...like he promised.

Scooting closer, she propped herself higher on her elbow and let one hand rest on his chest, which rose and fell in steady rhythm. She could do this.

Her lips brushed his, softly at first. Still, Cole hadn't moved, other than his deepened breathing. His eyes followed her with tenderness. When his lids closed for a long second, she allowed herself a deeper kiss. Everything around them slipped away.

~~~

Though desire swept through Cole with a force he'd never experienced, he pressed his arms to the warm concrete. Nothing in all his athletic career had required this much discipline. Her kiss meant more to him than a life of passionate encounters with girls.

Oh man, was he falling in love? Was this what it felt like? His heart squeezed inside his chest. Could he let himself fall in love?

The next kiss drove away any doubt or care. No way to block this blitz of emotion. He was down...sacked.

Audrey owned his heart.

Too soon, she relinquished his lips, and tremors ran through him. Maybe he should say something, but his mind buzzed. "Thanks." His voice cracked as he croaked out the word. *Thanks? That's all he could come up with? Smooth, Cole.*

Giggles gushed from Audrey. "You're welcome."

It was a rare occasion when this sweet girl laughed like that, and the sound of it made his goof worth the embarrassment.

Her finger ran across his cheek. "Thanks for keeping your promise. I can't explain how much that means to me."

"I know you're sweet and innocent, so it's worth the wait." He smiled. "You're worth it."

Audrey shot up from the ground and turned her back to him.

Had he said something wrong again? "What?" He stood and lay his hands on her shoulders. "Whatever stupid thing I said or did. I'm sorry. Please. I don't ever want to hurt you."

She rubbed her forehead, then covered her eyes. "I'm not what you think."

With a gentle touch, he turned her to face him and lifted her chin. "Look at me."

A tear carved a path down her cheek. He rubbed it away with his thumb. "You don't have to be anything for me. I love you exactly how you are."

More tears followed as her eyes searched his. What was she thinking? What was he thinking, saying that out loud?

"I love you, too." Her arms wrapped around his waist, and he held her close.

It seemed he could stand like this forever. But he shouldn't. He swallowed hard and slid away. "I need to get you back to your condo. It's getting late." And if he stayed much longer, he might lose all his discipline.

A smile rewarded him for his efforts. Audrey took his hand and started toward the gate. All too soon, their steps reached her door. If he held her close again tonight, he might not let go. Lifting her hand, he kissed her fingers. "Goodnight, Audrey. I meant what I said."

Her eyes shone in the glow of streetlights. "Me, too. Goodnight, Cole."

The door closed. He waited until the lock clicked, then crossed the lawn to his own place. Inside, he picked up the remote and threw himself on the couch. How could he sleep knowing she was right across the way? And she loved him.

Lord, help me. I'm trying to do this right. For once.

Chapter 9

Morning dawned with a heavy summer shower. Black clouds covered the skies as Cole sprinted from his car to the coliseum. He shook off the warm droplets. Not that it mattered since he came straight from the gym. All through his workout he'd relived Audrey's kiss until he'd dropped a forty-five pound weight an inch from his foot. He had to get his head together. No girl had ever affected him this way. The fact that he enjoyed being this whipped still threw him. But would the feeling last?

Across the room, he spotted Audrey talking with Sarah Beth. A glow lit her face when she caught sight of him. His eyes soaked in every detail. Her pink lips spread into that shy smile he loved so much. Love? He'd used the word. Another unexpected development. Of course, he hadn't imagined giving his life to the Lord either before a couple of weeks ago. Though he'd never possessed much intellect, one thing he could do—follow through with a plan and achieve a goal. Maybe that's how he should approach his spiritual life. And love life. With an exacting playbook. Because without a plan and God's help, he'd never win the battle for his soul.

Coach McCoy waved to Cole from the stage. "More lifting for you, Sanders. Get up here."

Cole's feet cut a path toward Coach through the crowd of volunteers and workers from the anti-trafficking organization—though he'd rather be across the room with Sweet Lips. Ugh. Had he really thought those words? What kind of goofball was he turning into?

Coach McCoy halted backstage at a mass of stacked cardboard boxes. "This is it. Instructions are taped to the top of each box explaining where to carry the materials and how to set them up. You and Grant can get started."

"Grant?" A quick survey of the area offered no explanation to where the big guy was.

"He was supposed to be here ten minutes ago." With raised eyebrows and a shrug, Coach McCoy disappeared.

Crud. Emma had probably sidetracked Grant.

Now he either had to text him to see where he was, or move all this junk himself. The cell phone in his pocket stayed put, and he scanned the lid of the first box. After reading the words twice, the instructions still made no sense to his brain. Maybe Audrey could slip away and direct him. The idea sliced through his annoyance about Grant. He pulled the phone from his pocket and sent the text to her.

Can you tutor me on how to set up these displays?

A second later she answered.

On my way.

Something even more pleasant filled his mind.

Once she joined him, the displays went up with ease. Her patient voice with that cute twang led him through the directions. Each time her eyes met his or her hand brushed his skin, any doubts about his feelings for Audrey fell away.

Together they knocked out all but a few containers by the end of the afternoon. Cole surveyed their work. The coliseum took on a different aura. Large, colorful exhibits lined the outer walls of the room. Rows of chairs in the center faced a podium and a colossal backdrop that read: Human Trafficking—Closer than You Think. A photo of a woman's bound hands filled the background. The picture nagged at Cole's mind. Had the images he'd seen on his computer been of women held against their will?

~ ~ ~

Working on the summit energized Audrey. Dozens of pamphlets filled her purse, and she'd read every word while Cole did the heavy lifting. Never in her life had she helped with something like this. At first, fear assaulted her at the thought of hearing about such a horrific topic, but a passion to help these victims soon overtook any misgivings she held.

She glanced at Cole's biceps as he carried out a stack of

trash. Okay, she had two new passions.

Cole smiled as he returned. "Almost done, and I'm starved. You like pizza?"

An hour ago, her stomach rumbled, now it thundered. She nodded. "Any kind of food will do."

"I like how you think." He closed the distance between them and slid his arms around her waist. Not in a million years had she envisioned a moment like this for herself. Being in love with a hot guy and him liking her back. He'd even said the L word. Could this be real?

Yet he held on and gave a gentle caress up and down her back. She could forget being hungry for a second or two or twenty.

Outside, the rain had ended, but humidity steamed up in billowy wisps from the scorching concrete, covering her skin with a layer of moisture. Summer in the South. Gotta love it, but hopefully she didn't stink. She made a discreet sniff at her shirt. Maybe he wouldn't notice if she smelled like the great outdoors, since he'd worked out earlier. "Where are you parked?"

"Right by your car." His eyelids lifted, revealing more of the honey-brown irises. "Even my car can't stay away from yours."

"You're so full of it." Elbowing him, she blew off the comment. "Do girls actually buy that?" She couldn't let her heart get too comfortable with all those pretty words.

His lips found her ear and nibbled. He whispered, "You better believe it."

Shivers traveled down her neck and spine. She lifted her shoulder to block his chin. "That tickles."

"That was the point." A smile as warm and inviting as Sardis Lake on a July day followed. Her reflection glinted off his eyes. Was she really what he saw? How could she bring about such words?

A rattling of metal interrupted her thoughts. Audrey turned and found a line of black trucks pulling into a nearby lot. On the side of each vehicle, an emblem centered the broad side. Red letters circled the seedy outline of a woman. *Freedom.*

Privacy.

The picture with those words made no sense. Especially at this gathering. From the front of one of the trucks, a man exited and directed the other drivers to encircle him. In a loud voice, he called, "We'll set up on the sidewalk. Remember to keep the protesters thirty-five feet from the entrance." The man turned his face toward Audrey, his eyes catching sight of her.

The bearded man from the Country Club.

Perspiration moistened Audrey's forehead further. Blood rushed, swishing to her ears, and every hair on her body stood on end. She swallowed hard and spun toward Cole, grasping at his arm to steady herself.

He caught her and held tight. "Are you okay?"

She forced a smile. "Need food."

"Leave your car and ride with me. Wouldn't want you passing out on the way."

She nodded and let him help her into the BMW. What was it about that man out there? Every time she saw him, a cold darkness washed over her. She'd read a book about using the innate sense of fear as protection right after her…incident. Was that what was happening? Some instinct giving her a warning?

The other door opened, and Cole slipped into the driver's seat. He leaned toward her and pressed his palm against her forehead. "You're not getting sick, are you? Your freckles are pale."

Probably just paranoid. She pressed on a smile. "I'll be fine when you feed me."

"Let's roll, then."

The luxury motor hummed when he pressed a button, and then he shifted into reverse. In no time, they sailed out of the parking lot toward the Square, leaving thoughts of the strange vehicles behind. The sleek leather interior of this car made her old hand-me-down look like the inside of a garbage can. Oh well, her little car worked, and she could enjoy Cole's ride. While it lasted.

Chapter 10

Rain splattered against the pavement as Audrey jogged behind Cole down the sidewalk toward the restaurant. He cradled her hand inside his. Too bad the brief reprieve from the summer thunderstorms hadn't lasted a few more minutes. The smell of garlic and yeast sent a growl through her stomach. Inside the Pizza Gin, she shook the water from her hair and wiped her arms.

Cole rubbed her shoulders. "I knew I should've dropped you off. You're drenched."

"A little water. I won't melt." Her eyes took in the damp strands of hair clinging to his forehead, the T-shirt sticking to his muscular chest. "Much." Had she said that out loud? She swallowed back her shock.

"Me either." A smile played on his lips. "Much." He took her hand again and led her to a booth.

Across the room, a group of guys waved. "Sanders, what's up? Why you sitting way over there?"

Cole waved them off. "Just chillin'"

The plastic bench pressed cold against Audrey's legs. With the AC blowing above, the wet clothes sent a shiver through her.

A waitress arrived a second later, eyelashes batting. "Hey, Cole. You want your usual?"

He shook his head. "I'll have water, and we'll look at a menu."

"Here ya go." She handed him the printed paper. "We made a new one." She leaned across him and pointed. "See, here's what you usually have." Giving him a direct look, she raised her brows. "But it's fun to try new things."

Audrey rolled her eyes. Was she invisible?

"Are you wearing purple mascara?" Cole squinted up at the girl leaning so close.

"You like it?" The lashes' batting speed accelerated.

Cole shot Audrey a look and shrugged. "I'm no fashion expert." He handed Audrey the menu. "I'll share whatever my girlfriend's having."

The batting came to an abrupt end, the waitress glancing Audrey's way. "The purple was an accident. Why is that color even an option?" She sighed. "You know what you want, or do you need a few minutes?"

If Cole was anything like her brothers, he'd want meat on the pizza. And a lot. "I'll have a water and the triple-meat, large."

"His usual." The waitress pocketed the notebook. "Except for the water."

Once she was out of earshot, Cole chuckled. "Not awkward at all. Are you cold? I can come sit by you."

"I—"

Another female visitor appeared. "Where've you been? It's like you fell off the planet since school let out." Clunky designer jewelry accented a pale blue tank top. The girl flicked her long, shiny black hair, and sat. On Cole's lap.

With one quick motion, Cole lifted her off and stood. "Been here and there. I was just moving over to the other bench to keep my girlfriend warm." With a hasty dip around the corner of the table, he dropped next to Audrey and hung his arm around her shoulders.

"Right. We'll catch up later." The girl's forehead creased before she walked to another group of students at a nearby booth.

Was this how things would always be? Girls throwing themselves at Cole everywhere they went? Not quite the dreamy date she'd imagined.

A second later, the guys across the room surrounded the girl. Apparently she had pretty friends, too, not far behind. Gathered beside Cole and Audrey's table, a large crowd joked and carried on. Near the bar, a band warmed up a bass guitar and drums. A heavy rock tune followed that Audrey had never heard, and three girls danced in place a couple of feet away.

Oh, gracious. When would food come? The sooner the better. A loud whoop erupted from one of the guys. "Beer pong at my place." The group rotated as one toward Cole. "You in, Sanders?"

Another guy laughed. "He has to give us a handicap this time. Last time Sanders played, I missed two days of class, I was so sick."

Cole shook his head. "Not gonna make it. Y'all be careful out there." The waitress wove through the midst of the crowd, delivering their drinks. He caught her arm. "Jules, can you box up our pizza to go? Maybe put our waters in go-cups?"

"No problem. Should be ready any second."

He glanced at Audrey. "You don't mind, do ya?"

Studying his pained expression, she shrugged. "Fine either way." But her stomach tightened. Was he leaving to escape the crowd or because he was embarrassed they'd seen him with her?

~ ~ ~

So much for a fun first date. Though the night varied little from Cole's old patterns before Honduras, it seemed as though he'd stepped into enemy territory. Adrenaline pulsed through his temples as he scrambled through escape routes in his mind. Leaving the restaurant was the only option that surfaced. Why couldn't everyone give them some space?

The takeout box arrived five minutes later along with the check. Audrey lifted her small purse, digging through a wad of one dollar bills. He caught her hand. "Put your money back. I'm paying for this disaster."

Her chin lifted as she smiled, revealing small dimples in her cheeks he'd never noticed. "I could at least tip our extremely friendly waitress."

A laugh erupted from his chest. "She did seem to like you."

"I know, right? She even spoke to me. Once." The freckles across Audrey's nose crinkled. That sweet face lifted his heart—made him feel at home.

He dropped thirty dollars on the table, then touched the tip of her nose. "I got it. Let's get outta here."

Scooting through the crowd with Audrey in tow, he made for the door. Almost there. "Whew."

In the breezeway, a hand caught his bicep. One of the guys from inside held on. "You're really not coming, Cole?"

Cole shook his head. "Not my thing anymore."

Grimacing, the guy shook a finger at Audrey. "Not cool."

Audrey's jaw dropped, then trembling, clamped shut.

Cole's teeth crushed together. No use arguing with a drunk. He'd been down that road too many times. "Later, dude." Cole pulled Audrey close with one arm and gripped the pizza box in the other. "Ready to make a run for it?"

Her head nodded, but her eyes brimmed with tears. He ran toward the car with her beside him. Why'd the night have to turn out like this? His fault, of course. If only he'd done a few things differently in the past.

Being a college quarterback delivered highs and lows. And tonight's attention drove him to a definite low. The funny thing was, not long ago, going along with the party would've been a typical night. A good night.

Now that they'd been drenched again, Cole flipped off the AC when he started the car. The pizza scent filled his nose. Man, he was hungry. "You mind if we get a piece now and eat it before I start driving?"

Audrey let out a small chuckle. "Go ahead. Just like my brothers." She cleared her throat. "Sorry if that offends you—comparing you with Grant and all."

"I can imagine the big guy scarfing down more than one on the way home. You'd probably be lucky to get any without getting your fingers bitten." He opened the box, pulled out a slice, and handed it to Audrey. "You need to eat, too." Then, he ripped off a big piece for himself and took a bite. The meat and cheese mingled with the garlicky sauce and sent a shudder of delight through his chest. Pizza. Thank the Lord for whoever had invented the blissful meat pie.

Before they left the parking place, they'd emptied the box.

Maybe he did more of the emptying, but Audrey ate a little. "That was good." He threw the box to the back seat and took a sip of water. "You want to call it a night or go see a movie or something?"

"I'm ready to go home." She sighed. "Work in the morning and all."

He reached for a strand of her hair. So soft. Even damp. He twirled the ends through his fingers. "Can we redo our first dinner out together? It kinda tanked."

After wiping her mouth with a napkin, Audrey chewed her lower lip. "Maybe we should cross the state line if we do."

If. His chest compressed so tight, it hurt. How much drama would she be willing to put up with? He shifted into drive and pulled onto the street. "In Louisiana and Alabama, I get some heckling. Got some fans in Memphis, but if we go too deep into Tennessee, they may throw a few oranges at me."

He'd meant the words as a joke, but silence weighed down the space between them, heavier than the moisture that clung to their skin. He glanced at Audrey, who seemed to be deep in thought, her arms crossed against her chest. He drove slower than his usual speed. Maybe she'd say something before they reached the parking lot.

The drive ended too soon, and the rain still sliced through the air. He parked and cut the engine. Nothing. She'd spoken not one word the whole way.

"Wait there, and I'll come around and walk you to your car door."

"You don't have to." She fidgeted beneath his gaze. "It's pouring."

His head fell back against the seat, and he ran his hands through his hair. How long would his mistakes dog him?

Her door hadn't opened though. Eyes closed, he waited for the sound of her leaving. Maybe for good.

The handle pulled with a clack, and the swish of rain splattering against the hood reached his ears. But, she hadn't left. "Cole?"

He lifted heavy eyelids. "You change your mind?"

Audrey offered a crooked smile. "Will girls be sitting in your lap if we go to Memphis?"

Warmth flooded his face and chest. She hadn't quit him yet. "Only you."

Chapter 11

Now she understood why her parents drank coffee. Audrey yawned. Between thoughts of Cole racing through her brain and thunder rattling the roof, she'd tossed and turned until the alarm sounded. Good thing the country club allowed the staff to have drinks free of charge. The hot brew couldn't be ready soon enough. As she filled her cup and set it behind the wait staff counter, another image troubled her. The man from the protest. Would he be among the golfers dining at lunch? No way the guy was from around here. Someone must've brought him to the club as a guest.

Dread tightened her muscles throughout the morning. To keep busy, she wiped down the baseboards and doors.

The manager stopped and smiled. "You know I can't give you a raise."

Audrey forced a laugh. "Just working off nervous energy."

"Tell you what. You keep cleaning like that, and I'll give you a freebie from the pro shop."

Scrubbing faster, Audrey nodded. "I do have my eye on a pair of shorts." She laughed. "But after last night, I may need to invest in a golf umbrella."

"Don't waste your money on an umbrella. Get one out of lost and found. We're up to about twenty." He waved her back. "Only the regulars are out on a muddy day like this, anyway."

Ten minutes later, the door chimed, the first of the lunch customers coming through. She needed to hurry. On wet days, only one waitress and the cook worked at the golf course café. She had seniority, and it was a good thing. If not, her gas tank would sit empty, and she'd be eating tortillas and beans like she had in Honduras. The mission trip left her savings at an all-time low. But she didn't regret going for one second.

The regulars gathered at the usual spot in the corner. No sign of the creepy guy from outside the symposium. Thank goodness.

After serving a round of sweet tea and taking orders, not that they ever varied, she breathed out a sigh that erased the strain of the morning. At least she got a pair of shorts out of all that anxiety.

Until the door chimed again.

She pressed on a smile and turned to greet the new arrival. Dark eyes under bushy brows met hers. Something menacing in his gaze set off alarms and left her with chill bumps that felt more like large welts.

Lord, I need You.

"Can I help you, sir?"

The dark eyes narrowed. "I'm sure you can." One side of his bearded lips lifted as he gave her a once over. "I could help you, too, if you like."

Her stomach roiled at his implication.

Stand your ground.

"Are you a member here, sir?"

"I was a guest the other day. I'm certain you remember me."

She swallowed a lump that felt more like a saucer stuck in her throat. "Is the member here, yet? Or do you have his name?"

After a large step closer, he pointed to the table of men in the corner. "Those gentlemen recognize me." His voice raised to a bellow. "Get out of my way, girl. You remind me of my ex-wife." He grabbed at his facial hair. "I have to keep a beard to cover the scar that crazy woman left."

A retired local attorney from the group in the corner rushed to her side. "That's no way to talk to the lady."

"You remember me, right?" The man's finger raised toward Audrey. "She acts like I'm not welcome here."

For the second time in twenty-four hours, someone had shoved a finger toward her, and again, her eyes brimmed with tears. She forced her legs to stand strong, though. "The club is for members. I have to make sure you are a member or with a guest, or I could lose my job."

The attorney stepped in front of her. "Who did you come with the other day? You said you were making a movie in town, but I never caught your name or the production company."

The man's face hardened, and he gave an exaggerated sigh. "I'm not making a movie here, but I make movies. Nado Productions." He reached in his wallet and held out two cards, handing one to the attorney, the other to Audrey.

The last thing she wanted was anything this man had touched.

"Maybe the young lady would like to leave her waitressing for an acting career." If the man didn't look so wicked, he might've been attractive with the dark hair almost matching his eyes. His build wasn't intimidating, but he exuded evil. Like slime oozed off him.

Audrey stared at the card and took a shaky step back.

The attorney read the card and raised his gray brows. "Berkley Long, Producer. Nado Adult Films." He shook his head. "Unless you come as a specific member's guest, I suggest you don't come back."

Angry shouting would've given her more peace than the silent malice covering Berkley Long's face. "Got it." His eyes met hers once more. "See you at the coliseum."

~~~

Something was wrong with Audrey. Tension crumpled her face when Cole caught a glimpse of her inside the coliseum. Was she still upset about how their dinner turned out? He raked his fingers through his hair. As soon as he could catch up with her, he'd find out. Since Grant had decided to show, Coach McCoy pulled them outside to set up a barricade before he'd gotten the chance to talk with her.

What kind of people protested at a summit on human trafficking? The summit officials wasted no time deliberating how to handle the situation. They'd wanted to make sure the crazies setting up their picket line stayed away from the conference attendees.

Scanning the group that lined the other side of the street,

Cole shook his head. "Coach, what are those people trying to prove?"

Coach McCoy set down an orange cone and turned to face Cole. "The sex trade is all about money. The signs read *freedom and privacy,* but they should sport dollar signs. I've read material Sarah Beth found about the keynote speaker for the summit. Her message is worth hearing, and she exposes the truth behind these groups of protesters. These *businesses* are not happy about being publicly laid bare." He glanced at Grant. "You both should come listen to the woman's story. She was forced into sex trafficking at thirteen. Her life of abuse, pornography, and prostitution will make your skin crawl." Coach's shoulders lifted and shook as if he was trying to rid himself of the image.

The muscles in Cole's stomach twisted. "I never knew."

Grant shot him a hard look. "Maybe you didn't wanna know."

Coach McCoy huffed. "Grant, how many times are we going to have this talk?"

"Fine. Sorry." The big guy rolled his eyes.

Coach wiped the grime from his hands. "I think we're done here. You guys can go."

Cole stood, scraping his foot across the pavement. "I'll go inside and see if they need anything before I leave."

The rise in both Coach McCoy's and Grant's eyebrows let Cole know he wasn't fooling either man. So they knew he was looking for Audrey. So what?

He stomped off to the building and entered the double doors. The room scurried with activity. He walked from one side of the room to the other. The conference started in a few hours. He'd like to leave to change clothes and eat before it started, but he wanted to see if Audrey would join him.

A soft tap landed on his shoulder. Audrey. Even in that small touch, he felt her gentleness, her hesitation. He turned.

Her lips lifted a fraction, but no one would call the expression a smile. He pulled her close to his chest and whispered. "I know something's wrong. Let's go talk and get some food. From a drive-through."

"Sure." Her voice little more than a whisper, she leaned into him.

Cradling her in the crook of his shoulder, Cole escorted her to his car. He opened the door for her and reluctantly released her. "We can come back and pick up your car later."

She fastened her seat belt. "Okay, just drive by and let me grab my purse. I didn't feel like keeping up with it."

"You don't need any money."

"I'm a girl. I like to have my purse."

Cole chuckled. "Got it. Driving to your car."

She pointed. "It's over—"

"I know where it is." He eyed her and grinned.

After needling through the parking lot, avoiding protesters and conference-goers, Cole pulled up behind her Honda. Audrey hopped out, opened the front door, and reached under the seat. Once she retrieved the purse and shut the door, she leaned across the hood and pulled a note from under the wiper blade.

Color drained from her face, and her gaze darted from side to side, eyes wide.

What had she found? Heart racing, Cole busted out of his door. When he reached Audrey, he braced her around the waist.

The handwritten note shook in her hands. Only three words on the paper.

I see you.

Chapter 12

Audrey wilted into Cole's arms. He led her back to his car and helped her in. Why would someone write that note? What did it mean? She curled her legs to her chest and hugged them tight. Thoughts swirled. Harrison. The man at the country club. Even the guy last night at Pizza Gin who'd wanted Cole to party with him. Why did she seem to bring out the worst in people?

She pressed her head to her knees and sniffed. The seat belt alert in the BMW chimed away. Not caring, she let the tears flow. Sobs wracked her breathing. Three years of pent up hurt bursting out. Again. Fear coursed through her veins. Again. Gasping, Audrey pressed her rib cage hoping to catch a bit of air into her lungs. Could a person drown in her own tears?

Cole parked, cut the engine, and rubbed her back. Kind words came in whispers. They rang in her ears, but she couldn't catch her breath.

He removed his hand, taking its warmth, and fiddled with his phone. "Coach, I need you and Grant back at the parking lot. Now. It's Audrey."

Strong arms wrapped tight around her. In silence, Cole held her and repeated a phrase over and over. "I'm here. It's okay."

A sharp rap on the window caused Cole's muscles to flinch as he held her. Her door flew open, and she stopped breathing all together.

Grant's voice bellowed beside her. "What did you do to her, Sanders? You're gonna regret it."

Audrey lifted her head and forced out words. "Not Cole." The lack of oxygen kept her from speaking more. She gasped for air. ·

Grant pulled her from the car and held her on her feet. "Are you hurt? What happened?"

Cole raced to their side, lifting the note. "She found this on her car." He shrugged. "I don't know what it means. She just freaked."

A wave of color, near purple, shaded Grant's taut face. "Here? Someone left that on her car here?"

Coach McCoy appeared. "What? Let me see." He held the note and stared. "It may not even be intended for Audrey." He rubbed her shoulder. "Sweetie, maybe they had the wrong car. I'll have Oxford PD check it out though. We'll all watch over you."

His words broke through her fuzzy mind. The fear clamping her chest relaxed. From the very start she'd liked Coach McCoy—he was the reason Grant chose to play in Mississippi rather than Alabama. And he knew something of her and Grant's past.

Breathe.

She sucked in air and let her rib cage spread.

Exhale.

She let it go.

Cole stepped closer, holding up his phone. "I'll call the police."

Coach McCoy raised an eyebrow. "I think they'll take things more seriously coming from me. If you know what I mean."

The grip Grant had on her loosened. "Can you make it to my truck?"

She nodded and let him lead her to the door. She stepped up on the side rail and climbed into the monstrous contraption. Once inside, Grant shut the door. Outside, Cole stood, confusion clouding his features. He had no clue about the nightmares that haunted her.

Audrey mashed her fist to her forehead. Why did crazy things happen to her? She had no desire to explain her past to Cole right now. Especially not now, not when she'd finally been able to overcome some of her fear. And she'd enjoyed kissing him. A lot.

The police arrived and spoke to Coach McCoy. After the

officers asked Cole a few questions, Coach McCoy sent him home.

Thank you, Coach McCoy.

Hashing out her past with the police would be hard enough without Cole listening.

~ ~ ~

What just happened? Cole's hands squeezed the steering wheel. He pressed the gas and drove toward his condo. Over and over his mind replayed the events. The fierce look on Grant's face. Coach McCoy's reaction. Calling the police.

The note only held three words. *I see you.* Why had Audrey fallen apart? He released a deep breath. But hadn't fear always lurked in her eyes? The way she struggled at first to touch him after the little boy's death in Honduras. The first night he'd asked to kiss her, she'd trembled. The past few days she'd been more…normal. But in an instant, this intelligent, kind girl all but curled into a fetal position.

Nothing about this made sense. In his gut, though, he sensed danger. And if someone tried to hurt Audrey…. He'd die before he let that happen.

He pulled into the condo parking lot and jogged to his place. Why had Coach McCoy sent him away? Especially after they'd talked the other day about his feelings for her.

Cole paced the living room. A beer would be nice, but he'd gotten rid of his stash. Trying to avoid temptation. If Audrey didn't contact him soon, he'd call until one of them explained. Or he'd get back in the car and find them. He'd never been a quitter, and he wouldn't let Grant push him out of Audrey's life.

After thirty more minutes of pacing, he picked up his phone. He placed his finger over Audrey's number. A knock on the door stopped him. Maybe that was her.

He flung it open. *Grant.* "Where's Audrey? Is she okay?"

"I'm sleeping on her couch for a few nights." His jaw flinched. "We need to take turns watching out for her. Like when she walks to her car. To and from work, at this summit. All the time."

"I'm on it. But what's going on?"

Grant hesitated. "I want to make sure no one's stalking her." His hand closed into a fist. "That's all you need to know. And don't ask her a bunch of questions. She likes you and says she trusts you." Eyes blazing, he shook his head. "Don't make me angry, Sanders."

The look on Grant's face would've scared away a hungry twelve-foot alligator. Cole would let his questions ride for now. And he'd help watch Audrey.

Chapter 13

After a hot shower and a good cry, Audrey dressed in gray slacks and a printed top. Her feet slipped into black flats as she grabbed the hair dryer. Once she combed through the wet strands and dried them, she exited her bedroom holding her stomach, still shaky from the afternoon. At least Grant's friends had brought her car home for her, and she hadn't had to deal with that.

Her brother looked up from his perch in front of the TV and lowered the volume on his hunting show. "Where do you think you're going?"

His question picked at her resolve. "Back to the summit. I want to hear the speaker tonight."

"No way." He stood. "I don't wanna go tonight. Emma's coming over here in a second."

Not Emma. Not now. Audrey sighed and continued to the kitchen. Juice might take away some of the lightheadedness. She poured a tall glass and slugged it back, the cold adding to the quaking in her midsection. If she hadn't found that note, she and Cole would be together now. Had he planned to attend the summit with her?

She fumbled for the phone in her slim pants pocket and sent him a text.

Still going tonight?

Bursting through the door without knocking, Emma bopped in, a cloud of sweet perfume surrounding her. "Hey y'all. Let's go do something fun for a change. There's a band downtown that's supposed to be awesome." She shook her hips and twirled. "It feels like ages since I've gone dancing."

Grant's face contorted like he'd sucked on a green persimmon, and he shook his head. "Dancing? I'm not really into that."

With a huff, Emma pooched her bottom lip. "You never want to do anything fun."

He wrapped his big arms around Emma and pulled her into a hug. "Isn't it fun just being together?"

The writing was on the wall for this relationship—in thick black Sharpie. Audrey swallowed back a chuckle. She shouldn't be so cruel, but Grant had no idea how to entertain a girl like Emma. If he thought sitting around watching sports or hunting channels would be romantic enough to keep his "girlfriend" happy, his bubble would burst sooner than expected.

Her phone vibrated. Cole.

Whatever you want to do. I'm ready and a short walk away.

Audrey pocketed the phone. "Grant, take your girlfriend out. She doesn't want to sit around my place. Or yours, either, for that matter. I'm fine and Cole's right across the sidewalk. Go."

His big shoulders fell a fraction. "I don't dance. How about a movie or dinner?" He glanced at Audrey. "You can go with us."

Emma raised an eyebrow and stared at her.

"I don't want you babysitting me for the rest of my life. Y'all go out. And I've shown you how to get by on the dance floor. Step from side to side, and move your arms a little. Oh, and avoid holding them up like a T-Rex."

A huge grin covered Emma's face, revealing perfectly straight, white teeth. She giggled and motioned toward Audrey. "Listen to your sister. She knows what she's talking about." Then she traced the edge of Grant's collar with her finger and looked up at him with puppy dog eyes. "Pwease, Grant?"

His lips pressed together as he looked down at the pretty face pleading with him. "Okay. I'll try."

"Whoop! Whoop! Yeah." Emma squealed and wiggled.

Audrey bit her tongue. Couldn't Emma save her dancing for the band? The more she traipsed around, the more her overpowering scent filled the room. "Y'all go on and have fun." Before she got a headache. Audrey stepped to the door and opened it. "Shoo, Grant. I'll see you later."

Emma literally pulled Grant out, and Audrey shut the door behind them. She pushed her back against the entrance and let her head fall. "Thank goodness." She sent Cole a text.

How about we leave in fifteen?

I'll be at your door then.

Warmth covered over the icy terror that had plagued her for the past couple of hours. She refused to let fear govern her life. Tonight, she'd go to the summit on human trafficking that she'd worked so hard to help set up. With Cole at her side.

~~~

Cole cradled his phone against his chest. Maybe things had settled down now. Still, he wanted to know what was going on, but Grant had been pretty firm about not asking Audrey a bunch of questions. Not that he'd let Grant dictate what he said or did, but he shouldn't pressure Audrey. She'd open up when she was ready. The way she had when she kissed him. The tender thought brought a rush of heat to his face, and he held the phone tighter. Looking down at the device against his chest, he rolled his eyes. "Man, I'm a weirdo."

His stomach growled. He laughed and grabbed a bag of chips. "A hungry weirdo." He ripped open the bag, inhaled every last barbeque chip, and then checked his phone. Still five more minutes. Plenty of time to brush his teeth.

When he finished, he crossed the lawn and knocked at Audrey's door. While he waited, he breathed into his hand. He'd done a good job.

The door pulled open, and the shy smile that had captured his heart peeked out. "Hey. Sorry about earlier. I totally overreacted." Audrey took his hand with a light grip. "You ready to see the fruits of our labor?"

Not really. "Sure."

Back in the parking lot where Audrey had fallen apart, Cole pulled to the opposite side, as far away as possible from the place they'd been when she found the note. People of all ages and races crowded the sidewalks near the entrance. At least thirty-five feet away, protesters carried signs. Cole picked up his pace and avoided looking at them.

Inside, he stopped. Where would Audrey want to go? She'd already picked up information from most of the booths earlier in the day. The keynote speaker wasn't for thirty minutes or more. "You wanna lead?"

Audrey shrugged. "Wherever we can find a seat."

"About midway up, there's a place." He pointed at a row and started toward the steps.

Once seated, he held her hand without speaking. The room buzzed with conversation making it hard to hear, and nothing came to mind to say anyway. At least nothing safe to discuss. If this counted for date number two, it'd likely be as awkward as the first disastrous one, considering the subject matter. Why couldn't they do things like normal couples?

A slender Asian woman came to the stage to welcome and quiet the audience. The crowd fell silent as the screen behind her came to life with photos of dirty basements and chains, hypodermic needles and bruised faces.

This would be a long night.

Next the keynote speaker took the stage. An average looking woman. Could've been anyone's neighbor or someone you pass in the grocery store. But as she unfolded her life story, Cole's stomach churned. He shouldn't have eaten those chips so fast.

At thirteen, this woman had been beaten, drugged, and raped. And the story only got worse. Cole squirmed in his seat. When would this be over?

The talk turned to money. The speaker explained that without demand by American men for prostitutes, the sex-trafficking industry in the U.S. wouldn't be expanding at such an alarming rate. She claimed that pornography not only drove up the demand, many times the medium was another way of trafficking victims.

The chips rose to the top of Cole's throat. He released Audrey's hand and got to his feet. "I'll be right back." He hustled to the nearest restroom and emptied his stomach. No one in school or his home ever explained this dark issue. If they had, maybe he'd have been more sensitive about the sites he'd visited on his own computer. Did people not realize what was going on in the world? *Ugh.*

At the sink, he brought water to his mouth and rinsed. Pressing a paper towel to his face, he stared at himself in the mirror. What kind of man was he?

He straightened his shoulders and tossed the towel in the trash. From now on he'd be a man that stood firm against this...evil.

~~~

Audrey's lungs expanded as the speaker concluded, and she jumped to her feet to applaud the woman's bravery. Standing before a crowd and divulging such a personal experience, a horrific experience, took courage. A lot of courage. If this woman could suffer all those atrocities and be this fearless, then she could learn to fight her own battles and move forward with her life, too. No more cowardly falling apart.

Where was Cole? She surveyed the steps where he'd exited, searching for a glimpse of him. Staying put seemed like the best option. Unless he'd left. Maybe he didn't feel the same way about the summit.

Her neck craned to look around the crowd. At last, she caught sight of him. His face had lost its color. Was he ill?

She waved and took a few steps toward him. Cole met her halfway down the concrete stairs and took her hand. His fingers were clammy as they clasped hers.

"Are you okay?"

He nodded without a word.

Something was wrong, but she wouldn't ask again, at least not until they were alone.

Once they reached his car and eased out of the parking lot, Audrey fumbled for words. "I noticed you looked pale when you came back earlier. Your skin felt cold." There. She'd asked without asking.

Cole faced straight ahead, his hands gripping the wheel. "I need to tell you... I need to be honest. Before Honduras, I had no problem with looking at pictures or videos, you know, like they talked about. After the trip I changed. Haven't gone there. But hearing about what happened to that woman and others like her. It made me sick. Literally."

At a stop light, he turned to face her. "You may not want to be with me. I've done a lot of stupid things—bad things."

Her stomach dropped as relief washed over her. *Guilt.* That's why he'd been sickened. He'd been convicted by the words he'd heard. "Thank the Lord. I thought maybe you didn't get why this summit is so important."

"I get it." Cole angled his head, those honey-colored eyes searching her face. "You still want to be around me?"

"More than ever."

Chapter 14

After night two of the summit, Cole drove toward the CSU. Beside him, Audrey sang along with the radio to warm up her voice. She'd promised Bryan she'd sing as soon as the conference let out, and Cole's promise to keep an eye on Audrey worked to his advantage. He'd keep an eye on her *and* Bryan.

The singer was a nice guy, and Bryan's voice would be his ticket to the big times, no doubt. But one other thing Cole knew without a doubt, the guy had a crush on Audrey. Was it because her voice blended with Bryan's as if they were made to be together? Or would Bryan like Audrey even if she couldn't sing a note because she was a nice girl?

Either way he'd monitor the situation.

Cole sighed. His own blah baritone, or whatever they called it, wouldn't woo a stray cat. He and Audrey had so little in common, maybe he should back off. The thought slid over him like a cold sweat. If Bryan and Audrey were meant to be, then it was what it was.

The BMW came to a halt near the edge of the lot, the last open spot. Bushes blocked Cole's sightline to the left. With muscles tightened, he rushed to open Audrey's door and lead her in the opposite direction. Maybe paranoia was getting the best of him, but another chill ran across his shoulders despite the steaming summer heat.

Inside the warehouse, a fluid guitar melody resonated through the room. Even without the great voice, Bryan oozed talent. The musician glanced up, and a smile blazed across his face, his eyes lighting at the mere glimpse of Audrey. Definitely a crush.

The song ended, and Bryan waved for her to join him.

Near the stage, Cole released Audrey's hand, but not before he planted a soft kiss on her cheek. "Break a leg. Or whatever I'm supposed to say."

Her face flushed, mouth tight.

Was she nervous?

His hands caught her shoulders and squeezed softly. "Go light up the night with your freckles and sweet voice." He swallowed hard and made the words come out that popped into his mind. "For the Lord, Audrey."

Tears brimmed her eyes. "Thanks. I needed to hear that."

Cole nodded. Never in his life had words like those come to mind, much less come to his lips. Was God nudging him to let Audrey go? Or to just fight her fears?

Once Audrey stepped onto the platform, Bryan's smile widened. How was that even possible? "You ready, my lady?"

Cole pressed his lips together. *My lady?* Both of Cole's hands squeezed into fists, and he held his breath.

Bryan spoke a few more words to the audience, but Cole's mind remained glued on the first comment. *My Lady.* Then Bryan introduced Audrey, and Cole focused.

"This is the latest song that will go on the demo I'm making in Nashville next week. The words were written by this sweet girl singing with me, and I'm trying to get her to join me on the trip. I know with her voice on the harmonies, we'll end up with a contract. Please say a prayer for us and give her some encouragement."

The students applauded and whistled. Cole's skin burned. It was as if someone had poured lighter fluid on him and struck a match. A bonfire of jealousy burst to life. Maybe he should go outside to get some air. Or just leave. He edged toward the door. As he did, Grant stepped in. Could things get worse?

At least if he left, Grant could take Audrey home.

Emma peeked out from the other side of the big guy, squealed and waved. "Hey, Cole." She blew him a kiss.

Yup, things could get worse.

The pick of Bryan's guitar began a slow, somber melody. Bryan sang and Audrey joined in.

Cole's feet halted, and he took in the words of the song Audrey had written.

Clarity, where are you?
Certainty, so far?
The pecking of evil
Tapping on a scar.
Open up, they beckon.
Let us take our fill.
No, I have a Savior
My soul you cannot kill.
You may not feed on me
Or fill me with fright.
This is not my battle.
The Lord for me will fight.
This battle was won
By God's Holy Son.
Victory proclaimed,
By the power of His Name

The music continued, and Cole's anger subsided. What would make Audrey write such a song? What filled her with fright?

The note on the car could be part of her fears, and he'd promised to watch after her. Good grief, he loved her. He'd plant his feet here and smile to support her because his feelings were sure, no matter what hers were. The girl either loved him, or she didn't. If God wanted to use her in Nashville, she should go. As soon as they finished the set, he'd tell her as much.

~ ~ ~

Audrey's nervousness fell away as she sang. The way Bryan had mixed the words and music, they flowed like a well of cool water inside her. He'd even printed off copies, now with notes, making it simple to join in. Most of the time, though, she closed her eyes or focused on the ceiling above her, imagining praises rising up like incense before the altar of the Lord. When at last Bryan announced the final song, she searched the crowd for a glimpse of Cole. Her eyes found him, and he rewarded her with a big smile and a thumbs-up. Her heart skipped a beat.

How did he do that to her so easily?

After the last note echoed away, she turned off her microphone and took a step toward the edge of the stage.

Bryan caught her elbow. "Have you decided about Nashville? The producer is a Christian, and we'd be staying with a couple from Chris's former church. No hotels. No expense on you." His blue eyes twinkled. "Or pressure."

"I'll think about it and pray some more. That's the best I can do. I'd have to miss work at the country club, so I'd lose income."

Beside her, Grant appeared, followed by Emma, then Cole. Her brother gave her an affectionate punch. "Good job, sis."

Bryan nodded. "I know, right? Now to convince her to try out in front of the Nashville bigwigs. Her only excuse so far is that she'll lose her income."

Grant's eyebrows met in the middle above his nose. "If you need money, I have cash in savings you can use."

That Grant. Sweet of him to offer. He'd been a mini tycoon all his life—cutting yards, splitting wood—and never spent a penny. Until Emma. Audrey chuckled. "I do have another excuse." She ran her hand across her damp forehead. "I'm terrified."

Cole stepped close and wrapped his arm around her waist. "Don't let fear ground you. Remember the words of that song y'all sang."

"What song?"

"The one you wrote, the first one y'all sang tonight."

Whoa. He'd paid attention. The thought both thrilled and alarmed her. Mercy. Everything scared her, and she was sick of it. "I'll talk to my parents. I promise I'll let you know soon, Bryan." She turned to Cole. "Thanks for the encouragement. You want to stay for coffee, or are you ready to go?"

"You should probably get some sleep." Grant interrupted before Cole could speak. "Uncle Phillip's in the hospital. Mom wants us to run home tomorrow and visit him. He's not doing well."

Her stomach sank. "What's wrong?"

"They think he has a blood clot."

Cole took her hand. "Sounds dangerous. I'll take you home."

They slipped out the back and walked to the car without speaking. Once inside, Cole switched off the radio. "Sorry about your uncle. Has he been sick?"

"Yeah. He was in the army, and deployed to Iraq. A mine blew up near him, and he lost a leg, plus vision and hearing on one side. He's had health problems ever since."

"Is your family close?"

She had to laugh. "Too close sometimes. My aunt and uncle live across the field from us. My cousins love to hang out at our house."

"That's cool. I hardly ever see my cousins. Maybe at Christmas, if at all."

"I guess it's all right. We live on family land, so it kinda worked out that way." Guilt nagged at her. "I shouldn't dread going back home. You never know when you could lose someone."

They reached the lot at the condos, and Cole put the car in park. The engine still ran, keeping the AC blowing cool air toward her. Should she open the door, or was he waiting to kiss her? Her right heel bounced on the floor mat as she glanced at him.

Cole's eyes burned into hers. "I hate to think of losing you for long." His hand cupped her cheek. He inched closer and gave her a tender smile. "You can kiss me again—if you really want to."

Could someone's heart literally melt? Because hers felt like it just liquefied. Audrey inched closer to his lips. The corners turned up as she neared. Her heart thumped against her chest as his breath tickled her chin. With a slight touch, she brushed her lips against his. Cole's fingers ran through her hair. Waves of warmth flowed through her, and fear melted away, allowing her mouth to fully connect with his. She lost herself in the kiss and the moment, no longer thinking of anything but Cole.

Breathless, Cole pulled his face away a fraction. His hand

continued weaving through her hair. "Whoa."

Why was he saying that? The fog lifted, and she studied his face. "What?"

His words came in a breathy whisper. "I love you, but it's getting steamy in here. In more ways than one."

Judging from the moisture on the windows and her own ragged breathing, Cole was right. "Thanks."

He laughed. "You're welcome."

Why did such stupidity escape her mouth? "So I guess I won't see you tomorrow since I'll be in Jasper."

His arms encircled her. "I hate to let you go, but I can't sit in the parking lot with you either."

"I hate to let you go, too." Audrey squeezed him closer.

"Hey, if you're not tired, and it won't ruin you for tomorrow, we could go for a ride. You know, out in the country."

Those words.

A country road.

A field. Darkness and dirt.

Her arms dropped from around him. Her chest seemed to explode. She had to get out of Harrison's truck. "No." She pushed away and swung open the door. Her feet carried her at a sprint. "No."

"Wait." Cole's arms caught her around the waist. "What? What's wrong?"

Audrey struggled, slapped at the hands. "No. Stop. Don't touch me!"

"Sanders, I'll kill you." Grant's voice boomed. He bounded toward her, a fierce look in his eyes.

Another scream ripped from her throat. "Harrison, no!" She struggled toward her brother. "Grant, help me!"

Grant's big arms caught her. "Audrey? Audrey? You're safe." He held her out and looked her over. "What happened? What did Cole do?"

Safe? Cole? She swallowed, allowing her thoughts to clear. *What did Cole do?*

A voice nearby said, "I asked her if she wanted to go for a

ride in the country, then she took off running and screaming. Man, I didn't—"

"Shut up, Sanders. I'm asking her, not you."

Sanders. Cole Sanders. No. She'd flipped out. Only worse. *Lord, why?* "Cole…" Audrey gulped for air. "I saw Harrison in my mind. It's never happened before."

Grant allowed one arm freedom as he lifted her chin. "Did Cole hurt you?"

She shook her head. "No." Tears blurred her vision further. "I'm going crazy or something."

Taking a step closer, Cole held out a cautious hand. "It's probably the worry about that note, the pressure of deciding about Nashville, plus your uncle's illness. And the kiss."

Grant's head shot around. "Go away, Sanders."

A long sigh blew from Cole's lips. "I'm trying to help. Could someone explain what's going on?"

"Now, Sanders."

"I love you, Audrey, and I'll see you when you get back." With those words, Cole turned and took the path toward his condo.

"Sorry." Audrey pulled away from Grant's grip after Cole disappeared. She should hit herself over the head with a shovel. Maybe she'd be more normal than she was now. She should just tell Cole. Wiping the tears from her cheeks, she hurried toward Cole's door, but then stopped. The day had already been so disturbing. Telling Cole now about Harrison would be too much.

She turned toward home. Sleep couldn't come soon enough. If it came at all.

Chapter 15

Harrison's face. Hands grabbing. The hard ground of the field. Dirt in her hair, on her back. Why was he doing this?

No. No. Help me!

Audrey sat up and gulped in a deep breath. Where was she?

Daylight crept in through the crack between the brown curtains covering her window. Morning. After tossing from side to side half the night, she'd turned on music, but it hadn't helped. Then she tried the TV. Even tried turning on the light to read the Bible. Still the nightmare had come when she closed her eyes.

She threw her legs over the side of the bed to the old shag carpet and pressed her feet to the floor. Her head ached, and pain radiated through her jaw. Where was the Advil? She must've been grinding her teeth all night. The doctor said it was stress that fueled the involuntary habit, but the plastic guard the dentist had given remained at her parents' house. She hadn't needed it in a year. Today she'd bring it back. Because the nightmares that ravaged what little sleep she'd managed last night might return. She shuddered at the vision and fought the urge to get back into bed and curl up under the covers.

She may as well face the world, though. After a shower, she threw on a casual skirt and top. Today was Sunday, and if she woke Grant up now, they'd get home in time to attend church with her family. She could drive, and he could sleep if he needed to. Except she'd need someone to keep her awake. And she didn't know if Grant had slept either. Was he at his own condo or Emma's? Another nightmare.

Sending a text could work. When he woke up, he'd read it. She pulled the phone from the charger on her night table.

Ready when you are. We might make church if we leave early.

She hit send and went in search of pain relief. After swallowing two ibuprofens, she emptied the dishwasher and folded a load of clothes, trying to pretend all was normal. That she hadn't gone crazy last night. Why did it have to happen with Cole? Heat rushed to her face. So embarrassing. Maybe she'd call her old counselor on Monday. She didn't want to tell her parents. Worrying them wouldn't help. Her mother had enough on her plate with Uncle Phillip in the hospital. Where was that book the counselor had given her? Audrey scanned her shelves. Nope. She hadn't left that one out where guests could see. It was under the bed.

After picking up a stack of clean towels, Audrey headed back to her room. Once she put them away, she bent down and lifted the dust ruffle. There was the book. She slid on her belly until the slim paperback was within reach. *Survivor Recovery.*

The counselor had reminded her over and over that she was a survivor. It was up to her not to continue being a victim. Not to give that power to her attacker. She read through the notes she'd scribbled in the margins. Therapy led her to start journaling and writing poetry—poetry that now might become songs played on a Christian radio station. Audrey allowed a small chuckle. God did work in mysterious ways.

Her phone beeped. Maybe Grant was up. She pushed up from the floor and read the text. Cole. Her heart skipped.

Couldn't sleep all night worrying about you. I love you. Are you ok?

Relief swam through her. Thank goodness he hadn't given up on her yet.

I'm fine. Sorry I'm so messed up.

We're a good match then. Still love me?

Aw. Tender strength wrapped around her heart.

Of course. I love you.

When are you leaving? Did I wake you? Can I help you somehow?

As soon as Grant gets up. I'd hoped to go to church in Jasper if we could. Pray for me. Are you going to church today?

Audrey stared at the screen. No answer. Maybe he had a call or went to get something to eat. If he was like Grant, he had to consume mountains of food first thing in the morning.

Five minutes. Still no answer. Had she said something wrong? She moved to the kitchen and made a cup of instant coffee in the microwave. Not near as good as what they had at the country club, but she couldn't afford a coffee maker right now.

Her phone beeped, and she grabbed it.

I haven't been to church in like three years. Your question caught me off guard.

Oh. That made sense. Too bad she couldn't be here today. They could go together. It would be hard to go alone for the first time in three years. What should she say? Coach McCoy and Sarah Beth sat in the balcony at their church. Cole could sit with them.

You could text Coach and go with him. He'd make it less awkward.

Another five minutes with no answer.

Maybe.

Obviously, the subject troubled him.

Don't stress about it or about me. We can go together if you want, next week.

We'll see. Be careful today.

She'd been too pushy. Audrey let out a pent up breath. Should she text back? His text seemed kind of final. Or was it? Navigating romance could be such a pain.

Romance. At least she had one after all this time.

A loud rap on her door ended her deliberation. Only Grant knocked that hard. Maybe they'd make it to church in Jasper after all.

~~~

Cole wiped his eyes and stretched his arms and legs across the cool sheets. The ceiling fan hummed above his bed, the AC blew, keeping the room chilly. Just the way he liked it. *Sleep. Gotta love it.*

Most nights he slept like a turtle on a sunny day at the reservoir. His thoughts turned to home. Jackson. He'd grown up in the state capital among the wealthy and highly-educated. His family attended church with that group. They were good people, nice, like his parents.

When Audrey asked about church, he'd run through the reasons he'd quit going. And sleep was number one. After partying on Saturday nights, he'd never even tried to drag himself from bed. After game days, he could be pretty sore, depending on the number of sacks Grant and the other guys allowed through. Most of the time, the big guy did a good job. Okay. He had to admit, Grant protected him really well.

Enough about Grant.

Church.

Growing up, he'd gone through all the motions. But when the other kids got excited about God, he'd never really understood. It was like they'd received a spark that skipped him. Sure, a lot of them fell away during high school or college, but some of them had stayed on course.

Maybe he was hard-hearted. Maybe it took going on that mission trip, seeing poverty, witnessing a child die, to get through to him. Maybe it took a shy, sweet girl to explain God's grace in a fallen world. His tutor in business courses became his tutor on grace. He chuckled. Funny how God had thrown them together.

Now she'd reminded him of church. He could go. The whole idea of church made sense, and he wouldn't feel like such a hypocrite sitting in the pew now. Maybe. He swallowed back a bit of anxiety and texted Coach McCoy.

Thinking of going to church.

His phone played its ringtone. That was quick. "Hello."

"Sarah Beth and I will be glad to pick you up. Say in about two hours?"

"I guess."

"I'm following orders. The wife doesn't want you to feel uncomfortable walking in by yourself."

"Okay, then. See ya in two hours."

"Yeah, see ya. Surprised you're up so early, though."

Cole sighed. So was he. Technically, he wasn't up. Just lying in bed wide awake. Thinking of Audrey.

Chapter 16

Cole garnered a few looks as he entered the church foyer, but Coach McCoy stuck by his side. They ambled up the stairs to the balcony, Sarah Beth speaking to every last member. Cole glanced around the cluster of benches overlooking the rest of the audience and nodded. "I like the idea of sitting up here."

Amusement crinkled Coach McCoy's eyes. "You and Sarah Beth." He pointed. "I'd like to sit up front." He clapped Cole's shoulder. "I hope you'll give this place a try for a few weeks."

Cole shrugged. "We'll see." Not making any promises.

Once they took their seats, Coach McCoy nudged him. "Eat lunch with us. Sarah Beth's learned to cook a roast in a Crock-Pot, and it's actually good. We always make enough for guests."

"I do like to eat."

Coach laughed. "I heard that."

As an older man stood up at the podium to welcome everyone, Sarah Beth took her place beside Coach. Cole scooted over a bit. Too bad Audrey wasn't at his side. After the speaker left the podium, a younger guy moved front and center. Bryan.

Cole held in a groan. Made sense the musician led worship. He pushed away jealous thoughts that attempted to nibble at his enjoyment of the praise songs and focused on the words.

In the center of the opposite wall, a stained glass window held the image of the cross. Light rippled through, reflecting colors of red and green around the room.

How was Audrey's day going? *Lord, help Audrey's uncle fight his illness. And Lord, something's wrong with Audrey. Help her, because I don't know how.*

The songs ended, and Chris took the pulpit. Cool. The student minister seemed like a normal guy.

Sleep weighed on Cole's eyelids, and he leaned back in the pew. Now he remembered what normally happened during church. He lifted his shoulders and straightened his back, trying to shake off the drowsiness.

The verses Chris read came from Isaiah. The verses spoke of a sinful nation. Cole's mind traveled to the summit on human trafficking. Definitely a resemblance.

Chris explained how Isaiah was a prophet who warned the nations of terrible punishment for their sins, but then God offered help if they would only listen, "Come now, let us reason together. Though your sins are like scarlet, they shall be white as snow."

The notion ignited in Cole's heart. That's what he wanted now. To be clean. For the filth, *his filth*, to be washed away. A clean slate. White as snow.

The rest of the sermon seemed to be preached directly to him. The words made sense. When Isaiah appeared before the Lord and cried that he was a man of "unclean lips," that was Cole Sanders. All his good deeds were but filthy rags before a holy God.

His toe tapped. He had to press himself into the chair to keep from running to the front of the auditorium and shouting, "That's me. I want to be clean."

He swallowed hard and swiped his hand across his forehead when Chris offered an invitation for anyone to come forward if they needed prayers. Was the guy staring at him? It sure seemed like he was.

Everyone stood to sing. There was plenty of room to get down his aisle with people on their feet. *Now or never, Sanders. Don't whimp out.*

Cole tapped Coach McCoy and pointed. "I'm going in."

Coach's eyes widened, then glistened. "I've got your back. Let's go."

The walk down the stairs, through the foyer door and into the sanctuary felt like miles. Cole's ears buzzed. Were people staring at him? He focused on Chris's smiling face. The minister took Cole's hand and shook it with a firm squeeze, then led him to the side. Another church leader took Chris's place at the front.

"What can we do for you, Cole?" Chris whispered.

What did he want? He took a deep inhale and spit out the words from his heart. "I want to get clean and make it official." He paused to gage Chris's reaction. "Does that make sense?"

A broad grin filled the minister's face. "It sure does. Is there something you want me to say to the congregation for you? Ask for prayers? Or do you want to speak for yourself?"

Hmm. That part hadn't entered his mind. His heart rate sped up. He glanced at Coach McCoy.

With a nod, Coach squeezed his arm. "You got this." The same phrase he used before a game.

"I'll speak." What he'd say, no idea. *Lord, help me.*

Chris grabbed a cordless microphone and led Cole back toward the center. He aimed a nod at Bryan. The musician shot a smile and a thumbs-up Cole's way and ended the song a few seconds later.

A hush settled over the room. All at once, the microphone in Cole's hand felt like a hundred-pound weight. He swallowed hard. Chris looked toward him with an expectant gaze.

Cole took a breath. "I'm Cole Sanders. A few weeks ago, I traveled with a group to Honduras. Until that point, my life had centered on myself, football, and good times. A lot happened on that trip, and I began to want to change how I lived. My eyes were opened to the reality of life and death. Of poverty and hunger." He took another deep breath. "When Chris spoke earlier of putting away the filth and becoming clean, I knew that's what I wanted to do today, what I needed to do."

He swallowed against his dry mouth. "Once when I was skiing in Jackson, out in the reservoir, I saw a group singing and baptizing people in the lake. So, I'm standing here before you putting my faith in God's grace, believing that I can be white as snow. And this afternoon, if Chris isn't busy, I'd like to take a plunge into Sardis Lake, like those guys I saw in Jackson, and start fresh."

Cole exhaled and handed the microphone back to Chris before he blurted out anything else.

Eyebrows raised, Chris turned to the church. "Amen, Cole. I'll be glad to go to the lake with you. I'm sure a few of these folks might like to join us."

Applause resounded through the room. An old woman near the front let out a loud "Amen."

Heat rose to Cole's face. His eyes filled with liquid. He stared at his feet. "Thank you, Lord."

Bryan led the church in one last song as Chris escorted Cole to a bench. He nudged Cole with his elbow. "You ever thought about going into ministry? You're pretty good at public speaking." The minister sniffed and swiped his eyes.

"Never entered my mind once." But he'd spoken in front of TV cameras for years and played to an audience for what seemed like all of his life. "If I'd have to read a lot or learn some ancient Bible language, count me out."

"Yeah, there's learning all that Greek. But maybe you can use your speaking gift some other way for the Lord. Stepping behind a pulpit isn't the only way to preach."

Cole shrugged. "Maybe." He never expected all this. Who knew what was next?

Only God.

~~~

Audrey yawned as Grant rounded the corner to the back of the church parking lot. Five minutes late wasn't too bad, considering. Once he cut the motor, she hopped out and took quick steps toward the back of the old red brick building. Grant followed close behind.

Almost to the sidewalk, Grant's feet came to a halt, and he threw out his arm to stop her. "Wait. Is that...?" His eyes fixed on a dark blue Toyota Tundra with a lift kit, fender flares, and a tool box. And a black antler sticker ornamented the back.

An icy chill clawed at Audrey's chest. That truck belonged to the Waldens, but Mrs. Walden never drove it. Why would Harrison or his father be here? "I thought just Harrison's mom came."

Grant pulled his keys from his pocket. "Let's go straight to the hospital. We'll get to spend more time with Uncle Phillip. No one was expecting us this early anyway."

"Okay." Seeing the truck seized a chokehold on her nerves. In all the years that Harrison's mother had attended, her husband had never darkened the door of their church. Maybe Mrs. Walden's car had broken down, so she'd taken his. Audrey glanced around. Could Harrison be here? She hadn't considered the possibility he'd ever show up again. Mom said he hadn't gone to church since the incident. Said he lived out of town. What timing. She'd hoped to enjoy worship with her family.

She joined Grant in his truck and buckled up. But questions battered her mind. What if Harrison and his father attended their little church? Could she ever go back? Could she forgive?

At the hospital, she shook off the bitter emotions raging through her and forced a pleasant expression. She should try to cheer up her uncle. He'd been through so much.

As they entered the room, the smell of antiseptic and waste blended, adding to her already shaky stomach.

A voice came from the thin man in the bed. Was that really her uncle? He'd lost so much weight. And he hadn't needed to lose any more. Once he'd been as big and strong as Grant.

"Hey, hey. Look what the cat dragged in." Her uncle patted the bed and took a raspy breath.

Forcing her feet forward, Audrey smiled and sat on the edge of the small mattress. "How are you?"

Oxygen tubes fastened around his unshaven face. "Been better." He struggled to capture another bit of air. "They say a blood clot made its way to my chest."

Grant pulled up a chair. "We've been praying for you. You want me to go get you a Payday or Pork Rinds from the vending machine before I sit?"

"Nah. Your momma's got me fixed up." He pointed to the night stand. An array of snacks and fruit crowded the inside of a basket beside him. "Tell me about what's been going on—" His chest struggled to catch a breath.

Audrey smiled, nodded, and sent a text to her mother, letting her know they'd arrived, while Grant droned on about football. Good thing. Poor Uncle Phillip could barely breathe, much less talk.

Two hours later, her mother flew through the door, arms open wide. "Come give me a hug. I'm so glad to see my babies." She planted a kiss on each of them, but her smile didn't carry the cheerfulness to her eyes.

Her father entered next, carrying two buckets of chicken. The scent of fried food overpowered the rest of the odors in the room. "Y'all got here early." He sniffled and crinkled his nose. "Figured Grant might be starving. Church ran late." Audrey studied her father's face as Grant reached to relieve him of a bucket. They'd probably bought that one just for him.

Were Daddy's eyes red? She glanced at her mother. Lines carved her pretty face, and a touch of mascara had smudged under her right eye. Audrey's stomach churned and growled at the same time. "Have you been crying?"

Her parents exchanged guarded glances.

What had happened at church?

Chapter 17

The smell of pot roast smacked Cole's nose before Coach even unlocked the door, and his stomach roared.

Coach chuckled. "A little hungry?"

"I'm glad we decided to eat before going to the lake."

Inside, Cole followed the happy couple to the kitchen. Their large dog licked his elbow the whole way while a fluffy black and white cat swished around his bare ankles.

Lifting the lid of the Crock-Pot, Sarah Beth sucked in a deep breath. "I'm hungry, too. Don't worry. Everything's in here but the rolls, and I bought the kind that don't have to be cooked. Safer that way. We'll be eating as soon as I get the table set." She went to the cabinet and pulled out six plates. "Here, Jess, honey. Set the table."

Seemed like more plates than they needed, but who was he to question how she did things? Maybe there was a big dessert.

Coach McCoy studied the stack in his hand. "There's a few extra here."

Sarah Beth's head made a quick twist toward him, and she bit her lip. "I didn't tell you? I asked Cassie to lunch."

"No. Why so many—?"

The cat let out a low growl, and the dog exploded into vicious, howling barks, tumbling toward the front entrance hall. Judging from the crash and thud that followed, it slid on something and hit the door.

Sarah Beth grabbed a basket of napkins and pushed it at Coach. "That's Cassie. I'll go let them in."

Them.

Cole held in a groan. Emma and Cassie were sisters. The smell of pot roast lost some of its appeal. Would Emma be one of *them?* Grant was out of town with Audrey. He shot Coach

McCoy a pleading look.

"I know."

"Here, kitty." A shrill voice clanked through the air like a cowbell at a Mississippi State game. "Let me hold you."

Definitely Emma.

A second later, Cassie and her sister stepped into the kitchen behind Sarah Beth.

Emma toted the squirming cat. "Hello, Cole. I didn't know you'd be here. Thought I'd be stuck with the old people, since my nephew Benjamin bailed on us and Dylan's filming in New Zealand. Not that Dylan's young, but at least he's hip and funny."

The girl had no filter. "Nice, Emma." Cole shook his head.

Her eyes widened, and she squeezed the writhing ball of black and white fluff closer. "This is perfect. Jess has been promising me we could get out the Jet Skis when he wasn't too busy to chaperone. And Daddy said I had to have someone responsible along." She rotated toward him. "They're docked near the lake. We could go right after lunch. Can we?"

Coach McCoy pressed his lips together and stared at Cole, as if the answer was up to him.

Cole's stomach dropped an inch or two. Wouldn't look good, but they'd be at the lake already. Both Audrey and Grant would deserve an explanation. He popped his knuckles. An old habit from when he got nervous about reading out loud in school. A habit he'd broken in tenth grade. At least the knuckle part. "Who else would go?"

Cassie shook her head. "I get seasick on anything that floats, so count me out."

Sarah Beth opened a bag of rolls and placed them into a basket lined with a cloth napkin. "I was thinking we'd send out a group text to invite everyone to your baptism." She shrugged. "They can all wear their suits, and Jess can tow the boat out, too."

"Baptism? Cole?" Emma allowed the cat to make an escape and squared off with him. "You're getting baptized?"

The first of many strange looks he'd no doubt encounter.

And she clearly hadn't been at church. "Going all in."

"Huh." Emma's lips parted a fraction, and she touched a finger to them, gazing toward the window.

Silence from Emma? Already a miracle. "Send the text, and invite everyone, Sarah Beth." Cole nodded. "Sounds like a good plan." And it sounded like it'd keep him out of trouble with Grant and Audrey.

Chapter 18

"Then we went under some low limbs, bank fishing. A snake dropped in the boat, and my sister, Nora, went spaz. She grabbed the pistol and shot three holes in the bottom of that boat." Emma set her iced tea on the table and made exaggerated gestures with her hands. "The snake may've survived, but the boat didn't." Her eyes widened. "We had to swim for it. I've never gotten in a boat with Nora since."

A small chunk of potato fell from Cole's fork as he laughed out loud. He had to admit Emma was hilarious. With one funny story after another about fishing with her father, who everyone called Big Roy, she entertained the whole table during lunch.

Obviously she and Cassie were as different as he and his own brother, because Cassie sat shaking her head throughout most of the meal. "Emma, you know Elinor Elizabeth doesn't like being called Nora."

The dog and cat set up camp beneath Emma's chair as she pinched off tiny pieces of meat and bread, feeding the animals under the table. Each time, Emma glanced around the room first in some vain effort to be discreet. What a trip. She wasn't fooling anyone.

Sarah Beth heaped another helping of roast beef and gravy over an open roll. "Emma, did your nephew tell you about when he brought Cassie's poodle over here with him after the mission trip?"

With a loud whack, Emma slapped the table. "No way. What happened?"

"You should've seen it. Benjamin brought that big poodle with all her bows and puffy hair circles. Jess had never seen a standard poodle and couldn't get over how tall she was. I could tell Benjamin was nervous because, as you can see, Gingie is a large dog."

"What kind of dog is she?"

"Some kind of weird mix. Anyway, Gingie and Hairy, the cat, were digging up the yard, as usual, when Benjamin came. I tried to catch Gingie, but she took off, flapping mud the whole way toward Cassie's poodle. Mimi gave one snappy bark, and both Hairy and Gingie rolled over on their backs. Like Mimi was royalty or something. So cute."

"Oh." Emma's cheeks dropped to a frown. "I thought you were fixing to tell us something funny. Maybe you had to be there."

"Emma Bosarge." Cassie's neck turned a dark shade of red, and she rose to her feet. "Think before you speak. I'm sorry. She's a prettier version of my dad, but with a mouth on steroids."

Shooting a haughty look at her sister, Emma wiped the corner of her lips. "Mimi is a snooty dog if you ask me. Like her owner."

Cassie scooped up her plate and walked to the sink. "Lunch was delicious. Let me help you clean."

Cole held in a chuckle and followed Cassie's lead. He was ready to get a move on. Antsy, even, to get to the lake.

"Leave your dishes." Sarah Beth waved them off. "And Emma's not the only one who blurts."

Coach McCoy laughed. "I did marry a blurter. Everyone can go home and change clothes. We'll swing by Cole's so he can get his car and meet at the marina. Sarah Beth, can you send the group text to the other students while I hitch the boat?"

~ ~ ~

Audrey couldn't get over what she was hearing. "You mean Harrison's dad confessed all that in front of the whole church?"

Her father nodded. "Yep. You could've knocked the preacher over with a feather when Riley came forward. Then when he talked about seeing prostitutes..."

A slap ricocheted around the small room as Grant's fist

punched his open hand. "It's his fault Harrison turned out like he did. When we were growing up, Harrison was a good guy. I should've beat the stew out of Riley, too. Where is Harrison anyway?"

"Nobody knows." His gaze fell on Audrey. "He's run off."

Her heart fluttered, and the room spun. She closed her eyes and covered them with her hand. "I can't talk about this anymore."

Her mother wrapped her in an embrace. "Oh, sweetie. We shouldn't have told you."

"It explains a lot, but I need to move on. I can't stay in the past." Burying her face into her mother's shoulder calmed the fluttering. She clung tighter.

A shuffle on the sheets reminded her of the reason for the visit, and Audrey lifted her head. "I'm sorry, Uncle Phillip. We came to cheer you up."

"And you are. You don't ever have to pretend about real life in front of me. I know the score." His chest rose and fell in short bursts.

Both Grant and Audrey's phones chirped. Audrey pulled hers from her small purse and checked the message. Sarah Beth.

If you're in town, meet us ASAP at the marina. Cole's getting baptized! Afterward we'll enjoy some watersports.

A thousand emotions and questions ran through Audrey's mind. Her Cole? Was there another Cole that came to the CSU? If it was her Cole, when did he make this decision? Could she borrow the oxygen mask from Uncle Phillip?

Grant grunted. "What? Cole's getting baptized? Is he doing this for you, Audrey?"

She shook her head. "I didn't know anything about it." If she had, she'd be at the lake right now. Warm tears filled her vision.

"Between this and the news about Riley, you'd think it was a cold day—"

"Grant." Audrey pulled away from her mother and stomped a foot. "Jesus said those that are strong don't need a doctor, and he came not to call the righteous, but the sinners." Giving him a sharp look, she pointed in his direction. "And we all do things we shouldn't."

A long, guilty breath blew from his lips. "Okay, okay. You were always good at Bible Challenge." He opened the tub of chicken. "Can we eat now?"

Dad nodded. "Yeah, son. Blessing first. Then I want to know, what is this Cole fella to Audrey? Are you talking about the quarterback?"

Audrey bowed and tried to focus on thanksgiving. But Grant had just opened another can of worms.

~ ~ ~

A group of twenty or so students sat on or around the pier. Cole and Chris waded through the rocks that edged the lake and into the warm water. Sun filtered through the small waves, dissecting and glimmering in effortless ripples.

Once they'd treaded waist deep, Chris stopped and put a hand on Cole's shoulder. "Today, the angels are rejoicing with us at your decision. Because you've told us you want to be all in." He made a wide sweep of his arm and smiled. "Now, you're going all in with Christ. You're here. Are you ready?"

Cole nodded and took a deep breath. He was doing this.

"I'm baptizing you today in the name of the Father, the Son, and the Holy Spirit."

With those words, Chris gave a gentle push, and Cole plunged beneath the surface. He sprung up a second later, water running down his cheeks to his shoulders. Christ died for him. The drinking, the girls, everything… All his sins washed away.

Clean. He felt clean.

Like a prayer drifting upward through the blue skies and white clouds, the day was perfect. Cole basked in the golden light as he and Chris swam back toward the shore. Emma let out an earsplitting whoop. No mistaking that noise.

Each student took a turn embracing him. Many offered kind words. Bryan stood among them and clasped Cole's hand. "Bro, I'm glad to call you a brother."

Sliding between them, Emma wrapped her arms around them both and yanked. "Group hug!"

Cole planted his feet. "I only huddle in football."

Her long lashes lifted as she rolled her blue eyes in a dramatic gesture. "Don't be a hater." She gasped. "I've got an idea. A challenge. You, me, and Bryan race on the Jet Skis. If I win, you get to kiss me."

"That's messed up on so many levels. No."

Bryan clucked his tongue. "I'll take the challenge. But when I win, you have to agree to ride to church with me and stay for the *whole* service. On the front row where I can see you, Em. You don't mind if I call you Em?"

A new respect and a healthy dose of fear for Bryan and his wellbeing ran through Cole. "Danger, bro. Grant could squash you like a bug."

Emma giggled. "Okay, then, Bryan. I see you've been stalking me." She glanced at Cole. "I tend to slip in and out of church because I have to send Daddy the bulletin to prove I was there. He never clarified how long I had to stay." She picked up three vests and handed one to Bryan. "Oh, and I like you calling me a pet name. You have permission to call me Em."

Oh, man. "Good luck, Bryan." *The boy better hope he wins.*

Emma slung a vest toward Cole. "Since you're a fraidy-cat, you can be the judge. Ride out ahead of us and pick a finish line."

Sounded safe enough. He slipped the vest over his shoulders, hitched and tightened all the snaps. A spin on the water would be fun. "All right. I'll call the race. No back-talking the ref, though."

They lowered and launched each of the watercrafts. Cole pulled up the choke and fired the engine. The machine rumbled beneath him as it warmed. He wrapped the wrist band around his arm and pumped gas through the engine. Three other shiny red Jet Skis roared to life, ready for other students to ride. Emma's dad must be loaded.

He couldn't wait to start a run. Maybe shoot a rooster tail

of water over Coach McCoy's boat.

After he'd cleared the dock, Cole let the three hundred horses go and hit it, wide open. The rush of speed and water sprayed across his skin. The feel of the open lake pumped his adrenalin. He leaned into a turn and made a circle. To his left, he caught sight of Emma.

And he only thought he was riding fast. The girl had no fear and busted out some unreal maneuvers.

For Bryan to beat this girl in anything related to water, it'd take a miracle. Where was the guy anyway?

Seconds later Bryan zoomed up on a lime green WaveRunner and stopped. He called over the engine's rumble. "Where's the race starting and ending?"

Emma spun back toward them at breakneck speed. She stopped inches from Bryan. "Where did that come from? That's not mine."

With a broad smile, he licked his lips and patted the machine. "This is my baby."

"Tricky." A perturbed expression darkened Emma's blue eyes. "No wonder you're so tan." She revved the motor of her Jet Ski. "I'll still win."

Cole laughed. The musician wasn't that stupid after all. He had a shot. "I'll be the judge of that." He pointed at a grouping of trees. "How about you start here, get even with the woods, and then come back. One lap. No redoes."

After a glance toward Emma, Bryan turned a mischievous eye to Cole. "I'm ready."

"Ready." Emma nodded.

"On your mark, get set—go."

The spray of the takeoff covered Cole's face. Emma and Bryan rode neck and neck. Neither giving an inch. They made the turn and headed back toward him. From the corner of his vision, Cole spotted Coach McCoy's boat speeding their way. *Uh oh.*

He focused his gaze back on the race. Emma bent low on the machine, wind whipping her hair. Like an extension of his body, Bryan rode the ski looking straight past Cole. A wave of worry rippled through Cole's stomach. This probably hadn't been a good idea.

In a flash both skiers passed him. Who knew who won? He'd call it a tie.

Coach McCoy pulled alongside and cut his motor. He waved at Emma and Bryan, then cupped his hands around his mouth. "Come here."

They glanced at each other and glided over.

"No more racing. There was a reason Emma's father said she had to have a responsible party along." Coach gave them each the evil eye. "Got it?"

"Yes, sir," they answered in unison.

After Coach McCoy cranked the boat and rode off a piece, Emma turned to Cole. "So, I won, right?"

Cole shook his head. "Tie. Neither wins. Sorry."

"That means we both win."

Bryan circled them. "You can have your kiss after the church service. Not before."

Grinning, Emma pulled out her phone. "Okay, okay. Smile. Let's take some pics."

The camera pointed Cole's way. He smiled and held up a hand to wave.

She pulled closer. "Cole, why didn't you wait until Audrey was home for your baptism?"

That came out of nowhere. Cole bit the inside of his cheek.

Bryan stopped his circling. "I think Cole had the right idea. The decision was between Cole and God. The way it should be."

Cole nodded, but the thought to wait should've crossed his mind.

Chapter 19

After explaining her new relationship to her parents, Audrey sank her head into her hands. "He's been very respectful. I…care about him." Would they be supportive?

"Have you seen this?" Grant paced by the window. "My newsfeed's blowing up with pictures of Emma jet skiing with Cole and Bryan. I mean, what's going on? When did all this get planned? You didn't know anything about it, Audrey?"

"I knew nothing, Grant." She turned to her parents. "Why don't y'all grill him about his new girlfriend, Emma, for a while?"

Grant shot her a dark look. "How about not."

"Honey, we're happy if you're dating a nice guy." Her mother wrapped her in another embrace. "Sounds like he had to go on a mission trip to find the Lord. Kind of ironic, don't you think?"

Being in her mother's arms gave Audrey the confidence to voice her insecurity. "Why do you think he didn't wait for me to be there? You know, to get baptized."

Her father rose to his full height. Only six feet two inches, he wasn't as tall as her uncle or brother, but still a big guy. "Each man has to come to God on his own two feet." He gave her a playful thump. "If he'd done it another way, someone might wonder if it was about you. This way's better."

Her father was right. She would've wondered if Cole was trying to please her. Her soul rejoiced, but a tiny part of her flesh envied that Emma had been there instead. Not to mention the pictures that had Grant freaking out. But she wouldn't let jealousy consume her. Audrey pulled out her phone and punched in a text.

Cole, I heard the good news! I'm so happy!

No answer came. He must still be out in the water. A picture of Emma in her minuscule black bikini with her blond hair blowing in the wind flashed through her mind. Not going there. *Not going there.* If Cole loved her, he loved her. If not...her heart would be shattered.

~ ~ ~

Waves bobbed below the clear blue sky with only an occasional puffy white cloud to block the sun's rays. Cole sailed over the swells, spray and wind whipping him, exhilarating his senses. Between the baptism and soaring speeds, his heart burst with happiness. One thought hit as he turned back toward the dock. He wanted to share a day like this with Audrey. He slowed and brought the Jet Ski around.

Someone else should get a turn. Once at the pier, he cut the engine and floated the machine to another student. "Have fun, man."

Behind him Emma and Bryan pulled up. Water streamed from Emma's golden hair as she let out a whoop. "That was fun. We have to do this again soon. Like tomorrow. And the next day and the next. Like every day." She hopped off onto the pier and faced Bryan. "What say ye, Bryan Freeman?"

With a laugh, he held up his hand for a high five. "It's a plan. As long as you get permission from your large new man Grant."

Emma slapped his hand with a bit less enthusiasm than she'd displayed a second before. "I do what I want, when I want. I learned a long time ago not to trust anyone and not to give up anything for anyone."

A puffy cloud drifted in front of the sun, and a hot breeze cut across the marina. Or maybe only the mood had changed with Emma's statement. Words obviously borne from a dark place. Cole waited for Bryan's response.

The guy never took his eyes off Emma as he stepped toward her. He took her hand. "Who hurt you, Em?"

Cole swallowed back his surprise. The guy didn't pull out any stops.

She said nothing. For the second time in one day, Emma

had been left speechless. Another shocker. She took her hand back and removed her vest.

With her face toward Bryan, white lines running down Emma's spine caught Cole's eye. "What happened to your back?"

She spun around. "Cheerleading accident. I hate those scars. At least I can't see them."

"Cheerleading accident?" A chuckle escaped from Cole before he could stop it.

The way her forehead wrinkled above angry blue eyes let him know he shouldn't have laughed.

"It can be a dangerous sport." Bryan ruffled her wet hair with his fingers. "That must've been some tough accident and recovery. What happened?"

The anger dissipated with his words. Bryan was good with Emma. Who would've thought? They walked toward a picnic table under a grouping of trees, discussing a freak fall from a pyramid of cheerleaders. Emma had broken her back.

Here was a girl who'd endured two surgeries and months of physical therapy and who still bounced over waves, full speed with wild abandon. Emma could be more substantial than she appeared. Or maybe she was just plain nuts.

Chapter 20

Circling the trailer, Cole wound the boat strap tight to secure the boat before Coach McCoy pulled the truck up the dock. Gravel crunched under the tires, and water dripped from underneath the hull.

Once the vehicle moved on, Cole stretched out his arms to loosen his muscles. A light shade of pink started at his wrists and traveled upward to his shoulders. He slipped on his shirt and headed toward his car. Pads on top of the burn wouldn't be fun at practice tomorrow, but it had been a good day. The sun lowered toward the horizon, waves dancing on the gentle breeze. A great day, really. Maybe later, he'd get to see Audrey. The perfect ending to it all.

But he wouldn't hold his breath for that one. The way she'd reacted so strangely the other night didn't make sense. If only she trusted him enough to tell him what was going on in her head. Or maybe Grant could shed some light.

Like that would ever happen.

No. It was up to Audrey to explain what triggered those…spells.

From across the lot, Emma sent a furious wave. "Come eat with us at Pizza Gin."

Not that fiasco again. With Emma, there'd be double trouble. "No thanks. I'm wet."

Bryan's Jeep pulled between them. "Dude, I'm buying, and it's a celebration for you. Come on."

The roast from lunch a distant memory, Cole's stomach joined the begging. "Maybe."

Bryan covered one side of his mouth. "I'll run interference with Emma."

The guy must've sensed the dilemma. "You're brave, bro."

"God's got my back." Grinning, Bryan pulled away.

By the time Cole jerked into a parking spot on the Square, his body demanded to be fed. He jogged toward the entrance of the restaurant, lightheaded from hunger. Should've brought a protein bar. Could he stay upright until the food came?

His clothes, damp from lake and sweat, clung to him. Gross. Maybe his odor would keep Emma away. She and Bryan already sat at a booth, and the crowd looked thinner than it had the other night. Good. Their table was near the exit, too.

Cole slid in beside Bryan. Kind of a weird move, but it seemed safer. "Did you order, yet?"

Emma nodded. "We got appetizers to start and one pizza with all the meats for you, one pizza with veggies for Bryan. I'll take a bite or two from you both." Cocking her chin, she eyed Cole. "From both the pizzas, 'fraidie-cat."

Already with the relentless flirting. Where was his phone? He'd meant to check on the way to see if Audrey had called. Maybe he could use that as an excuse to go outside.

Bryan pushed a glass of water in front of him. "We didn't know what to order you to drink." The musician inclined his head across the table toward Emma. "So, Em, tell us who or what shut down your trust for all mankind. A dishonest guy?"

The straw in her Coke became the focus of her attention. She swirled it in her soda, sending little bubbles to the surface.

"We're not all bad, Em." He leaned further toward her, resting elbows on the dark laminate. "Maybe you haven't met the man God has in store for you. Are you praying for His will? Or running after your own?"

The dude was bold.

Emma removed the straw with her finger over the end, then released little droplets into her upturned mouth. She swallowed, twisted her lips, as if deciding whether to answer. "On my sweet sixteen birthday, my best friend hooked up with my boyfriend. I could go into all the details, but I've seen the same happen over and over again. Not just the time it happened with me. People screw each other over all the time. Lie to each other. My goodness, look at my sister. Cassie, the saint and perfect wife. Her husband cheated with anything that moved." Her chin jutted forward. "Not happening to me. If someone's gonna do the hurting, it'll be me."

Bryan's hand crossed the table to catch Emma's. "Then you become the person you hate."

Bold and honest.

Cole pictured the *relationships* he'd had, if he could call them that. He'd been plenty careless with people's emotions. Had he wrecked hearts like someone had destroyed Emma's?

~~~

The long drive home gave Audrey time to think about all that had happened in a day's time. Her uncle on death's door. Harrison gone missing, and his father going forward at church. Then hearing secondhand about Cole, seeing the pictures Grant forced in front of her eyes.

The thoughts jolted her. What had she expected? Cole would sit in his house twiddling his thumbs until she got back? Slim chance. And he'd given his life to God. She should be happy.

Meanwhile, like a pot of her grandmother's turnip greens, Grant stewed the whole way back to Oxford. He seemed to think he and Emma were in a committed relationship. Even slimmer chance of that. What would he say to Emma?

After sitting for hours, her legs itched to walk. At last, they were nearing the city limits.

"I'm hungry." Grant slowed and turned toward town. "Daddy gave me twenty dollars to buy supper. Let's pick up a pizza."

Could the guy not eat something at home? She was ready to see Cole. "I have a frozen pizza in my freezer you can have."

"Those are too small."

"You ate a whole bucket of chicken for lunch."

"I have to keep up my weight. We run it off in this heat."

If he was running any size off, it didn't show. "Can we get it to go?"

Five minutes later, they hustled toward the entrance of The Pizza Gin. They'd called ahead but still could expect a wait.

The place wasn't known for fast food, but they had great pizza. The last disastrous trip here with Cole came to mind. What a disappointment that had turned out to be. All the more reason to hurry in and out.

Grant flung the door open and held it for her. Inside the dim light, her eyes adjusted. Oh, mercy. Cole. Emma. And Bryan with his hand on Emma's. Could she block that view from Grant?

She shoved Grant toward the bar. "Can you get me a drink in a go-cup?"

He nodded and headed over to add a Coke to their order. Her nails embedded into her palms as she rushed to the table to warn poor Bryan.

"Hey, y'all. Small world."

Cole looked up, brown eyes landing on her. He jumped to his feet. "Have I got news for you." His arms drew her close. "I'm so glad you're back."

His warmth helped her fight the urge to barrage him with questions.

Emma pulled her hand from under Bryan's in the nick of time as Grant's voice rattled behind her.

"What's going on, Emma? I called you like…a few times." Her brother caught himself toward the end of the sentence. Thank goodness. But he'd made another mistake. He'd punched in Emma's number way too often.

The waitress saved Emma from answering. At least it wasn't purple-mascara-girl again.

Grant eyed their steaming hot pizza and took a good whiff.

Cole pointed to the booth. "Have a seat. I need to run out to my car and get my phone. I left it in the trunk all day. It's probably way overheated." He met Emma's eyes as if trying to send her a message—an excuse, and then grabbed Audrey's hand. "Come with me?"

Emma brought a finger to her cheek. "I know, my phone almost melted. Well, except when I had it out to take pictures. But then I put it away. Probably why I didn't get your texts or calls." She patted the seat beside her. "Sit, Grant. Tell me everything about your day. How's your poor uncle Phillip? I've been so worried."

No. Emma wasn't stupid, but why was Cole helping her cover? For that matter, why had she bothered to help?

~ ~ ~

Once outside, Cole spun Audrey in a circle, and then caught her back up in his arms. "I missed you today." He planted a kiss on her soft cheek. "Guess what?"

"I heard." Her eyes darted from his to the sidewalk. "You were baptized at the lake. I'm so happy you wanted to make a public confession of faith at church, too."

Did she doubt his feelings for her now? "I really did leave my cell in the car all day."

"I figured when Grant showed me the pictures from Emma's newsfeed of you all on the water."

Guilt gnawed at his nerves. That had to have made her feel left out. "Sorry."

She shook her head. "Looked like you had a nice time. By the way, what was going on with Bryan and Emma?"

"He's trying to convert her. I think."

Cole popped the trunk and retrieved his phone. She'd texted him. Once. Despite, or maybe because of, the pictures. "The day would've been perfect if you'd been there."

"We can go to the lake another time."

She kept her tone light, but guilt still assaulted him.

"I feel like we need to talk. Clear the air about a few things. When you… I'm confused by what happened, you know, but I want to help."

"I can't. Not tonight." A pleading look crossed her face as if she knew the exact subject matter, and it pained her. "It's already been a hard day."

He shouldn't push. After all, her uncle was sick. "Okay. But soon." Her sad expression tugged at him. "You think they'd notice if we left?"

A smile. Finally. "One can dream."

"How about we grab a couple of pieces of pizza before Grant eats it all and tell them we're outta here?"

She nodded. "Better hurry, then."

Inside, they snatched a few slices and threw them in a go-box. They said their goodbyes, leaving poor Bryan in the hot seat. Cole pushed aside any responsibility for that one.

Shoving pizza in their mouths kept them busy on the way home. A girl happy to eat in the car with him. Perfect.

As they entered the parking lot beside the condos, a fluttering, white piece of paper caught his eye on Audrey's Honda. Had she seen it? Oh, please, don't let it be something weird.

"Wait. Stop right here." She pointed with a stifled sob.

Too late. He shifted into park. "Want me to get it?"

All she seemed to manage was a weak nod. He busted out of the car, and lifted the wiper. Another note.

Easy to find.

The world shifted beneath his feet as fury shook his hands. He swiveled looking for any sign of movement. Squeezing the life out of someone came to mind—if he found out who was threatening Audrey. And he'd do his best to figure out who did this. Why would they want to scare her? Some creep, no doubt.

That must be what Audrey was so afraid of. Someone had been stalking her. Was the someone named Harrison? The name she'd screamed the other night? Maybe he'd chased her down a country road. That would explain a lot.

~~~

"I don't want to read it, and don't tell Grant." Audrey sank onto the couch and drew her knees up to her body, shock and exhaustion numbing her mind. "I can't deal with it right now."

"What about the police? Coach McCoy? We need to let them know. That's what y'all did last time." His hand moved behind her head, caressing, comforting. "We can't ignore this." He twisted in front of her to make eye contact. "I'll be here for you. You can trust me."

His eyes captivated her, slowed her pounding heart. Wouldn't she love to trust Cole? Trust herself? Trust life not to hurt so much? So far, experience had proved otherwise.

"Audrey."

The way he spoke her name, quiet but firm and full of emotion, gave her a glimpse of hope. She let out a long sigh. "Call Coach McCoy. He can ask the Oxford PD for no blue lights. No drama."

His lips pressed against her forehead. "You're brave."

If only that were true. If only she could absorb some of his confidence and still the quaking inside.

An hour later, the police and Coach McCoy cleared out of her living room and the parking lot. Only Cole remained. No sign of Emma or Grant, thank goodness, and luckily, she didn't have to rehash everything like last time. They'd only searched her condo and the grounds, finding nothing but a few crushed beer cans. No surprise in a college town.

Cole rose to his feet. "Um, I'm a mess from the day in the lake. Mind if I grab some clothes and shower? I'll be fast."

"You can go home. You're probably exhausted, and you have practice in the morning."

His hands crossed in front of him like a ref. "No way. I'll stay at least until Grant gets home next door." He pointed to the door. "Lock up. It'll only take me five minutes or less."

She nodded. A quick shower sounded good. Maybe she'd run down the hall and rinse off the smell of hospital and fried chicken while Cole was gone. "Okay."

After he left, she sprinted to the bathroom. While the water heated, she grabbed fresh clothes. In no time, she was in and out, dressed in a clean T-shirt and gym shorts. She grabbed a brush and took quick steps back to the living room. A knock on the door made her jump, even though it was probably Cole. She peered through the peephole to be sure. What a beautiful sight he was. Wet hair and all.

After he came in, she wrung her hands—a different kind of nervousness filling her. Now what? She motioned toward the bookshelves lining one wall. "Wanna watch a movie?"

"Got any comedy?"

"Laughing would be nice." She smiled. "Yeah, mostly. I don't own any horror flicks or anything like that."

He perused the videos until he settled on one. "This one's

great. Comedy and football."

"Figures. My brothers love that one." Taking the DVD from his hand, their fingers grazed. A lump caught in her throat. She swallowed at it. Three times.

Cole's eyes stared at her neck, then moved to her lips. His proximity, the look, zapped currents of longing through her. Longing to be held. Longing to trust. Longing to be brave. Her fears dropped away, and she fell into his arms, her lips reaching up to find his. She soaked in his strength, ran her hands across his shoulders. The softness of the skin covering solid muscle.

"Audrey." His voice broke as he relinquished her lips. "We should put the movie in."

A key turned in her doorknob, and Grant traipsed in.

Audrey took a quick step away from Cole.

Not Grant. Not now.

Grant's jaw fell open. "What's he doing in here and why do both of you have wet hair?" In three long strides, he covered the distance and shoved Cole's shoulder.

Popping her brother's hand, harder than she meant to, Audrey moved between them. "Stop, Grant. You don't understand."

His eyes blazed. "I think I understand well enough. Don't say I didn't warn you about him. You're on your own." Spinning toward the door, he stomped away. The walls shook as he slammed first her door, then his.

"I'll talk to my brother and straighten him out." Audrey sighed and returned her gaze to Cole. Why would any guy want to deal with their crazy baggage?

"Let it go for now. He'll cool down." He pressed a kiss on her forehead before turning toward the door. "Goodnight. Lock up after me. And if you hear *anything* weird outside, promise you'll call me."

Chapter 21

Cole's green jersey rippled in the light wind as he took the sidewalk toward the indoor practice field. Thank the Lord for any movement of the stale hot air after running drills in the sun. The other players in red and blue jerseys taking the hits had it worse, though. Only a chosen few got to wear the green that signaled a *no-hit* player.

Wade Simmons, a wide receiver, gave Cole a light shove as they entered the building. "Who's that girl that's got you wrapped, man? You never go out anymore."

Grant's head twisted their way so fast he might've blown a disk.

Better to be careful answering. "Since when are you interested in my love life?"

"Gotta keep us entertained, man." The receiver laughed. "She must be pretty good to keep you home at night."

Cole's posture stiffened. He'd never much worried about a girl's reputation until now. "Watch it, Wade."

Another player stepped forward and slapped the top of Wade's head. "You must be trippin'. You're talking about Vaughn's sister. That's why Cole's keeping his trap shut." He shoved a thumb Grant's way. "Y'all don't want none of that."

With wide eyes, the receiver stepped back. "Sorry, Grant. I didn't mean to start nothing. I mean, I didn't know him and your sister—"

Rushing the guy, Grant grabbed hold of Wade's jersey. "Him and my sister what?" An air horn sounded, and Grant released his shirt. "Shut up if you know what's good for you." Grant shot a seething look at Cole and grunted.

Or was it a growl?

Cole pulled on his helmet. *Gotta keep my head in the game. Gotta keep my head, period.*

Coach McCoy addressed the group. "Men, wake up and smell the football. No time to mess around. We gotta keep the foot on the pedal. All the way to August." He tossed a ball toward Cole. "Don't get lazy with it. Keep your feet moving."

The defensive coordinator directed his team of players. "Don't just stand around. Take it to 'em." With a clap, he sent them sprinting to their places.

At the signal, Cole ran the assigned play.

Coach McCoy yelled. "Run it again, Cole. Play like you mean it. Be strong. O-line, protect your quarterback."

Sweat dripped in Cole's eyes. He rubbed away the burning salt.

Though he wore an undershirt, the pads still rubbed against the sunburn from the day before. At least when he ran, air blew across his face. Man, he was hot.

"Watch your stance, Cole. Run it again. Vaughn, get your man."

Grant grumbled. "I got a man I'd like to take out of the game."

"Bring it. Or shut up." If Cole didn't face this challenge head on, the whole season would be a mess. It was his responsibility to keep the offense focused.

"You'd love to get me sidelined."

"I'd just love for you to play some football. Check yourself. Let's run the play right this time. Down. Set. Sixty-four. Hut. Hut."

The center made the snap. The leather secure in Cole's hands, he shuffled his feet and launched the ball to his wide receiver. Out of nowhere, a force like a travel bus knocked him to the ground. Flashes of light exploded and floated in front of his eyes, and his face grew numb.

Where was he?

The defensive tackle scrambled off of Cole and held out a hand. "Sorry, man. Grant rammed me right into you."

Cole ignored him, pushed to his feet, and staggered, blinking. Around him, sounds ricocheted, clacks and clattering of plastic, grunts and thuds and yelling. Then a loud buzzing noise.

He'd been hit hard.

Players around him traded punches. Most of the team joined the brawl with shouts and clatter reverberating in the large room. Probably his friends against Grant's. He blinked again to clear the fuzziness. His helmet must've really smacked the turf.

He wouldn't let Coach know, though. No sidelines for Cole Sanders. The air horn sounded again and again as the coaches broke up the fights.

Coach McCoy held Cole's shoulder pads with one hand and lifted his chin with the other. "Look at me. Cole. How many fingers am I holding up?"

"I'm fine, Coach. What's the next play you want me to run?"

Coach held his chin a moment longer. "We'll let the doctor decide if you're running a play."

His fists formed tight balls. If Grant cost him his starting position... "Can I run the play again and see how I feel?"

"Nope. Go see the doc."

This could not be happening. On the sidelines, Grant and another player stood with the head coach, receiving a blistering speech. Good. They deserved it. Cole marched on. He had to focus on getting things straight with the doctor. No concussion.

He spent an hour or more in the medical office. An hour he could've been practicing. Finally the doctor escorted him to Coach McCoy.

Leaving the cool of the air-conditioned office back to the practice field had him dizzy again.

All this because he'd fallen for Grant's sister. And he hadn't said anything bad about Audrey. Why'd Grant have to be such a jerk?

Maybe that was the problem. He hadn't defended Audrey, either. Cole mashed his palm to his forehead. But he hadn't had time. His brain swirled trying to make sense of things.

Coach McCoy eyed them both. "What's the verdict?"

The doctor shook his head. "Sorry, Coach. He took a good hit. Mild concussion."

The coach's mouth twisted, part frustration, part sympathy. "Get some water, Cole, and let one of the trainers take you home. Leave your keys with me. We'll bring the car to the house later." Placing his hands on both of Cole's shoulders, Coach McCoy squared off with him. "Chill tonight. You don't need to go out. And no paybacks. That's my job, and I'll handle it."

~~~

The contents of Sarah Beth's SUV spilled out when Audrey opened the passenger door.

"I'm sorry. I'll get it." Audrey fought to catch the stack of folders. Papers drifted in the light wind and floated across the condo parking lot.

After putting the vehicle in park, Sarah Beth hopped out of the driver's seat and jogged over to help. "My fault. I was dictating a letter on the phone before I came. I should've cleaned out the car instead. With all this volunteer work on the summit, I've had to stay up late and get up early to do my paying job." She giggled and shoved a file under her arm. "Who am I kidding? My SUV's like this all the time."

Once the clutter had been captured and relocated in Sarah Beth's back seat, they climbed in the car. Sarah Beth turned from side to side, leaning forward and back. "Now, where's my phone?" She buried her head under the steering wheel, searching.

Audrey held in a laugh. "Um, Sarah Beth?"

Sarah Beth lifted her head, grazing it on the dash and wheel with a thump. "Yes?"

"It's in your left hand."

"Oh, my stars. Since I've been pregnant, I do that all the time. It's like my left hand isn't part of my body. I call it preggy brain." She placed the phone on the console and fastened her seat belt. "You're probably scared to ride with me to the summit now."

Audrey shook her head as they pulled forward. "I just hate that you had to go out of your way. The police took my work schedule and patrolled here and the country club. They didn't see anyone suspicious."

"It's not a lot of trouble. Besides, you're helping out at the conference, and I'm excited you wanted to meet the speaker with me afterward. Katerina Long has an amazing ministry in Nashville that helps to rescue and restore victims of trafficking. I'd love to see the CSU get involved somehow."

"How do they help the people they save?"

"First they give medical care, clothing, and emotional counseling. Many times the women come with only the clothes on their back. Then they offer to help them find employment, but they also have an apparel shop where they can work until they find the right job. They make clothing and accessories from recycled T-shirts, old beads, all kinds of things. You know, kind of a vintage look."

"In Nashville?" The trip with Bryan might allow her to check into the ministry, even see the shop. "Bryan keeps inviting me to go there with him to meet with the agent and all. Maybe if I do, I could check it out."

They pulled into the lot, and Sarah Beth glanced at her. "Oh, Audrey. You should go."

The nagging in her stomach returned. "I don't know."

"What's stopping you? Is it too expensive?"

"He seems to have that part worked out."

The SUV came to a stop in a parking place. Sarah Beth's eyes met hers with a small smile. "Cole?"

"He says go for it."

A wrinkle formed between Sarah Beth's brows. "What is it then?"

Audrey lifted one shoulder. "Fear. Lack of confidence. Never having left home without a big brother beside me. A lot of things like that." She pulled at her door handle and exited the car.

Outside, the protesters staked their claim across the street again. A news reporter held a microphone toward the leader.

Berkley Long. But he'd shaved, revealing a jagged scar along his chin and cheek. His eyes found and followed her as he spoke. "Tonight's speaker's nothing but an old prostitute looking to find a new way to take people's money. You can't buy this load of bull she's selling." His hand ran across his face. "Look what the crazy woman did. She tried to kill me. I'm just a man who believes in freedom and privacy. Those are our rights."

That was the reason the man worked so hard to fight this summit. He'd said his ex-wife gave him that scar. She must've been spilling his secrets.

And he said I look like her.

"How does that creep live with himself?" Sarah Beth took Audrey's elbow. "He's so pervy, he freaks me out. Let's hurry."

~ ~ ~

As the conference ended, Sarah Beth led Audrey backstage. Goodness, the woman knew and spoke to everyone and their brother along the way. Who could help but love the quirky beauty that was Sarah Beth McCoy?

Once they reached one of the smaller offices, Sarah Beth came to an abrupt halt and tapped on the door left ajar. "It's me."

A second later, the door opened wider, revealing Katerina Long. "Come in. Pull up a chair so we can talk."

Up close, exhaustion etched Katerina's features, but she still exuded a quiet strength. A scar ran across her forehead under the edge of her brown bangs. Freckles covered her nose and cheeks below her brown eyes. Audrey touched her own face.

We do look alike.

An hour later, Katerina finished telling the story of life under the thumb of Berkley Long. Exploited as a young girl in Russia and trafficked to the U.S., the poor soul married the evil man after some kind of monetary trade he made with her pimp. She'd hoped to escape life as a prostitute. Living with an abusive husband proved to be just as dangerous.

Audrey had to know more. "How did you escape, Katerina?"

"One night, I fought back, not caring if I lived or died. I knew I must be free one way or another. When I tried to leave, he struck me across my forehead with a broken beer bottle. We struggled, and I ended up with the jagged broken glass. I did what I had to do to escape his grasp. We both bear the scars." Katerina lifted her bangs to fully reveal the mark.

"I took evidence with me that may eventually convict him. I handed it over to the FBI. They are building a case. With help from a church and God's grace, I started a new life and later a ministry helping other women that had been through similar traumas."

Audrey sat up straight. In that moment, the realization fell on her like a pine tree in an ice storm. She could use the bad in her life to help others. "I've lived in fear so long because of something that happened in high school, but I want to be like you. Strong. Able to help others."

"God is my strength." Katerina pressed a hand on Audrey's forearm. "When will you graduate from the University? I could use someone on the business side of the ministry, perhaps to find grants and promote fundraising, run the social media."

Clapping her hands, Sarah Beth stood. "Audrey would be perfect, and I can help her get started while she's still in school here." Her clapping slowed. "If she decides to work for you and vice versa. Sorry, I get excited." Her stomach rumbled. "And hungry." From a large bag on her arm, Sarah Beth pulled out a package of sour gummy worms and pushed a wad into her mouth. "Mmm. Y'all want some?"

Katerina laughed, a beautiful, strong laugh. Then she rose and retrieved her wallet. "No, thank you, but I'll give Audrey my card. Come to Nashville, visit, and pray about God's plan for your life."

"I will." Audrey read the card. *Empowered Hearts.* Exactly what she desired. To be empowered.

If they were leaving soon, she needed to text Cole. There was no sense having Sarah Beth drive her around.

Are you still picking me up? I'll be ready to leave soon.

After hugs, Sarah Beth and Audrey left the coliseum. A new

bounce lifted Audrey's steps.

Cole hadn't answered, so Sarah Beth stood with her, waiting.

Darkness covered the almost empty lot, but freedom from fear bolstered her heart and mind. She would be free one way or another, like Katerina.

Sarah Beth jangled her keys. "Let me drive you. It's not like Oxford's that big."

"Sure. Cole may've fallen asleep. We stayed up and talked for so long, plus he said he took a spill at practice. Which seems odd considering he's a no-hit player."

Once inside the SUV again, Sarah Beth turned to her. "What are you thinking about Empowered Hearts?"

Audrey met her friend's gaze. "I want to check it out. Do research. This may be the type of career I've been looking for."

"Going with Bryan next week would give you the opportunity, right?"

"Will you pray for me to make the right decision?"

"Of course, I will." Sarah Beth turned the key and put the vehicle in gear. "Because I know all about running off and doing things my way. You're smart to pray first."

"Thanks. Then I need to be willing to listen to the answer."

With a snort, Sarah Beth slapped the wheel. "There's that, too. I've tried to run from the answers. I'm so stubborn. If it weren't for people like my good friend, Juan, and a few others, I'd have missed the chance to see God making beauty from the ashes of my life."

Beauty from ashes. The scripture sounded familiar. "Does that come from Isaiah?"

"Chapter sixty-one."

"I'm going to read that tonight and pray."

They rode with only the quiet background of the Christian music station the rest of the way. Lost in thought, the gentle roll to a stop near the sidewalk took Audrey by surprise. "Oh. We're back. Thanks for the ride. I'm not sure why Cole didn't show up. Or Grant. His truck's right there." She pointed across the lot.

"I enjoyed hanging out." Sarah Beth parked and cracked her door. "I'll walk you in. I have my stun gun under the back seat."

"I'm not letting a pregnant woman protect me." Audrey held up her keys and twisted the top of the pepper spray. "Grant bought me this, and I'll run to the door."

"I'll watch until you go inside."

With that, Audrey opened the door and jogged down the sidewalk. She waved as she entered the condo, and Sarah Beth drove away.

As soon as the door closed, she threw her purse on the table. Her wallet spilled out. But, where were her check and tips from this morning? Her head must've been in the clouds when she left work. The envelope probably still lay on her front seat. Good gracious. She needed that money. She wasn't leaving it in plain sight all night for someone to steal.

Grabbing the key ring and her phone, she ran back out toward the parking lot

Chapter 22

The room spun, and Cole gripped the arm of the couch to pull himself into a sitting position. What time was it? Was his car back in the lot yet? He'd texted Grant about bringing Audrey home from the summit just in case. Or had he? The ache in his head reminded him to take it slow as he rose to his feet. He must've fallen asleep. Exactly what the doctor told him not to do. Why did Grant have to pull that mess?

He checked his phone.

Audrey had texted.

Are you still picking me up? I'll be ready to leave soon.

Crud. That was forty-five minutes ago. He scanned his other texts. He did send the message to Grant. Hopefully, he'd made it in time. What if he hadn't and some creep had attacked Audrey?

Cole scrambled to yank open the nearest blinds. Thank goodness. A light shone in Audrey's window, but he still needed to check on her and explain what happened.

Outside, the change from light to dark threw him off kilter. It took a bit longer than normal for his vision to adjust. When his sight cleared, movement in the parking lot caught his eye. Better not be that stalker. Concussion or not, the guy would get a butt-kicking if he found him.

~ ~ ~

The sound of crushing aluminum sent a chill through Audrey, and her ribs froze in place, holding her breath midway as she inhaled.

"You do look like Katerina. Only younger. Innocent." The voice held a bitter edge. "And afraid."

Audrey spun to find Berkley standing between her car and the condo. Her paycheck and tips fell from her hand, but she squeezed the key ring with the pepper spray. "I'm going inside now."

"Yeah. Inside my car. Let's go." He dropped a crushed beer can and reached toward her with one hand. "You can't believe the lies Kat told you. She's crazy. I took good care of her, gave her all the money she could ever need, and she threw it back in my face. Right along with a broken beer bottle." He traced the line of his scar with the other hand.

Audrey stepped backwards. "I'm not Katerina, and you need to leave." Her fingers fumbled with the lid of the pepper spray. She should've practiced with it. Her heartbeat pounded in her ears as the smell of sour beer reached her nose. She pivoted to run, but arms clamped around her waist, tore her from the ground. He carried her toward a polished black car.

Her scream ripped the air as she kicked and clawed to break free.

Throwing her back on her feet, he spun her around and backhanded her across the mouth. "Shut up if you want to live."

Her neck jerked left, the ground spinning beneath her as he grabbed her up again.

Then as quickly as he'd attacked, he released her. She pressed one hand to her mouth and looked around.

Muscular arms encased Berkley's neck. "Run, Audrey!" Two men wrestled and punched. What was happening?

Her heart pumped, and her vision blurred.

Hands grabbing. The dirt. The field. The humiliation, shame, and pain. She couldn't breathe.

No!

Lord help me. I won't be a victim again.

Her phone. Where was it? She fell on her hands and knees and searched the warm asphalt. Her fingers held a cylinder. The pepper spray.

Save Cole.

Cole. That's who was fighting with the man. She needed to help him.

Call 911.

Her hand landed on her phone. Her fingers shook as she pressed the numbers, then she stood.

"911. What's your emergency?"

"Send help to the parking lot of Old Colonial Condos. Quick!"

Adrenaline soared through her as she dropped the phone and ran toward Berkley and Cole. How could she spray one without hitting the other? The bodies slammed against her car. Cole's head bounced against the roof. He groaned and slumped to the ground.

A laugh surged from Berkley. Pure evil. Then he turned to face her. "Now. Get in my car or my foot's crushing your boyfriend's head."

She took one step toward him. Was she close enough? She lifted the canister, aimed at his eyes, and pressed as hard as she could.

The liquid sprayed between them and nailed the mark. Berkley cursed and covered his face with his hands. Audrey pressed the pump again and again. She didn't stop spraying his head until every drop emptied. He grabbed blindly for her, spewing obscenities.

When would the police arrive?

Please, God, we need help.

A second later an Oxford taxi pulled into the lot. When the door slid open, Grant stepped out, and Emma tumbled behind him, giggling.

He staggered over. "What in the world?"

"Grant! The notes on my car. This man attacked me. Cole tried to stop him, but he needs help. I sprayed the pepper spray and called the police."

"I'll kill him!" Grant roared.

Somehow Berkley opened his eyes to a squint. One look at Grant and he stumbled toward his vehicle.

Emma jogged over to Cole. "What happened? Should I call an ambulance?"

Audrey bent to her knees and touched Cole's face. "Cole, are you okay? Can you hear me?"

He groaned and opened his eyes.

A few feet away, Grant lifted the attacker off the ground and banged him against a car.

Blue lights approached, sirens blaring.

Audrey held her phone to her ear. "Cole, I'm calling an ambulance."

He pushed himself to a sitting position and clutched her arm. "No. You can't. Football. No doctors."

"But, Cole. You hit your head."

"No. Please. No. And don't tell Coach. Please, I'm begging you."

Chapter 23

Four officers restrained Grant as he bellowed at Berkley Long. "Mister, you messed up when you crossed a Vaughn. Not only do you have me, my brother, and my father who'll haunt you the rest of your life, I've got friends from football in every state around here. You better not show your sorry self in the South. And let me tell you something else. Next year, I'll be pro, and I'll use every dime I have to make your life miserable."

The police handcuffed the horrid man and put him into the squad car, but Grant kept yelling. "Real men don't have to hurt women to prove they're men. I hope you find out what that's like in prison."

Audrey touched Emma's hand. "Can you go settle him down? Tell him I'm fine. That he and Cole saved me."

She took a step away but stopped. "Audrey, I'd say you saved Cole, too. Looks like you about turned that snake's skin two shades redder than scarlet with that pepper spray, girl."

"I never meant for this to happen. Grant's got to learn to control his temper and the guilt that eats away at him. Learn to forgive."

With a pitying look that flattened Audrey's defenses, Emma chewed her lower lip. "I know. Grant told me about—"

"Not now, Emma." How could Grant tell this girl? It wasn't his business to share, especially with her. Audrey clamped her jaw together, then winced with pain from Berkley's blow to her mouth.

"Sorry. I won't mention it again." Emma turned and jogged to Grant.

Audrey refocused her attention on Cole. She ran her hand across each arm and leg to check for injuries. Her hands moved across his chest and back. "Does any of this hurt?"

"No. He didn't land any punches worth mentioning. Only my head hit the car." His voice registered little more than a whisper.

"You need to get checked by a doctor. You were out cold." She touched his cheek. "Do you feel nauseated?"

"No."

Another whisper. His head must hurt something fierce. Dread and guilt squeezed at Audrey's gut. He'd been injured fighting for her. She couldn't let him ignore it.

Grant and Emma appeared beside them, and Grant held out a hand to lift Cole from the ground. "Thanks for saving my sister."

"Thanks for finishing the job. That guy's scum." He tottered as he caught his balance.

Maybe Grant could talk some sense into Cole. "Don't you think Cole should go to the hospital and get a CT or MRI? He hit his head really hard."

"No. I can't." Cole's voice rose, but not without pain pressing his lips and eyes into narrow lines. "I already fell today, and I don't want to be sent to the sidelines for any longer than I already have been."

Strange glances passed between Grant and Cole, and then Grant took a step closer. "Cole knows what he wants. The doctor's gonna be looking at him the next few days anyway. Keep an eye on him all night tonight. Keep him awake. If he throws up or something, come get me. Better yet, watch him at my place. Y'all can hang out on my couch."

"I know." Emma giggled. "Let's stay up watching movies all night."

Still feeling shaken from the attack, the idea of watching movies beside Emma sank in Audrey's gut like a brick in a fish pond. "Um, I don't know. Cole's bound to have an aching head. Better to keep things quiet."

~ ~ ~

The headache that plagued Cole earlier in the day didn't hold a candle to the one pounding against his skull now. He steadied himself by leaning against the hood of the car and assured the EMTs once more he didn't need to go to the hospital.

A dull halo wrapped the streetlights in the parking lot. Audrey's gentle hold on his arm gave him strength. Somehow, with God's help, they'd saved each other. And thank goodness she'd turned Emma down on the all-night movie marathon. The sad puppy look on Emma's face almost had him feeling sorry for her. Almost.

The policeman who'd taken their statements came by. "We'll need y'all to come to the station and press charges. Sorry. I know it's been a rough night and you boys have practice in the morning. I'll make sure it goes as fast as possible." He tapped his phone with his index finger. "I have to call the coaches and the chancellor. The media will likely get wind of this." His rough voice sounded apologetic.

Sweat rolled down Cole's back. Could he fake it another hour? He'd have to.

Audrey rubbed his arm. "I'll drive all of us to the station in my car. I've got my keys and wallet out here in the parking lot somewhere."

Grant and Emma searched the ground. Popping up, Emma held a handful of bills. "Ooow money."

"That would be my tips from work. I'll share, though, if you find my paycheck."

Cole bent his head forward to try to help. It felt like his brain hit his eyeballs. Never mind the search for a few bucks. "I'll give you double the amount if we don't have to look for it."

A second later, Grant lifted a piece of paper. "Got the check. Let's go get this done. Maybe we can get in and out before the coaches show up." Grant opened the back door of the Honda, letting Emma in first then squeezing beside her. The big guy filled the back of the small car.

Audrey opened the front passenger door for him. "Here, let me help you." Her hand never left his waist until he was seated, then she buckled the seat belt for him.

"Thanks." Doubtful they'd beat anyone as slow as he was

moving.

Even the gentle motion of Audrey's driving nauseated him. Finally, they came to a stop. Another mile, and he'd have hurled.

The bright lights of the station slashed at Cole's eyes. He squinted as he walked. *Please let this be over soon.*

The officer presented them each a hard, straight-back chair. He'd almost rather lie on the tile floor. Especially if he could shut his eyes.

"Let's start at the beginning." The policeman's gravelly voice echoed in Cole's head. "The young lady went outside first, right?"

Audrey nodded. "I'd left my tips and paycheck in the car. I grabbed my phone and keys which had the pepper spray on the ring. I ran and retrieved my money but found that man standing between me and my condo. He grabbed me." She paused and swallowed hard. "I screamed, then he hit me—"

"That's when we got there." Grant stood and paced. "And I got hold of that creep."

Cole leaned his elbows on his knees and rested his head against his hands.

Behind Grant, Coach McCoy took quick steps to reach them. So much for leaving before the coaches arrived. "I got here as soon as I could. Audrey, are you injured?"

"No, sir."

His eyes turned to Cole. "Anyone else hurt?"

Grant stepped between them. "I took care of the guy before he could do any real damage."

So Grant was covering for him. Interesting turn of events after the guy threw a two-hundred-fifty pound human on top of him earlier in the day.

Not easily convinced, Coach McCoy looked to the officer. "Is that how it went down?"

"Yep. That fellow'd be a fool to mess around in this town again. We have him held on multiple charges, including attempted kidnapping."

Coach McCoy sniffed twice and whispered. "Did one of

you drink a beer?"

I guess I owe Grant for not telling about my second head injury of the day. "The obvious choice would be me on that one." He hadn't lied, but he hadn't told the truth either.

"You can't drink after a whack on the head like you took at practice."

Cole ran a hand across his forehead. "Not even one beer?"

"None." Coach McCoy pulled up the chair Grant had vacated. "Look at me, Cole. The scouts are watching you. And Grant, too, of course. There's pressure with that, but playing around with a head injury is serious business. You take care of yourself or not going pro will be the least of your worries. There is life off the field."

Cole forced a smile. "Right, Coach. I'll take it easy and follow the doctor's orders."

~ ~ ~

Audrey sighed and fell onto Grant's couch. The police had been true to their word and gotten them out quicker than expected. Of course, not before Coach McCoy had questioned them. Grant did most of the talking, leaving out the part about Cole's blow to the head.

Boys. Why did football have to be more important than their health? And why would those two cover for each other? Maybe she'd never understand their species. One thing she understood. Freedom found her tonight when she fought back. The hope of freedom released her from the fear that haunted her.

Was it God nudging and directing her to help Cole? It had to have been. The timing for Grant and the police to arrive seemed orchestrated by His hand as well.

Thank you, Lord.

Cole took a seat beside her, and she placed a throw cushion on her lap. "Lay down and rest. I'm going to watch over you tonight. No objections allowed."

"I give. Hold me." Kicking his feet around, he let his head mush into the pillow.

She met his gaze. "Until the sun rises, I won't let go."

Grant trudged in, threw his keys on the table with a clack, and disappeared down the hall. "Wake me if you need me." His door squeaked and shut.

Thank goodness. Maybe the Grant drama was over for good. She and Cole sighed in unison. She laughed and touched his lips with her fingers.

Neither of them would have to talk to stay awake. The currents running between them as they gazed into each other's eyes, so near to each other, could've lit up all of Oxford.

Now might be the time to tell him about Harrison. But the night had already been so mentally exhausting for them both. *No.* She'd wait until he felt better. Getting upset would only make things worse.

She swept back the strands of golden brown hair from Cole's forehead, the softness igniting her fingertips. How could she love him so much, so quickly? Seeing him on the ground tonight cut as if a razor had sliced right through her heart. A sight she never wanted to see again. How would she make it through football season? She'd have a little talk with her big brother. He'd better keep Cole from getting sacked.

"Audrey." His voice cracked.

"Yeah. What's wrong?"

"Grant's right about me. I've done all the things he's accused me of. Partying, hookups, locker talk…looking at porn. Before Honduras, anyway."

"Cole, don't—"

His golden eyes glistened. "No, Audrey. You have to go into a relationship knowing the truth."

Her heart quickened. *Relationship.* She needed to tell him her own truth and soon. "I understand, but you've given your life to Christ, and His grace covers all that. You're a new creation in Him."

"So long as you know what you're getting into."

Tears pressed in the corners of her eyes. Her voice caught in her tight throat. "I know."

Cole caught her hand and brought it to his lips. "I love you. Thanks for taking care of me."

"I love you. And I love taking care of you."

The night passed with a few short naps. She set a timer and checked Cole over and over to make sure he was okay.

Wouldn't it be nice to hold Cole Sanders every night for the rest of her life? But why would she think he was ready to settle down? With her?

His eyes blinked, then opened. "Do you ever think about the future? Us?"

So freaky. Did I say settle down out loud? "Yes." Better to keep the answer short.

The corners of his lips rose a fraction. "Okay. Where're we going?"

Was that a trick question? "Today?"

His eyes never left hers. "You know that's not what I mean. Where do you see our relationship going?"

Audrey scrunched her face. "Oh, have mercy, boy. You first."

A tremble shook his chest as he laughed. "Don't make me laugh. It hurts." His palm cupped her cheek. "Okay. I'd like a future with you. Tonight, when I saw that man grab you, I knew I couldn't live without you. I mean, we graduate in May. To be together after that might require some planning because I'm hoping to go pro."

More football. More seeing him get clobbered. "Every boy's dream—professional sports."

"What about you? If I'm drafted..." His eyes studied her, searching, penetrating. "Would you be willing to follow me from field to field? I'd make enough, you wouldn't have to work if you didn't want to. Of course, I'd support you pursuing a career, too, if you like."

Audrey's heartbeat zoomed into overdrive. Was he saying he'd marry her? He hadn't said the words. "Depends on what you mean."

"I mean—"

A door creaked open down the hall. "How's the invalid?" Grant walked in and stared at them. "Have y'all not moved?"

Oh, Grant. Why now?

Chapter 24

Morning came, and Grant drove away in his big red truck with Cole riding shotgun. A strange sight. Audrey ran her fingers through her hair. Exhaustion wracked her every move. A ponytail and no makeup would have to do for the meeting with Bryan. He was just a friend. Why fix up?

Beside her car, four quarters rested on the concrete near the back tire. An angry reminder of last night's reality. A few feet away, Cole had collapsed to the ground. A shiver tore through her. *Thank you, God. Things could've been so much worse.*

Leaving the quarters on the ground, she eased into the car to head toward Bryan's. Those quarters made her sick. They weren't worth what they'd almost cost her.

The drive passed with thoughts of her conversation with Cole this morning. Did he want a future with her? Could this be real? Could her dream of love come true? Her breath hitched. Oh, but she loved Cole. So much it hurt.

She checked the address. Bryan lived on a street she'd never had reason to travel her three years in the town. The dead-end road lined with ramshackle and mismatched wooden houses held little of the quaint charm surrounding the Square.

She pressed the brake and stared at the duplex corresponding with the address. Dilapidated would be a compliment. The green color of the panels covering the exterior reminded her of something her little brother's black lab threw up. A ripped screen covered one of the windows near a dangling light bulb on the front porch. And the shape of the building. Was it round or octagon? At least the yard appeared cared for. She pulled closer to the curb and parked with a chuckle. What would Emma think?

Bryan burst through the front—and possibly only—door, a

broad smile brightening his blue eyes. He *was* a cutie, and Grant would much rather she go out with a guy like Bryan. Too bad for her big brother that her heart didn't flutter for the singer.

"You found my pad." Bryan gave a broad stroke with his hand toward the structure. "I call it retro-seventies-time-warp. Or the ugliest architecture ever created by man."

Audrey took in his lean form. Plain white T and straight jeans topping black sneakers. So different from the jock style she'd grown up with. But still masculine.

When they reached the door, he swung it open and waited for her to enter. "Welcome to my humble abode. Not to be confused with a commode."

She couldn't help but chuckle. An old leather couch full of cracks sagged under the window, flanked by two lop-sided laminate end tables. A huge lamp in the shape of a leg graced one of them. "Is that, like, from that movie about the little boy and the BB gun?"

"Yep. Couldn't pass it up at a garage sale." Bryan cocked his head and smiled. "You know that movie? One of my favorites."

"I have two brothers who think it's hilarious. We watch it every year at Christmas."

"Us, too." He nudged her elbow. "We're like soul siblings, you and me."

Was he hitting on her? She was only here for singing. "So where are we practicing?"

He pointed. "Dining room."

Until then, she hadn't noticed the veritable music store in the room beyond—piano, keyboard, electric guitar, bass, acoustic guitar, and more. All lined up where most normal people would place a kitchen table and chairs. "Do you eat on your piano?"

"The couch is easier to clean. And replace." One shoulder lifted as did one corner of his mouth. He nodded toward the couch. "Found it on the side of the road last May. Find one every year."

"Saving all your cash for those?" She eyed the instruments.

"Every last penny. Hence the dump you've been brave enough to enter. Plus the fact that my parents believe us kids appreciate college more if we pay for it ourselves."

At the piano bench, he picked up sheet music and leaned it against the rack. "Have a seat. Or stand. Your call."

She situated herself on the bench, and he stood next to her. For an hour they sang and laughed. His quiet manner and stunning voice soothed away thoughts of her harrowing night. Only worries for Cole's injury nagged at her peace.

At the end of the last printed music sheet, Bryan clapped his hands. "And a good time was had by all. I'd say that's a wrap." He paused. "That's a wrap."

Audrey took him in. What talent. And funny. "So, it's a wrap then?"

After leaning his guitar against the wall, he joined her on the piano bench. "Except, I'd love to chat if you have a sec."

Was this where things turned bad?

"An awkward silence ensued." He chuckled at his own joke while his fingers hovered over the keys. "What happened to your face? I couldn't help but notice the bruise. Everything okay with you and the studly jock?"

Her hand went to her mouth. No wonder he wanted to talk. She'd forgotten about her swollen lip. "It wasn't Cole who did this."

"Whew." Bryan shook his fist in the air. "I'd hate to have to go kick his behind."

The vision sent a chortle through her chest and out her mouth before she could stop it.

His jaw dropped. "Don't laugh about it in front of me. Although we both know how that fight would end." He flexed his bicep. "I'd give it my all for you, though."

"Sorry and thanks for caring. I think Grant's got all that covered." Her eyebrows shot up. "And speaking of my big brother, what's up with you and Emma?"

His head shook so hard, a strand of hair fell down over one eye. "Whoa. Nothing. It's just...I can tell there's something going on with her. Everyone has a story, baggage that makes them who they are. Emma's no different, and I sense she needs help." He placed his hand on hers. "Not as much as you, though."

"What?" How could he presume to know her? She slid her hand away.

"Your music. The words. Something dark and evil hurt you. Almost broke you, but you didn't give up." His eyes locked with hers. Could the guy read minds? "Although you're not finished healing yet. That's why you write these." He nodded toward the sheet music. "Maybe you need to share your pain with others to mend."

Hadn't she wanted to do that? After talking to Katerina, she'd wished she could use the evil for good. To be like Katerina and share her story to help others. Maybe Bryan was a good person to start with. He always made her feel safe.

She took a deep breath and let it blow through her lips. "Okay. The only person I've talked about this with is my counselor. But I'll try."

"Would it be better if I moved across the room?" He stood and took a step away.

Her throat tightened. "I don't know." What difference did it make? "The short version is I lost my virginity to date-rape. Grant's best friend. Graduation night."

Bryan's usual smile vanished as his eyes darkened. "I'm so sorry. No one deserves that. Especially not you." With cautious movements, he sat beside her again. "Do you feel like sharing the long version?"

Her hands rubbed across her eyes and forehead. She wouldn't cry. "I want to be able to share. To help others. I'll try."

"Take your time."

She mashed her eyes shut as she went back to that place. A bonfire blazed, lighting up the dark night, reflecting off the silent Warrior River. The smell of wood and smoke and mud mingled with the laughter and voices of classmates.

Harrison stood across the crackling fire. His eyes found hers. For years, her face had warmed when those eyes turned her way. She dreamed of what it would be like to kiss the hottest guy in school—her brother's best friend, Harrison Walden. "After graduation, we had a bonfire by the river. I'd always had a crush on a friend of Grant's." She opened her eyes and turned toward Bryan. "Every girl did. He was the star quarterback and Mr. Everything at our school."

Bryan's eyebrows shot up. "Kind of like...?"

"Yeah. Like Cole." Audrey stared at her fingers. The memory of her excitement when Harrison walked over sickened her. "He asked me if I wanted to go for a ride in his truck." She swallowed back a bitter taste in her mouth. "I did. I hoped to kiss him."

"You did nothing wrong. You know that."

"I sent Grant a text that Harrison was taking me home." She took a shaky breath. "We all lived down the same country road out in Walker County. But Harrison pulled off onto a dirt road that led to a field. We used to mud ride there sometimes." Her hands wrung around each other, squeezing. "I knew he was taking me parking. I was even excited." Pain slammed her twisting stomach. What an idiot she was. Why had she let him take her home?

"Still. People go parking, Audrey. It didn't give him the right."

The dark. The field. Hands. "As soon as he turned off the car, he...changed. There was nothing romantic. All animal. Grabbing." Her chest filled with a strangled breath. "I said no. Stop." She squeezed her hands into fists. "I opened the truck door and started running back toward the main road, pressing Grant's number in my phone. Harrison grabbed me. Tackled me, really. Dirt. Hands everywhere. I fought. I did."

Bryan's hand clutched the ball her fists had made. "You said no. He was wrong."

"I guess the call to Grant went through." Her breathing slowed. "Grant and this girl fishtailed down that road. Their lights on us." Hot tears ran down Audrey's cheeks. "Grant punched Harrison over and over. I laid there. Just watching. No feelings about any of it. Like a movie playing with no sound. It made no sense."

Bryan's arms wrapped around her. Warm and kind. And safe. "Oh, Audrey. You were in shock."

"A shotgun blast ripped through the air. Blue lights. The girl with Grant had called the sheriff. Ambulances came and our parents...so humiliating."

"None of it was your fault." He squeezed tighter. "You are innocent, Audrey."

A heavy sigh pressed through her lips. "No one is innocent. Not completely. I was stupid then, and I'm probably deluding myself again."

"Look." Bryan released her hands and lifted her chin. "Just because one guy was a sicko doesn't mean every guy you meet is like that." He smiled. A genuine sort of smile. "Not even every quarterback. I like you, Audrey. I won't lie. And I'd like to get to know you as more than a friend, if you're ever free." He shook his head. "But Cole isn't a rapist. Don't let that be an excuse to run from him."

Excuse? That wasn't what she was doing. "I won't." She wiped her wet cheeks and gave an awkward chuckle. "You should be like a counselor or a minister."

He blinked twice. "Maybe like a singing therapist?"

Her laugh came easier. "Yeah."

"It could work. Concert psychotherapy with Bryan and Audrey. Nice."

"And original." She searched his face for any trace of awkwardness or judgment. Nothing. Why did she trust this guy so much? "I should go. But thanks."

"I'll walk you out." He followed her through the door to her car. "Let's sing the songs we worked on at Chris's tonight."

She nodded, but she'd forgotten about family night in all the drama.

"Can you leave for Nashville Thursday?"

"Yeah. I've already asked Ivy to take my shifts at the Country Club." She glanced at him. "And you're sure you don't mind if we visit the ministry I told you about?"

"I'd love to. Now it all makes sense. God can use you to

help others through your music and your testimony."

As she shut the car door, the scripture Sarah Beth had quoted came back to her. She'd looked it up this morning after Cole left. Two phrases stood out. *Beauty for ashes and to proclaim freedom for the captives.*

A stirring in her heart washed over her. Was her mission to proclaim freedom for the captives of sexual violence and exploitation?

Chapter 25

Standing on the sidelines never settled well with Cole. He paced, ignoring the pleas from the trainers to be still. No matter how many times he asked, they still said no when he begged to run a few plays. Didn't they understand his brain might explode if he had to stay off the field all week? Or maybe even for thirty more minutes.

The lack of activity grated on every nerve. All Grant's fault. No doubt the stalker never would've gotten the best of him last night if he hadn't suffered the first ridiculous injury. Cole let his eyelids close. Tired didn't begin to describe how he felt. But the memories of his talk with Audrey soothed away some of the pain and fatigue.

He'd admitted he wanted a future with her. An audible call. And he'd meant it. They were both adults—old enough to marry. A small shiver ran across his shoulders. Such a scary word. *Marriage.* Despite only dating her a few weeks, he wanted to marry Audrey, no matter the fear commitment roused in his mind. He'd never meant for this to happen. Never meant to fall in love. But holding Audrey was like holding life, and he wasn't going to fumble that away.

Dr. Marlow caught Cole's elbow. "You okay?"

"I told y'all, I'm fine." Even though his head still drummed, and dizziness swarmed his sight every few minutes. Still fine enough to play football.

The doctor held Cole's chin between his thumb and index finger and stared at him. "You have a funny expression on your face."

Laughing, Cole pulled his chin away. "Thinking about my girlfriend."

"Girlfriend? Unexpected concept for you. Serious?"

"Very."

One side of Dr. Marlow's mouth curled upward. "That explains the bizarre expression. No medicine to cure you. Good luck."

After three more hours of pacing and brutal frustration, the coaches sent the players home. Grant strode up, his hair plastered to his head, sweat and grime covering his practice uniform. Cole sighed. If only he could be the one covered in all that sweat and dirt. He missed looking through the bars of his helmet, being in the huddle with his teammates, analyzing the defense, then leading the charge. The adrenaline. The battle for the field.

They trudged to the truck without talking. Once inside, the motor rumbled to life, then Grant turned and faced Cole. "I shouldn't have..." His teeth clamped together.

Almost an apology. Had to be hard for Grant, and probably all Cole would get. "You love Audrey, but I do, too."

A grunt came from Grant's side of the vehicle. "Yeah. I see that now." He shifted into drive and pulled out of the lot. "Still wouldn't have picked you out to date my sister. She deserves to be treated special—by a nice guy. But she chose you. So..."

An insult tucked inside the acceptance, but he'd take it. "So you won't try to scramble my brains anymore?"

"Nah." His massive shoulders shrugged. "Not the Christian thing to do." He cut his eyes toward Cole with a hint of a smile. "Not good for the team either. Backup quarterback doesn't have your speed."

Cole nodded. "I noticed. He's got a good arm, though." The muscles down his trunk tensed at the thought of his replacement. The pro scouts would evaluate come August first, and he needed to be at his best. "I'm ready to get back on the field."

~ ~ ~

Telling Bryan about the rape both cleansed and pained Audrey's soul. The memories of the days right after the attack plagued her thoughts. Not eating. Showering over and over. Wearing baggy sweats even while the temperatures soared outside. Locking herself in her room with the guilt and blame that wore heavy on her, like a blanket of dirt.

Did she deserve what happened? She'd asked herself time and again. Her head told her one thing, but another accusing voice whispered something different.

Worst of all, for the longest time, she couldn't stand to be touched. Not even by her mother and father. Months of counseling helped, for the most part.

How long would the poor women who came to Katerina's ministry need counseling after years of abuse? Audrey flipped open her laptop to search for information on helping victims of heinous crimes. She scanned a few sites. Too bad she hadn't majored in psychology.

Katerina said counselors were already in place. Empowered Hearts needed business and fundraising help. Strange that God could use Audrey's business and marketing skills in this way. No. Not really strange. He was good like that.

She checked her phone. The guys should be back from practice. Rushing to the full-length mirror in the hall, she ran her fingers through her hair. After leaving Bryan's, she'd taken the time to straighten her boring brown mane and apply makeup. This was as good as it got.

Ten minutes later, Grant's door shut with a thud, vibrating the connecting wall. They were home. When would Cole call? Would he need to rest, or was he planning to go to Chris's for family night? He had to be exhausted.

At least three times she peeked out the window. She needed to take a deep breath and chill.

The Bible lay open to the page she'd read earlier. She looked back through Isaiah sixty-one, lingering over the last part of verse one.

He has sent me to bind up the brokenhearted, to proclaim freedom for the captives and release from darkness for the prisoners.

Therapy served its purpose, but ultimately God would set the wounded soul free.

A knock on her door sent her heart fluttering. She forced her legs to take slow steps. Sucking in a deep breath, she turned the knob and pulled.

Cole's penetrating stare stole the air from her chest—literally took her breath away. Then he smiled. Those full lips. She couldn't wait to kiss them again.

His fingers slid through her hair. "Hey. You look pretty."

Breathe, silly, and speak. "Thanks." Staring at his face never got old, but she should probably say something else. "You need to skip out on Chris's tonight and rest?"

"No way. I want to be with you before Bryan steals you away for a whole week." He pulled her into his arms and leaned his forehead against hers. "I hope he doesn't steal you away all together."

"He won't."

A few feet from them, Grant's door opened, and he stepped out. "Y'all can ride with me and Emma since you didn't get any sleep."

Not what she had in mind. But arguing with Grant when he was being civil to Cole made no sense.

Cole gave her a knowing look, so she pulled away and nodded. "We're ready."

Five minutes later, they loaded into the truck, and Emma launched into an update on her sister, Cassie, and her fiancé, actor Dylan Conner. "Dylan's coming back from location to meet our extended family. My parents, my other weird older sister, and more relatives will be here this weekend. Y'all *have* to come to the party with me. I'll be bored if you don't. Cassie said I could bring a guest. Or two." She eyed Cole.

Would the girl ever give up? How could Grant miss her obvious flirting?

Audrey clicked her tongue. "I'll be in Nashville for a week, so I can't make it."

Emma turned her lips down in a pout. "Oh, pooh. I hate that. How about you guys?"

"I'm in." Grant grinned and chanced a glance at Emma.

Which Emma didn't notice because she stared at Cole. "You know Dylan would love to see y'all again. He talked on and on about the mission trip. The three of us can ride over together."

No answer came from Cole. It looked like he smothered a yawn. Poor guy. Tired and put in an awkward position.

"It's cool if you go," Audrey whispered. "I'm sure Dylan would like to see you."

Cole leaned close. "What about Grant? We're finally getting along."

His breath fluttered her hair, sending chill bumps down her back. Her brain fogged. What had he asked her?

The truck rolled to a stop at the CSU. Grant shut it down and then turned to face Cole. "Come with us. I've never met Emma's dad, but I hear he's called Big Roy and carries a pistol."

Perspiration beaded on Grant's nose. Was he suddenly nervous about his relationship with Emma? Served him right.

Audrey chuckled. "You could be Grant's human shield."

Surprise flickered across Cole's face. He shrugged. "If that's what everyone wants, I'll go. Anyone got a bulletproof vest I can borrow?"

Emma giggled. "He's not that bad. If you don't cross him."

Audrey kissed Cole's cheek before she exited. What Cole needed was an Emma-proof vest. They all did.

~ ~ ~

Inside the old warehouse, Cole's eyes took a second to adjust. The lights were dimmed, and Bryan was warming up his guitar already.

Cole gave Audrey's hand a squeeze. "Go get 'em."

Her eyes sparkled in the low light when she smiled. "Thanks."

As she walked away, a thought sliced like a razor through his mind. Tonight's songs might be the ones that launched Audrey and Bryan into a whole new world—professional music in Nashville and touring around the country. Could a marriage work with Audrey traveling to sing while he played pro football and was on the road, too? Seemed like they'd hardly ever be together.

Nashville had a team. If somehow he ended up getting

picked by them in the draft... The chances of that seemed slim. With this head injury, he might not get drafted at all. What then? Where would his business degree take him? Maybe some kind of job in Nashville could work.

The music started and quieted the room. Audrey's voice had picked up strength since the last time. Confidence covered her. The sound gave him chills. So beautiful.

He'd not stand in her way if this was God's calling on her life. Even if he lost her.

Chapter 26

Cool iron felt good on Cole's fingers. He gripped the metal bar and lifted. Finally, the doctor relented and allowed a light workout. Better than standing around all day. As Cole raised the weight, the quick goodbye kiss from Audrey the night before stayed on his mind. A nice kiss, but not nearly long enough. Tonight would be different. Before she left in the morning, he'd plan something special. But what? Nothing in his playbook, so he might need advice.

After counting out his last allowed number of reps, he replaced the weights. Coach McCoy talked with Zach Garcia in the corner. The backup quarterback. The guy could have the job, just not until next year.

Cole made his way to the pair. "Hey, Coach. Zach. I'm feeling on top of my game, ready to run some plays tomorrow."

With a jerk of his head, Coach McCoy shot Cole a hard look. "Give yourself until Monday. Work up to it gradually." He motioned toward Zach. "Cole can tell you about a few drills that might help you pick up speed."

The dark-eyed freshman flashed a humble smile at Cole. "I could use the help. The mike's on me a lot faster than any I played in high school."

"Yeah, the middle linebackers in the SEC are tough. Let's set up a time tomorrow." Offering a fist bump seemed appropriate. "Coach, can we talk a sec before I leave?"

"Sure. Let's walk."

Outside the walls of the performance center and the ears of his teammates, Cole cleared his throat a couple of times. How to start? "Um. I wanted to… You know Audrey's going out of town tomorrow." Cole stared at his hands and popped his knuckles. "Before she goes, like tonight, I wanted to do something."

A cross between a cough and a laugh emitted from Coach McCoy. "You're asking for advice? Ideas to do something special?"

Heat inched up Cole's neck. Not awkward or embarrassing. He nodded, glancing at the man he considered his mentor.

"Hmm. Good idea." Coach McCoy rubbed the blondish stubble on his chin. "For me and Sarah Beth, Sardis Lake was special, so I proposed there. Where is someplace special for you and Audrey? Not like you're gonna propose or anything." He turned to face Cole with brows drawn together.

Cole swallowed hard. "Not tonight."

"Thank goodness. You and Grant are getting along so well since y'all throttled that weirdo. I'm thinking dinner and a little gift. So, is there a special place? Name a few options. Brain-storm."

Couldn't be Grant's couch. Definitely not Pizza Gin. Cole's mind blanked.

"Come on, Cole. Start at the beginning."

"Um, we met when she tutored me last year, but I didn't really pay much attention to her. I fell for her in Honduras."

"That's a bit too remote for tonight. Keep going."

Cole blew out a long exhale. "CSU, Chris's house. The sidewalk between our condos."

"You're really not very good at this. How about your first kiss? Where was that?"

Warmth spread from Cole's toes to the top of his head. The kiss he'd never forget. "I got it now. Thanks." He couldn't hold in a grin.

"Good luck." The end of Coach's elbow snagged Cole's bicep. "And be a gentleman."

"Right. I may need to borrow a few things from Sarah Beth."

"My wife will be hysterically happy to help." Coach released his arm.

While taking off toward his car, Cole saluted. He had little time to get everything set up. His first stop entailed being recognized and probably gossiped about, but right now he was letting all that go. For Audrey.

After circling the Square twice, he found a spot near a jewelry shop. He exited his car and hurdled the small wrought iron fence between the street and the sidewalk in front of the store. A bell chimed as he opened the old wood and glass door.

A young woman wearing a slim black dress and high heels looked up from near a display. "Can I help you?" She grinned and pointed, sporting three narrow bracelets on her arm. "You're the quarterback."

At least only one other customer was in the store, but of course her head turned at the announcement. "Yes and yes. I need help finding something nice for my...girlfriend." There, he said the word. Not all that hard. He kinda liked the way it sounded. "Something with maybe a heart or a cross?"

One lined eyebrow rose. "Price range?"

"Something nice." The credit card Dad provided left him with plenty of room for large purchases, especially since he'd given up partying lately.

"I have just what you want." With a voice that oozed sweetness, she led him to a locked glass case and retrieved a key from behind the counter. The lock clicked as she opened it. "Each of these necklaces is from a line that you can personalize, adding pieces and engraving if you like. What do you think? Can I show you one or two?"

The jewelry sparkled in the display lights. So many choices, but not much time. "The silver one. Can you engrave it now?"

"Good selection. We're not too busy, so depending on how much engraving, I should be able to deliver." Her eyes traveled across his shoulders then back up to his face. "What do you want to say to your girlfriend?"

His fingers tapped one at a time against the glass, leaving prints all across the shiny cabinet. What did he want to say? She had his heart? No. Too long. "How about my heart. You know, as in, I'm giving her *my heart*."

"Whoa, you are serious about her." She lifted the necklace

and fastened the cabinet. "I'm jealous. She's a lucky girl."

"No. I'm the lucky one."

~~~

Will you save time for me tonight? Cole's short text left Audrey with so many questions. Between fear and excitement, her emotions rose and fell like the bus on the bumpy Honduran roads. Like the beginning of her relationship with Cole.

A large suitcase sat by the door, ready for Nashville. What do people pack for an audition? Or for recording a demo? Bryan had been no help. His uniform of solid tees and straight legged pants worked for him but weren't quite her style.

The phone chimed with another text from Cole.

What's your favorite food?

Her fingers tingled on the face of the phone. So he must be taking her to dinner?

Pizza and chocolate chip cookie dough are a close tie. I could eat them every day.

But hopefully, he'd skip the Pizza Gin after the last two experiences in the restaurant. Oh, gracious. What should she wear tonight? She'd already straightened her hair three times. The sleeveless navy shirt and jean shorts she wore made sense for most of the places she'd been in Oxford, but Cole might travel in a higher social circle.

The phone sounded off again.

Pizza and cookie dough. A woman after my own heart. Meant to be together. Dress casual. Close your blinds. I'll knock soon. No peeking. Yes, I've seen you looking over here.

Cheeks burning, Audrey pulled the cord to lower the blinds. So embarrassing.

An hour later, the knock happened. There'd be no slowing her steps this time. She was ready to be with Cole. As the door slung open, her heart flipped at the view.

Clean shaven, caramel-colored hair cut shorter, he wore a red polo that hugged his shoulders and biceps. No looking at his legs. Not now anyway. "Hey." She stepped out.

"Hey, you look pretty. I like your hair." His fingers ran through a few strands. "Ready?"

Tackling the Fields

The urge to touch his hair simmered in her own fingers. "Yes. You look nice, too. Hair cut?"

"For you." His hand still lingered near her cheek. A slow smile spread across his face. "If it makes you want to kiss me or anything, I'm willing."

Hadn't she been thinking about that all day? Her eyes fell to his mouth, unearthing a bit of timidity and at the same time sending sparks through her entire body. Her face burned. She probably looked like a human sparkler. "You can kiss me this time." She swallowed at her tight throat. She'd miss him this week.

His lips met hers, and she closed her eyes, pushing out the sadness that threatened to spoil the perfect moment. Minutes passed in a blur of emotion and craving. He smelled clean and woodsy, like a spring day. Maybe she wouldn't leave, after all.

At last, he released her lips, holding her face in his hands. "Whew." He whistled. "Your lips make me forget why I came." He dropped his hands and picked up a picnic basket she hadn't noticed until now. "Come on."

A dreamy numbness still embraced her, but she followed him down the sidewalk. "Where are we going?"

"A surprise."

147

Chapter 27

Audrey followed Cole down the sidewalk, past the pool. His free hand took a light hold on hers. The tennis courts had to be their destination. She snuck a glance at him. His expression reminded her of her dad on Christmas Eve. Cole clearly enjoyed planning a surprise. And for her. How could she get so lucky?

"Almost there. Stop and close your eyes. I'll be right back." He held his hand over her face. "No peeking."

She scuffed the concrete with the toe of her shoe. Music started nearby and joined the summer choir of frogs and crickets, and then a scraping sound. Another loud scratch. What was he doing? "Are you ready yet?"

"Coming. Keep your eyes closed." His light Southern drawl licked at her ears, heating her face. Then his fingers covered hers. "Okay. I'll lead you."

"With my eyes closed? I'll fall and bust it."

His other arm wrapped tight around her waist. "Do you trust me?"

Did she? Good question. "This time."

With a gentle nudge, he took her forward. "Have some faith."

"We'll see." She took three more steps. "Are we there yet?"

His warm breath tickled her ear. "I see I'm gonna have to prove myself to you. Keep your eyes closed."

With one swooping motion, Cole lifted her into his arms.

Her cheek rested against his shoulder. "Should you be lifting me with your head injury?"

"I'm fine. Got to lift weights today. Besides, you're light."

Seconds later, he set her on her feet. "Open."

A small table covered in a red and white tablecloth stood

before her. One large candle sparkled in the center. His phone played the music through a small speaker. Audrey blinked twice, and her breath caught. Her mind buzzed with wonder. "You did this? By yourself? For me?"

His eyes glimmered amber, reflecting the candle's light. He pulled out a chair and motioned for her to sit. "Sarah Beth helped. I borrowed this stuff from her." He lifted the lid of the picnic basket. "My idea, though. Sorry it's kind of hot out here. I brought bug spray for the mosquitoes." His brow angled as he fumbled around in the container. "Pizza didn't fit in here very well. I had to take it out of the box in pieces and wrap them in foil."

Audrey smiled as he retrieved paper plates, two canned drinks, foil-wrapped pizza, and a whole tub of chocolate chip cookie dough. "You think you have enough?"

A hint of amusement flashed across his face. "Be nice, or I'll have to kiss every last one of your freckles."

The way he held her gaze unleashed at least a dozen big butterflies to flutter around her chest and stomach. Beautiful, happy butterflies.

He filled a plate with pizza and placed it in front of her. "Here you go."

"You know that's more than I can eat."

He took a seat at the table with his own full plate. "I'll finish your leftovers."

Hadn't she lived that one all her life with her brothers? One bite of pizza made its way down. How could she eat with him looking so adorable across the table with his short hair? And he'd been so sweet to try to do something romantic.

Already two pieces had disappeared from Cole's plate. Apparently nothing kept him from eating. He paused and swallowed. "You know why I picked this place, right? I mean I could've taken you out to a nice restaurant. Maybe I should've?" Face scrunched into a grimace, he ran his fingers across his forehead. "Is this a stupid idea?"

Audrey's heart squeezed at his insecurity. "Of course, I know why you picked here. Our first kiss. It's not stupid at all.

I love that you went to all this trouble." She glanced around and smiled. "And that no one's playing tennis tonight."

A smile smoothed his frown, and he raised his brows. "I reserved all the courts with the property manager. Being a quarterback has a few privileges. May as well take advantage of them every now and then." Abruptly, he stood and rubbed his hands together. "But I can't take this anymore."

A jolt of fear coursed through her. "What?" Was he doing all this to break things off? It didn't make sense.

He rummaged through the picnic basket again. "Here it is." In two quick steps, he knelt by her chair.

What was he holding? A little wrapped box? Her chest froze in place. "What's that?"

~~~

Audrey's eyes grew wide as Cole held out the present he'd purchased for her.

"Wait. It's not a ring." He was kneeling by her chair, after all. She was probably freaking out. "Not yet anyway."

Her chest fell as she exhaled. "Oh. I didn't—"

"Just open it."

Shaky fingers took the small package. Audrey untied the bow, and with slow, delicate rips, she removed the shiny paper. Her hands stopped once she'd set the wrapping aside.

"What are you waiting for? There's not a springy fake snake in there."

The corners of her lips lifted as she tucked her chin, letting her brown hair fall in her face. Was she trying to hide? "Is something wrong?"

Audrey shook her head. "No. I've never gotten a present from a guy. Well, except in kindergarten, a boy in my class gave me a red teddy bear on Valentine's Day. But he moved away before first grade." She held the package toward him. "You open it."

Cole let his head drop back. "Really? You want me to do it?" He took the box and held it near her face, then lifted the hinged lid. "Here's my heart to take with you to Nashville. So you don't forget me."

Glossy tears filled Audrey's eyes. "Thank you." She blinked, wiped a finger under her lashes, and sniffed. "It's beautiful. I'll treasure it like I'll treasure this night." Her eyes met his. "And your heart. Will you put it on me?"

Cole stood and stepped behind Audrey's chair. Why did he feel as though he'd just sprinted eighty yards? His heart raced, thudding in his ears like a distant train. Audrey lifted the hair at her neck and swept it to the side. Fumbling with the velvet cardboard to remove the necklace only made things worse. Big hands were great for football but not for something this small.

Finally the necklace fell free of the packaging. As he circled her delicate neck with the silver chain, her hair brushed against his arm. Desire swept through him like a wildfire in a lumber yard. And she wasn't even touching him. He swallowed at his dry throat and took a breath. "There. Got it." When she turned around, any last doubts about his feelings for her melted away. This was love. "Perfect. Like you."

~ ~ ~

Audrey stiffened. "I'm not perfect, Cole. You can't think that."

"To me you are."

Now was the time to tell Cole what he was getting into. A girl with struggles—perhaps messed up for life on more than one level. Audrey opened her lips to speak, but closed them again as he returned to his seat, grinning. Eyes bright and looking so happy. If she told her story, it would ruin the special evening he'd planned.

She brought pizza to her mouth and forced herself to chew, glancing every few seconds at the hammered silver heart shining up at her. Cole's heart. Could she really trust that she held his heart? How long would he be happy with her? Maybe this was just a phase after his Honduras experience and all. The week away in Nashville would be the perfect time to pray and settle her doubts about a relationship with Cole Sanders. Time and space.

After three more pieces of pizza, Cole popped off the lid of the cookie dough and offered her a spoon. His chair scraped the concrete as he scooted around the table to sit beside her. "You're not eating, just picking at the pizza. Feeling okay?"

"Fine." But was she? "Saving up for dessert." Fingers squeezing the spoon, she dug into the cookie dough. A huge glob dangled. She caught it in her mouth, the semi-sweet chocolate warming and melting on her tongue with the sugary dough. Closing her eyes, she moaned a little. Oh, but chocolate soothed the nerves sometimes.

Laughter rumbled from Cole. "Man. I'm a little jealous of the cookie dough. You really like that stuff."

A giggle caught in her throat as her face heated. She pushed back the rest of the dough with her tongue to swallow the mound. "I—"

"There they are." The court gate opened with a screech, accompanied by a screechy female voice. "I knew they had to be somewhere on the grounds. Both their cars are here."

Emma and Grant. There went the romantic evening.

"Look at y'all having a big ole picnic. How adorable. We wanted to ask y'all to watch a movie with us." Emma nudged Grant. "You should take me on a picnic sometime."

Grant nodded and squinted. "What're you eating, Audrey? You've got something on your mouth." He stepped closer. "Cookie dough. Can I have some? Looks like you have enough to spare a bite or two. Oh, and I bought you more pepper spray for Nashville."

Audrey swiped her mouth with her fingers. No sign of any napkins. Cole must've forgotten them. She looked up at her date. "Got another spoon?"

He gave her a crooked smile, nodded, and dug into the basket again and handed Grant a spoon.

Quickly, Audrey shoveled another glob of dough out for herself. "Cole, Emma, better get what you want in a hurry now that Grant's holding a utensil."

Would she get another moment alone with Cole before she left for Nashville? She studied Cole beside her. His full lips curled up into a smile as he returned her gaze. Her breathing quickened. Was steam rising from her face?

Maybe having company for the rest of the evening was for the best after all.

Chapter 28

Audrey pressed her face against the pillow that was squeezed between her head and the Jeep door. If only she could sleep, the trip to Nashville would pass so much faster. But constant thoughts of Cole stole her chance to rest.

She couldn't help remembering his warmth beside her on Emma's loveseat. Laughing about that ridiculous movie Emma picked out. She'd pretended to pay attention to the plot, but who could think with Cole that close?

One thing had caught her attention besides Cole when she'd been in Emma's condo. The place oozed money. Furniture and décor that looked as though Emma had emptied the Pottery Barn. Maybe Emma and Cole's lifestyles matched better than her own. Raised out in the country, she and Grant had all they needed, but certainly not a life so full of luxuries.

She glanced at Bryan in the driver's seat, his eyes matching the blue sky surrounding the Jeep. They'd sung for an hour or so when they first left Oxford. Then talked about their childhood. His in Tupelo, Mississippi, less than two hours down the highway from her hometown outside of Jasper, Alabama.

Bryan's middle class upbringing had been similar to her own. His father worked as a supervisor in a manufacturing plant. Couldn't be too much different than Daddy's management position in the coal mines.

Church played a major part in their family's lives. Being present for every single function was never questioned. It was part of life.

Bryan paid his own tuition. She'd gone on an academic scholarship and worked to make her spending money.

Audrey lifted the silver heart on the chain Cole had given

her. How much had the purchase cost him? She'd been in that store, and there was nothing cheap there.

"Can't sleep?" Bryan smiled and slipped his eyes her way for a second.

"Nope. Mind won't shut down."

"You nervous? Scared? The people we're staying with are great. You'll love them. They pastor the church where Chris used to serve. A real nice family."

Rolling green hills filled the view out the windshield. Such pretty country. But a sliver of doubt stabbed at her stomach. "I am a little nervous. You'll probably think I'm such a baby, but I've never traveled without family. Even church camp and youth trips, Grant or my younger brother were along."

"That's kinda sweet. You can consider me your scrawny big brother, if it helps."

Audrey's stomach loosened. As usual, Bryan eased her fears.

~~~

He could do this. He needed to talk to someone. Coach McCoy would understand.

Cole tapped on the open door of the office. "Coach. You got a minute? Or two?"

The phone on his desk rang, but Coach pressed the button to silence the noise. "Yes."

"You can take your call if you need to."

"They can leave a message." Coach McCoy waved toward a chair. "Sit. Talk. Is this about Audrey and the surprise dinner?"

"In a way."

Leaning back in his chair, Coach McCoy pressed the ends of his fingers together. "Did it go well?"

"Yeah. I think." Cole scanned the desk in front of him, his eyes landing on a glass jar of gumballs. A weird gurgle sounded from his stomach. What was that? The protein bars he'd eaten for breakfast should've kept him full.

"You want a gumball?" Coach McCoy pushed the container forward and plucked off the lid. "Sounds like you're hungry or nervous. Either way, it could help."

Cole popped one in his mouth and chomped into the chewy ball. Why did he think he could talk about this with anyone? He chewed harder.

The coach's eyes narrowed. "Just spit it out."

Cole stopped chomping and pushed the gum between his lips.

"Not the gum, knucklehead. Whatever it is you want to talk about." He stood and stepped across the office to shut the door, then returned to his seat.

The gum slid back between Cole's teeth. "Okay. Here goes." He swallowed back the syrupy sweetness. "How do people wait? You know? Till they get married. Seems like...impossible."

Coach McCoy clucked his tongue. "With man it might be impossible. With God, all things are possible." He laughed. "In other words, it ain't easy. You know, I wasn't perfect before I became a Christian—before I met Sarah Beth. Then we spent a long time getting to know each other as friends." He lifted his head, clucked his tongue again, and shrugged. "And we had a short engagement."

Cole smiled at the honesty. Where did that leave him? Could he back off and spend more time with Audrey as a friend? A different approach, for sure.

"Desire is not a bad thing in and of itself. With marriage, it's a beautiful thing—God's design. But the world is bombarding us with a different message. The truth is, it takes a strong man to reign himself in. A weaker man gives into all kinds of urges. Pretty much the opposite of what we see in the media."

"Thanks, Coach. I know you're right." Didn't make his life easier, though.

"Has Chris offered to do a Bible study with you? He did when I first became a Christian."

Cole nodded. "Yeah. Kinda been putting it off, but I'll call. With Audrey gone for a week, it's a good time to start."

"Good thinking. Don't—"

A knock on the door interrupted. The head coach stuck his head in. "Hey, Cole. You better?"

"All good, Coach Black. Ready to get back in the huddle on Monday."

"Glad to hear it."

Cole stood. "Thanks. I'll see you on the field."

On the way out, he paused in the hall to check his phone. No word from Audrey since her text to tell him they were leaving. His chest filled, thinking of her at his side the night before. He drew in a deep breath and let it out slowly. He missed her already. He punched a message to her. *Counting the hours until you bring back my heart.*

Chapter 29

What a nerve-wracking day. A long day. Audrey flung herself onto the bed at the minister's house. How did performers take this? Repeating, redoing, meetings…so many opinions. If this was the life of a professional musician, someone else could have it. All she could think about during the long hours was when could she go home. The sweet text from Cole only worsened her aching to be back in Oxford.

Her eyes closed. Maybe she'd lay here like this until morning.

When they had to go back to the studio. Ugh.

Thirty minutes later, a tap on the door pulled her from her pity party. She stood, straightened her cotton dress, and opened the door.

Bright blue eyes and a huge grin greeted her. "Wasn't this the greatest day of your life?" Bryan gushed and glowed like he had the whole day. Like he was made for this life. "There's food saved for us downstairs. Come on."

"I'm tired. I'll just turn in."

"No one's around. They're out at a baseball game with the kids."

The food sounded better if she didn't have to make conversation. "Okay." She trudged forward and down the stairs.

Bryan glanced back, furrowing his brows. "Are you feeling okay?"

"Tired. What time do we have to be back downtown in the morning?"

His lips pinched together before he answered. "Seven-thirty. But isn't it cool how Dylan and Sarah Beth hooked us up with all these industry insiders. A chance of a lifetime. I won't be getting any sleep tonight."

"Are you kidding? Aren't you exhausted? I am."

On the counter in the kitchen, a slow cooker simmered with a note beside it. *Make yourselves at home.* The smell of potato soup escaped as Bryan lifted the lid. He smiled. "She knows I'm not a big meat eater. I hope it's okay with you?"

"I like soup. It's better than the peanut butter crackers I'd planned on eating."

Bryan ladled soup into two bowls and handed one to her. "Drink?"

"Water's fine. That's what I drink at home."

"Me, too. We're so much alike, it's scary." His eyes widened as he made a goofy face.

Audrey chuckled and followed Bryan to the table. "We are way more alike than…" Why was she comparing Bryan and Cole?

"Than?" Bryan placed his bowl on the table, then filled two glasses with water and sat across from her.

"Nothing." The warm creamy soup hit the spot, but too bad there was no cookie dough. She smiled at the memory.

His spoon clinked against the green-and-white china bowl. "You're smiling for the first time in hours. What's on your mind? Or should I ask? I noticed the shiny new heart necklace you've been studying since we left."

Talking about Cole with Bryan didn't feel right. "I was thinking about cookie dough." Not exactly the whole truth.

"I like it. Give me some oatmeal cookie dough any day."

"Oatmeal? Wrong. Chocolate chip is so much better."

Bryan's hand went to his heart. "That hurts." His face became serious. "Can I ask you a question?"

Oh, mercy. Someone asking if they can ask a question was never a good sign. "Go ahead."

"Were you shut up in your room because you were nervous about being here alone with me?"

Good question, but the thought had never crossed her mind. Why hadn't it? "No. I was exhausted. Anyway, I trust you."

His gaze pierced hers. "Would you be nervous with Cole?"

The question and his look unsettled her. "You don't hold back, do you?"

He didn't answer. Just waited for her response.

Would she feel comfortable here alone with Cole? "I'd be a little nervous. But I'm not sure why." Maybe it was herself she didn't trust with Cole.

"Do you trust him?"

Was Bryan reading her mind? He'd asked the million-dollar-question she kept asking herself over and over. "I'm still trying to figure that out." Cole said he'd given her his heart. But for how long?

~ ~ ~

Thirty minutes into the small party at Cassie's, and already Cole smelled trouble. At no time did Emma move more than a foot away from his side. And he'd tried to get away. She was harder to shake than the Alabama defensive line. The bathroom might be the only safe place in the house. Might be safe. A better strategy would be to slip out the back, jump the six-foot fence, and walk home.

Emma's nails dug into his bicep. "You're not even listening."

He winced. "Sorry, I was thinking." Those nails were sharp. Cole focused on the blue-eyed blond. Her lip gloss glistened as she gave him a seductive smile.

"Thinking too much, if you ask me." She laughed as Grant returned with a drink for her. "Y'all come meet my other sister, Nora. She's just come down from her room. No doubt she's been up there writing one of her cheesy love stories."

"Love stories?" That sounded strange.

Emma led them to the parlor near the grand staircase of the Victorian home. "She's an author, but she writes her novels under a pen name. Liz Hart."

Cole shrugged. "Never heard of her." Why wasn't Grant talking? He just stared at Emma like he was under a trance, that stupid grin on his face. The girl had dressed in a low cut silk dress the color of Florida orange juice which probably explained Grant's oblivion. Poor guy.

"Here she is." Emma waved at a woman seated on the couch. Her bright red hair matched the older sister Cassie's, but Nora was taller with striking blue eyes like Emma's. "Nora, these are my new hot friends—Grant and Cole. They're football players for the university. Cool, huh?"

Nora squinted and glared at Emma, then pointed her sharp stare at Cole and Grant. "First. My sister knows I do not care to be referred to as Nora. Emma decided to call me that when she was too little to say Elinor or Elinor Elizabeth, which is my proper name." The redhead's brows lifted. "Second. Haven't you boys heard about the concussion studies on football players? You should remove yourselves from the sport now before you incur a brain injury. If you haven't already."

Hands on hips, Emma pooched out her bottom lip. "Be nice to my friends."

Cole chuckled. The Bosarge family had more than one blurter. The tension between Emma and her sister might give him a way out. "I'd like to hear about the study, if you want to tell me about it, Elinor Elizabeth." He took a seat in a nearby chair. If he sat there long enough, surely Grant and Emma would disappear.

A groan came from Emma. "Fine. Come on Grant. You may as well listen, too. It could be important. She researches all kinds of obscure information for her books."

Grant and Emma sat together on the loveseat. Good thing he'd chosen the one-person chair. Cole smiled and nodded while Elinor Elizabeth began her spiel. Like he hadn't heard this lecture from his parents and his genius brother enough times. His thoughts traveled to Audrey. What was she doing at this moment? If only he could send her a text right about now, but that would be rude. He nodded again to make sure it looked as though he were listening.

"Cole, my man, how's the arm?" Sam Conrad, the former backup quarterback and one of Coach McCoy's best friends, entered the parlor and stood in front of Cole's chair, blocking the view of Nora—Elinor Elizabeth.

Cole rose and offered Sam a firm handshake. "Arm's never been better."

"You want to go throw a few in the yard? I've got a football in my car, and I'd love to catch some of your perfect spirals." Sam waited, oblivious to the fact he'd interrupted.

"Excuse me, sir. I am in the middle of a conversation with these young men." The redhead's blue eyes fired at Sam like a flamethrower.

Outside sounded like a good idea. This woman might be as dangerous as her sister. Almost.

Sam's mouth opened to speak, but Cole took his elbow and turned him around. "Let's go get that ball." Cole waved. "It was nice to meet you, ma'am. Grant can fill me in on the rest of your lecture."

"It was not a lecture." The huff and, he assumed, another prickly glare followed him out.

Cole's steps sped up almost to a jog. "Hurry, Sam, before they get us. How about you give me a ride home, and we ease away early?"

"Sounds like a plan. Were you on a double date? That redhead seems rude."

"No way. Cassie's sister Elinor is, like...your age."

Sam flexed his bicep, then gave Cole a playful punch. "Hey, I'm not that old. The redhead's no Cassie. That's for sure."

He had that right. Neither was Emma. "I'm pretty serious about someone anyway."

They reached Sam's red Mazda, and he opened the front door to grab the football. "Better you than me, buddy. I was engaged once. Not making that mistake again." Sam tossed the ball to Cole. "You gotta watch out, or your heart will be crushed like a three-hundred-pound lineman stepped on your chest."

Sam should know. Enough linemen had stepped on him. "I'll keep that in mind." But Audrey wouldn't hurt anyone. He trusted her.

Chapter 30

A gospel tune played from the speakers in the craft room of Empowered Hearts. The chatter from earlier in the day dissipated as one by one the women cleaned their area and left. A florescent light bulb flickered above while Audrey organized leftover beads into containers.

Across the shiny laminate counter, Bryan reached toward her and dabbed at her cheek with a paper towel. "Just a bit of glitter." His eyes searched her face. "You look happy. Is Empowered Hearts everything you'd hoped?"

Her chest seemed to expand as she nodded. "And more. I finally feel like I've found my niche, my calling. God's working miracles with these women. Not all make it through the program, but enough. I love Katerina, too. She's amazing."

A crooked smile ran across Bryan's face. "So, I gather the music industry doesn't give you the same joy?"

Truth time. Audrey wrapped the leftover cord around a plastic cylinder. "Not so much. I enjoy singing, like at worship, but not for a living. I mean, I gave it a try, but if I'm sick of it at the beginning, I can only imagine what I'd feel like months or years from now. I get that music is ministry for you. It moves people. It moves me. But—"

He held up a palm. "It's not your calling. Don't feel guilty. Like you said, you gave it a fair shot." He ran his finger across the edge of the table. "I didn't want to tell you until after you'd checked out the nonprofit world, but we were offered a contract last night. And a gig. Opening act for the opening act, you could say."

Her empty stomach churned. Disappointing Bryan was the last thing she wanted to do. "I don't know what to say. Will they sign you? Alone?" Why did she say alone? A terrible word choice.

A smile played on Bryan's lips. "Yes."

Audrey's heart skipped a beat. "Yes?"

Bryan's eyes sparkled. "I told them from the start you were iffy. And I could tell from the first day, this wasn't your thing. So I'll accept the offer. Alone." He pretended to pout.

"I'm really happy for you. Your dream is coming true."

With a deep breath, he made a slow nod. "One of them."

What did that mean? Did she want to know? "When will the tour start?"

"In September. I'll have to take a semester off college." His fingers toyed with a necklace, sliding the beads back and forth. "You know you'll still make money for the songs you wrote, and you could make a living singing backup harmony on recordings. You're good."

"Thanks." The extra money from the songs might help her with moving costs after college if she decided to take a job with Katerina in Nashville.

"Either way, sounds like we might end up in the same city in a year." His blue eyes shone a little too bright.

Could she move to Nashville? On her own? No telling where Grant might end up if he was drafted like everyone predicted. And what about Cole?

~~~

At least he'd gotten to practice with the team, but this stupid dizziness still dogged him. Cole paid for his order at the drive through. How long would the problem last? He'd covered well enough, but it took every ounce of strength he possessed to keep his balance.

He opened the bag before he drove away, unwrapped a hamburger, and took a bite. Onions. Yuck. Why couldn't they get it right? He'd taste the smelly things all night now. Not helpful when he already felt nauseated.

Wouldn't he love to clobber Grant for starting this? And where'd the big jerk disappeared to this afternoon? The coaches hadn't said.

By the time he pulled in the parking lot of the condos, he'd finished both burgers, the jumbo fries, and the last sip of his milkshake. At least he was full for a while. He stared out the car window. Audrey's car sat in the same place, a sad reminder she was still out of town.

Where was Grant's truck? If he'd gotten sick at practice, his truck should be here. Unless he'd skipped out with Emma somehow.

Nope. There she was, sitting in front of her condo in a yellow bikini reading a magazine. A foot from his only entrance unless a side window was unlocked. Which it wasn't.

He took a deep breath before he exited the car. Ready position. Defenses up. Go.

The door creaked when he pushed it open. Was there any way he could get inside without her seeing him? If only there were such a thing as invisibility. Or a cloaking device. Should he walk fast or slow? Fast seemed best. Like he had something important to do.

Halfway between the parking lot and his condo, Emma sat up straight. "Hey." She'd made the small word into three or four syllables.

The cloaking device failed. Not invisible. His feet kept up the fast pace. "Hey."

"Got any plans tonight?"

To stay out of trouble. "Shower. Watch film." He inserted the key and opened the door.

"Shower sounds good. Film sounds dull."

Why was his mouth so dry? And how fast could he get inside and lock the door? "Sounds safe. See you later."

"Wait."

His feet froze in place. What now?

She jumped from her folding lawn chair and ran closer. Really close. Her lips parted and her blue eyes opened wide. "Have you heard the news about Audrey and Grant's uncle?"

His gut tightened as if ready for a heavy blow. "No. What happened?"

Janet W. Ferguson

Chapter 31

"Is that Grant's truck?" Audrey spotted the monstrous hunk of metal the instant Bryan turned the corner onto their host's street. "Why in the world would he be here?" Her stomach dropped. "Something's wrong."

Bryan tucked his head and squinted. "Maybe he's checking up on us?"

"No. He wouldn't miss football practice. Hurry." Her heart beat against her chest, and her ears rang. What could be so bad that he'd driven all the way to Nashville? The Jeep rolled to a stop, and Audrey jumped out, running to the front door. Inside, Grant stood in the kitchen with Pastor Reed. "What's happened?"

A grim look covered Grant's face. "Uncle Phillip."

The pastor moved to her side and offered a weak smile. "Let's go sit in the living room together."

With heavy steps, Audrey followed Grant and the pastor through the archway into the other room and eased down on the couch next to her brother.

Staring at the floor, Grant shuffled his enormous athletic shoes across the hardwood. Why wouldn't he just spit it out?

Though her mind buzzed numb, she knew. Uncle Phillip was gone. Audrey smashed her lips together and took a shaky breath through her nose. That's what Grant wasn't saying. "When's the funeral?"

After a slow nod, Grant turned to face her, tears brimming his eyes. "Day after tomorrow. Visitation's tomorrow night at the funeral home." He brushed at his eyes and sniffed. "Mom said we had to wait to leave till first light in the morning. The long drive and all."

The pastor pulled his chair closer. "Would you like me to

166

pray with you, or would you like time alone? Something to drink?"

Audrey swallowed back the sob that threatened to spill out. "I—I'd like a few minutes alone. To take this in." Her chest shook, and her voice cracked. "Thank you." Burying her head in Grant's arm, the torrent of tears and loss escaped.

When her crying slowed, she lifted her head. "Was it the blood clot?"

"Yeah." Grant sniffed. "Coach got the call at practice. I grabbed my suit from the condo and came straight up here."

They sat in silence for a while, staring at nothing. She tried to smile. "Good thing you thought to get your suit. Mom would get your goat if you forgot your custom-made big-and-tall."

"She reminded me. Said you had clothes at home, though." He elbowed her. "Not like you're big or anything."

Her big brother could be sweet when he wanted to. "Thanks. You mind if I go pack and turn in? Bryan can let you bunk with him in the basement and show you—" Another sob escaped. "This is hard."

"I know." Big arms encircled her. Grant squeezed her with a bear hug, pushing the air from her lungs.

"Oh, mercy, it hurts when you do that." A halfhearted laugh made its way out. "I hope you don't hug Emma that way."

"I'm not a complete idiot." His voice grew stronger. "Go on, and I'll see you early in the morning."

Halfway up the stairs, Audrey's phone played a tune too cheerful for the mood she was in. Cole. Her fingers shook as she answered. "Hey."

"I heard about your loss. I'm sorry."

"Thanks."

"I want to come be with you at the funeral. I can ask Coach McCoy to excuse me from practice."

What? How could that work? Where would he stay? On the fold-out couch in their living room? "No. You don't need to." Her voice wobbled more than she intended to let it. "There will be a lot of family and all, and there's not much room at the house as it is." And Grant would likely be in a foul mood if Cole were there, even with their newfound peace treaty.

"If that's the way you want it. But if you change your mind, I'll be there. I love you." His words were soft and warm, even across the miles.

Audrey's heart pinched at the sound. "Love you, too."

"Call me whenever you want, no matter how late. Or early."

She smiled at his attempts to soothe her. "I will. Goodnight, Cole."

"Goodnight, Audrey."

If only the warm phone in her grip was Cole's hand. She pictured his fingers cradling her own. She lifted the necklace he gave her with the other hand and kissed it. Weird, but comforting. In her room, she packed her clothes, dirty ones on one side and clean on the other. She'd have to let Katerina know what happened, too. She sent her a quick text, explaining. They'd planned to meet again before the week here ended. This wasn't the way she'd wanted to leave Nashville.

~~~

Two o'clock. A knot twisted Cole's stomach. Audrey would be at the funeral now. He ran the play Coach McCoy called for, but his heart wrenched. He should've gone even though Audrey told him to stay away. He should be at her side.

She was supposed to be in Nashville another two days this week. Would she go back? It wouldn't hurt his feelings if she skipped out on the rest of that trip and came back to Oxford.

"Cole, get your mind back to the here and now. Run it again." Coach McCoy signaled the play once more.

At least the dizziness had let up. The center poised to snap the ball. *Head in game.* No more thinking about things he couldn't change.

After practice and a quick dinner with a few of the guys, Cole turned his car toward home.

A sea of vehicles filled the condo parking lot and lined the street leading in and out of the area. Somebody was having a party. A big one. Great. Where was he supposed to park?

He eased up onto the curb and into the grass. If his BMW

got messed up, somebody was gonna hear about this. The parking lot should be reserved for residents.

Music blared ahead as he walked along the edge of the road. Sounded like a band. So much for a quiet night. Who threw this big of a party on a weeknight in the summer?

The parking lot held students sitting on their cars and tailgates. He pulled down his hat to cover more of his forehead. Once he reached the sidewalk leading to his condo, his feet stopped. Hordes of students lounged on the grass near his door, danced on the sidewalk, and a band played only a few yards away from Emma's. Was this her doing?

"Cole, what's up? You ready to party?" A guy held out his fist to greet him.

Crud. Recognized already. "Just passing through, man." Cole bumped his hand and kept going.

"Woo-hoo! Cole's home!" Dancing his way in short cutoffs and a hot pink halter, Emma parted the crowd. He had to admit the girl wore it well. "I'm having my first party in Oxford. Don't you think it's time?"

Good grief, her voice was loud.

When she neared, she sprang on him, arms out, catching Cole around the neck. "I'm so glad you're here." She dangled from him, so he caught her around the waist.

He stiffened and sniffed. Her pupils seemed small, her eyes glassy. She didn't smell like beer or weed, but the girl was drunk on something. A flock of guys eyed her like vultures waiting to swoop on a half-dead possum in the road. Not his problem though.

Cole looked down at her. Red lipstick covered her full lips, and her long blond hair fell down past her shoulders. She did look good. Too good. He untangled her arms from his neck. "What's the party for?"

"My very merry un-birthday." She giggled and motioned toward the band. "I got a call from these guys in Tuscaloosa, and they wanted to come check out Oxford, so I sent out the message on my social media. Didn't you see it?" The red lips pouted.

"No. I quit checking that lately." Cole glanced around. "You got all these people here with a message last night?"

Her fingers ran up and down his chest. "I have my ways. Aren't you gonna wish me a happy un-birthday?"

Must leave now.

"I'm really beat from practice. See you later." He spun around, threaded his way to his door, and slipped inside. "Whew." The last thing he needed was a drunk Emma. The sober one was dangerous enough.

Chapter 32

Audrey leaned by Grant against the counter near the sink. He held a spoon and the remnants of a Mississippi Mud Pie. Casseroles, cakes, and congealed salads filled both refrigerators and covered every table and laminate countertop in their parents' home. Friends and neighbors and church members came and went after the funeral, offering condolences and food. Small towns took the loss of one of their own to heart and showered their family with all kinds of gifts and plants.

She eyed her brother and the dessert, not his first one today. Probably not his last. "Are you gonna eat all that, too?"

His mouth swirled as he savored the fluffy chocolate and whipped cream. "Yeah. It's good. Funerals bring out the best cooks in Walker County. There's gotta be something to help people deal with loss." He shoveled the rest of the pie into his mouth.

She let out a long sigh and wiped the counter with a wet rag. "I guess. I'm not very hungry, though. The service was nice. Seemed like Uncle Phillip had all his business planned out in advance. Made it easy on Momma and Aunt Renee. And fast. Almost too fast. I miss him already."

Without warning, Grant put down the pie and slapped the counter. "Let's go back to Oxford tonight once everyone clears out. I want to see Emma. I miss her, and I haven't even had time to check in with her."

Why'd he have to bring up Emma when they were talking about family? And if Emma was his girlfriend, which she doubted, had she offered to come to the funeral? "We have to help clean up."

Hours later, after the straggling visitors left and Audrey helped pack away the last of the banana puddings in the refrigerator, she and Grant trudged out to the truck. When she opened the door, she shook her head. He'd loaded every available nook and cranny with leftovers.

With the drive from Nashville, the visitation, the funeral, the visitors, her bones were weary. She flopped into the truck like a soggy towel. A quiet ride would be nice, but she should make conversation to keep Grant awake. He had to be tired, too. The boy's body operated like a well-trained machine so often, sometimes she had to remind herself he was flesh. "Okay, tell me everything that's gone on since I left. Football practice. Emma. The party at Cassie's. All of it."

One side of Grant's upper lip lifted. "All of it? That's a lot of talking." His voice held a bit of a whine.

"Come on. It's late, and it'll keep you awake. Start with your favorite part." Hopefully, not Emma.

~~~

Heavy bass vibrated the walls of Cole's condo. The sheets crinkled as he turned over and pressed the pillow over his head again. When would the band stop playing? If not soon, the police would be showing up.

Thump, thump, thump.

Cole sat up. Was someone beating on his door? Maybe they were in Emma's condo. A vision of the vulture-guys crossed his mind. The girl could've got herself into a big mess by now.

With a groan, he pushed off the covers and pulled on gym shorts and a T-shirt. Not like he was sleeping anyway. He stomped down the hall and out the front door. He knocked at Emma's. No answer. Turning the knob, he called in. "Emma? You in here?" Nothing. "Emma?"

The thump hadn't come from there. Must've been a drunk knocking. He turned toward the sidewalk, but his feet came to an abrupt halt as a sour smell assaulted him. "Yuck." Someone had thrown up.

Cole squeezed his eyes shut a moment and covered his mouth. That mess would have to wait. Lifting his lids, he pivoted right and marched through the remaining dancers toward the drum set, watching the ground for more puddles.

He stood in front of the band and made a signal to cut it.

The long-haired guys eyed each other and brought the song to an abrupt end. The dancers grumbled.

The lead singer spoke. "Dude, what gives?" They gave an expectant look at Cole.

He puffed out his chest and straightened to his full height. "The neighbors may've called the police. You should pack it up before they get here." Not precisely true, but it could be.

A crowd of drunks stared at him, so he smiled his best television smile and ran his fingers through his hair. "I'll call the Oxford taxi service to send a few vans so you don't get arrested driving home." He lifted his phone, found the saved contact number, and made the call.

Now where was Emma? He should be able to hear her if she was anywhere nearby. He circled around the band, scanning faces in the dark, garnering strange looks and more than a few high-fives. No Emma. His abs tightened. Maybe he should've stayed to watch out for the girl. But was that his place? For once, he'd love for Grant to be home.

He followed the sidewalk to the pool. Voices carried and the sound of splashing water drifted through the humid air. Emma did seem to spend a lot of time laying out in here. The gate squeaked as he swung it open. Where was the lock when they needed it? A shirtless guy sat on the side while another stood in the water. They turned to check him out.

Emma swam in her halter and shorts. Thank goodness she was wearing clothes, at least.

"It's time to end the party. The cops may be coming. Come on, Emma. Let me walk you home." He rolled his hand in an exaggerated movement.

One of the guys waved him off. "We got it. You can go back to wherever you came from."

Flames sparked in Cole's belly. The guys' intentions were all too obvious. Fighting already had him in a mess, but he wouldn't let them take advantage of a drunk friend. Even Emma. "Not leaving without her."

The guy on the side stood, while the dude in the water

moved closer to Emma.

The one standing asked, "Is she your girlfriend? Cause she doesn't act like she has a boyfriend."

"No."

The guy took a step closer. "Who do you think you are then? Her daddy?"

The heat turned into a blaze rushing up to his cheeks. "Back off."

"Or what?" Another step closer. The guy wasn't big, but pretty drunk. His friend in the water held a little more weight.

Think. Something to talk a drunk guy into backing down. A fight would hit the papers. "Look, I'm trying to help you out." Cole lowered his posture and his voice. "You ever heard of Grant Vaughn, the linebacker?"

The guy cocked his head. "Yeah. What about him?"

Cole pointed with his thumb. "That's his woman." He shook his head real slow. "The guy's got a temper and a jealous streak. He's on his way here—mad as all get out. If I were you, I'd hurry and leave." Another possible half-truth. But who knew? Grant could be on his way.

"That guy don't scare me… but if that's his woman." He turned and called to his friend in the water. "Dude, let's go. The cops are on the way."

Cole's shoulders sunk. Thank goodness. Now the really dangerous part. Getting Emma back inside her condo.

Chapter 33

"Emma, come on out of the water. Please." The smell of beer and chlorine permeated the night air. Cole raised a hand to the back of his neck. He dug in with his fingers and massaged the knots forming there. At practice tomorrow, he'd pay for this late night. And he wasn't even having a good time.

Swimming on her back in the glow of the pool lights, Emma laughed. "Get in. It feels great."

"No. I'm ready to go home and go to bed."

"Hmm—that could be fun."

"You know what I mean."

"You can go home. I'm fine." She spun to her stomach and dove under, swimming toward the deep end.

Cole sighed. Why was he doing this anyway? He should've stayed out of this whole thing. He took a step back. Could he leave her? Swimming alone at night...drunk? An image of Emma drowning flashed across his mind. No. He couldn't leave her.

Her head popped up at the other end.

"Hey." He yelled and waved her in. "Emma. I mean it. Let's go."

She ducked back under and swam toward him. When her head surfaced again only a few feet from him, a mischievous smile danced on her lips. "You come get me."

Infuriating. That's what Emma Bosarge was. He stared at her. The water rippled and bounced with small hypnotic waves around her form. The wet shorts and pink halter clung to her skin. Her blue eyes glittered, matching the turquoise walls that reflected through the water. Old Cole pounded to come out, not caring about the consequences. To dive in and live according to the flesh—a term he'd heard in a sermon sometime in his past.

Cole ground his teeth. He wouldn't live like that anymore. But he had to get Emma out. Setting his jaw, he stripped off his shirt and stepped into the water, climbing down the steps. "I can't leave you out alone. It's dangerous. Let me get you home, Emma."

She swam to him and latched her arms around his neck. "See how nice it is in here."

Warm water caressed his skin, drenching him. Her fingers ran through his hair, bringing chills to his scalp.

Get out now.

In one fluid motion, Cole lifted Emma and carried her up the steps and kept going. Forget the shirt. He'd get it tomorrow. This had to end.

Emma giggled. "Woo. You're so strong."

Once he reached her condo, he stood her up and opened the door. "Go put on dry clothes. Do you have a coffee pot and coffee?"

She shook the water from her hair, splattering on Cole's chest. "You can help me change if you want." She tugged on his arm.

"No." He gave her a stern look and pulled his arm free. "Stop. I mean it."

Her lower lip poked out. "You're a party pooper."

He studied her pouty face and slumped shoulders. She looked like a sad little girl. But not. "What'd you take tonight? Or drink?"

"Who says I took anything? I'm going to change." She spun on her heel and staggered down the hall toward her room. "There's an expresso maker on the counter by the stove."

Expresso maker? In the kitchen, Cole fiddled with the fancy machine and small shiny pellets of coffee. No clue how to make the contraption work.

A door opened and shut in the hall, then opened again, and Emma emerged, wearing a thin, light blue nighty that matched her eyes. She may as well have been in one of those lingerie commercials. She moved near, and Cole stiffened.

"I can't work this thing." He inched away, toward the door. "Anyway, sleep on your side in case you get sick or something." His heart fluttered. He had to leave.

~~~

Random cars dotted the street leading to the condo. Once Grant found a parking space, Audrey threw her purse over her shoulder, grabbed a sack of food, and got out of the truck. Someone must've had a big party.

Beer cans littered the parking lot and the landscaped flower beds, looking and smelling like a brewery had blown up. Another obnoxious odor hit her the further she went. She glanced down at a blob of something on the sidewalk. Something gross. What happened?

Though it was really late to knock, Grant couldn't wait to see his *girlfriend*. The lights glowed in both Emma and Cole's units, but neither Cole nor Emma had answered their texts on the way into Oxford.

At the entryway to Emma's, the door swung open. Cole barreled out into Grant. Shirtless. Behind him, Emma stood, hair wet. In some sexy nightgown.

No. Can't be.

A bitter taste filled Audrey's mouth. She blinked hard. As she took in the full picture, it seemed her insides ripped open, and her heart took a dive, shattering along with all the other disgusting refuse littering the area. How had she been such a fool? Why had she let herself believe in love? "How could you? You said you loved me."

Grant slammed a palm against Cole's bare chest. "What's going on here?"

"It's not what you think." Cole didn't budge and pushed back against Grant, then gave Audrey a pleading look. "Audrey. You have to believe me."

His words buzzed in her ears, and tears stung her eyes.

Emma gawked at Grant, mouth wide. "What are you doing here?"

Grant slapped the wooden frame around the entrance, causing a loud whack. "I did my best to hurry and get back to you...to find this." His voice exploded to a scream. "I guess trash attracts trash. You two deserve each other."

"Audrey, please. Let's go talk." Cole tried to push past Grant toward Audrey.

Her brother grabbed both of Cole's arms. "We've heard enough of your lies."

~~~

Running into the dark parking lot, Audrey disappeared.

"Wait." Cole broke from her brother's grip only to have Grant tackle him. They landed on the grass with a thud. "Get off me." Cole kneed Grant and climbed back to his feet.

Grant sprang up and grabbed Cole again, fist cocked to punch. "Leave Audrey alone. She's too good for you."

Emma jumped on Grant's back, screaming. "Stop it, Grant! Listen."

"Stop, Emma, before you get hurt."

"Let me tell you something. My daddy is an attorney. You lay a hand on Cole again, and I'll be a witness for a lawsuit." She inhaled, lowered her voice. "Big Roy will kick your behind in the courtroom, and he's big as you. You reminded me of him. Maybe why I liked you, but he's not a hypocrite. Like you."

With that last jab, she slid down and inserted herself between them. She pointed her index finger in Grant's face. "Look here. My family reads the Bible. I remember a story about getting things from your own eye first, and do not judge, lest you be judged. All it took was one smile from me and all your goodie-goodie, high-and-mighty rules flew out the window."

"Stop it. I don't want to hear your excuses for what you and Cole did."

She shook her finger in his face. "I did all the coming on, but he wouldn't go for it. Cole loves your sister. Doesn't make me look good, but truth is truth. For that matter, you should know I left Alabama to go to rehab for an addiction to pain-killers, and this is what it looks like when an addict falls off the wagon. Cole was trying to help me."

Grant let his fist fall, and his big shoulders wilted. He turned, walked to his condo, and slammed the door.

After dusting the grass, dirt, and who knew what else from his chest and legs, Cole shook his head. He almost felt bad for the guy. This was so messed up. Poor Audrey. He looked at Emma, standing there in her negligee. He almost felt sorry for her, too. But not right now. He was too angry with both her and Grant.

Where would Audrey go? Her car was gone. He had to get to his phone and call her. Inside his condo he dialed her over and over. No answer. She must've turned her cell off.

He threw on dry clothes and flip flops, picked up his keys, and headed to the car. If she was in Oxford, he'd find her. He had to. Both of their hearts depended on it.

~~~

Sobs choked Audrey. She mashed the gas pedal hard and headed toward the highway. The dark miles passed in a blur. Her phone played happy tones in her purse. "Shut up, phone." The sound ended and began again. Her chest shook. "Leave me alone." With shaky fingers she dug through her purse until she found the device. She flipped the switch to cut the thing off, then slung it to the back seat.

Always an idiot. That's what she was. And she'd thought *Grant* was being played. She'd fallen hook, line, and sinker. Tears blurred her vision, and she swiped at her eyes. She gripped the wheel harder. Where was she going? Not back to her condo. That was for sure. She couldn't.

A highway sign indicated she was traveling north on Highway Seven. Nashville. She'd go back. Bryan was there. A nice guy who wouldn't...

The torrent began again. She needed to stop all this blubbering. She'd known all along this would happen—Cole would break her heart. More miles passed as she tore down the dark road into the night.

Without warning, a deer leapt across the highway.

Gasping, she jerked the steering wheel to the right. The car skidded off the highway, caught air, and landed with a hard clunk that jolted Audrey's neck forward. A scream ripped from her mouth, and she pounded the brake while she sailed toward a pine tree.

Chapter 34

"Oh, Lord, help." The car slid on the damp dirt, and Audrey yanked left, then right, to gain traction. She kept her foot on the brake.

An inch from the tree, her car slid to a stop.

She released a pent up breath. Whew. "Thank you." Her head fell back to the headrest. That was close. Was this a sign? Maybe she should go back home. Hear what Cole had to say.

The wheels of her Honda spun in the mud. Thank God, she'd missed the deer and the tree, but now what? She turned on her phone. Dozens of missed calls and texts from Cole and Grant caused it to chime over and over.

No. She wouldn't listen to Cole's excuses. *Silence.* She slid the button over to turn the sound off again. But the stupid cell made a decent flashlight, so she held onto it. After pushing open her door, she stepped out to survey the area. The mud wasn't that bad. She bent down to gather sticks to shove under the tire that needed a better grip, then walked the path back to the highway. She'd gone mud riding enough with her brothers to figure this out. No calling for help. She didn't need anyone.

Back in the car, she pressed the gas easy and inched the car away from the tree. The tire slipped a bit but finally held. She kept the speed level as she drove up the embankment. At last she reached the gravel shoulder of the road and stopped. Breathe. She'd done it.

Now on toward Nashville.

~~~

Cole's eyelids drooped heavy as he turned toward home. He'd driven through town for hours. The sun would be coming up soon. Maybe Audrey had a friend she'd gone to stay with. There was that girl from her work, Ivy.

With any luck, she'd be back at the condo, and he could talk to her before practice. Why hadn't she stayed long enough to listen? Didn't she trust him at all? It had to look bad, but he could've explained. If only she'd let him.

Figured. He'd finally done the right thing, and no one believed him.

In the lot, he scanned for Audrey's Honda. No luck. He parked and trudged back through the sea of trash leading to his door. The sour smell sickened his already churning stomach. Inside, he showered and dressed for practice. There was no way he'd sleep. His heart hurt too much.

~~~

Pink strands of light pierced the darkness over the eastern hills. Audrey slapped her cheeks to keep herself awake. She was almost there. Just a few more turns. She picked up her phone. What would Bryan or Pastor Reed think about her showing up at the crack of dawn? Literally.

At the next stop sign, she punched Bryan's number.

"Hey." His voice, though gravelly from sleep, was kind. "Are you okay?"

"Yes. I'm pulling into the neighborhood. Think you can let me in?"

"Of course, but what's going on?"

The quiver in her chest returned. "I can't. I'll see you in a minute." She sniffed and blinked her eyes. Just another mile, and she could forget Cole Sanders for good.

~~~

Seated on the floor outside of Coach McCoy's office, Cole let his eyes shut. He pictured last night's scene from Audrey's perspective. If he'd come up on her and Bryan like that, what would he have thought? Would he want to hear her out? His heart wrenched, and his stomach growled. Great. He'd forgotten to eat. One more addition to the crummy day he was fixing to endure.

He checked his phone for the zillionth time. Nothing from Audrey. No sense calling or texting again this morning. If she hadn't answered by now, she wasn't going to. His abs tightened. Unless something terrible had happened to her. How would he know?

The obvious answer came to mind. Grant. Oh, man. How he hated to ask him. But to rest his mind, he'd text him. Cole searched the number and punched in a message.

Worried about Audrey. Just want to know she wasn't in a wreck or anything. Please.

He sighed and hit send.

A second later his phone signaled a text.

Nashville. Safe.

Nashville? Cole let his head fall to rest on his knees. His eyes stung as he clamped his jaw shut. She'd run to Bryan. Any part of his heart, mind, and soul that didn't ache before, screamed with pain now. How could she?

Footsteps approached. "Um, Cole? Are you okay?"

Cole pressed his index finger across each eye before he lifted his head to look up at Coach McCoy. "No." He hated the quiver in his voice.

Concern filled his coach's face. "Come on. Let's talk. And pray, if you want." He held out a hand to pull Cole to his feet.

Cole followed Coach through the door and sunk into a chair.

Instead of taking a seat behind his desk, Coach McCoy pulled up another chair diagonal to Cole and waited.

The words jammed in Cole's mind.

"Say something. Just start at the beginning." Coach's voice was filled with compassion.

Cole swallowed, his mouth dry. "Last night...Emma. I tried to help her..." How much should he say? He didn't want to get anyone in trouble. "Nothing happened, but it looked bad when Grant and Audrey got home late last night." Covering his face with his hands, he rubbed his forehead. "Audrey wouldn't listen. Took off back to Nashville and won't answer my calls to let me explain. I did the right thing for once, Coach." Cole propped his elbows on his knees and kept his head down. He couldn't look at him right now. He still had a little pride.

Coach McCoy squeezed his shoulder. "I'm proud of you. I don't know what happened last night, but it sounds like the other team is pressing in an attack for your soul. Do you mind if I pray for you?"

Cole's throat constricted when he spoke. "Okay."

"Father God, Cole's hurting, and I imagine Audrey, Grant, and Emma, too. Ease the heartaches. Bring truth to light. Bolster Cole's defenses against evil, Lord. Block the path of anything that turns Cole away from You, and show Cole Your love and grace. In Jesus' name, amen."

"Amen." The fatigue and pain weighing down Cole's shoulders lessened. Not gone, but bearable. He lifted his face and sniffed. "Thanks, Coach." He shook his head. "I don't know what else to do. She won't answer her phone. Should I drive to Nashville?"

Rubbing the stubble on his chin, Coach McCoy looked toward the window. "Audrey's got to learn to trust you if you're going to build a relationship. Communicate. She can't run off and hide when hard times hit. Because bad stuff will come, and this won't be the last time. Does Grant know the truth now?"

The image of Grant's sunken posture as he trudged to his condo came to mind. Cole shut his eyes, as if he could block out the thought. "Yeah. I think he's got the whole picture now. Poor dude."

"Whoa, compassion for Grant. Must've been a really bad scene."

"You don't want to know."

Coach McCoy nodded. "You're right. I don't. Let's go play some ball."

Playing ball, doing the right thing, and leaning on God. That's all he had. With no control of the future, he'd tackle the field of today.

Chapter 35

Falling around Bryan's neck, Audrey held onto him as if to absorb his strength. His warmth comforted the wounds bruising her heart, the fatigue, the fear. "Oh, Bryan." She wanted to forget last night. Forget the last couple of months. Forget Cole.

Her hands moved from Bryan's neck to his cheeks. She pulled his face to hers and pressed her lips to his, eyes closed, blocking out everything else.

With a quiet groan, Bryan pushed away. "Audrey, no. This isn't how…" He lifted her chin, and his blue eyes met hers. "Come inside and talk. Tell me what you're thinking. Driving all through the night to get back to a place I know you were ready to leave?"

"I don't want to talk." Her stupid voice cracked again. "I don't want to think. I want to move forward, sign the contract, and sing with you. Leave school, live here and all of that." She buried her face in his shoulder.

Bryan's arms held tight, and he caressed her back. "I care too much for you, Audrey, to let you make those kind of decisions right now. Maybe if you feel the same in a week or so, but not right now. Let's get you inside."

Fine. Her spine ached after the long day and night, but that pain was nothing a hot bath and a nap couldn't cure. She'd wait a week, and Bryan would see. She was starting a new life now. Without Cole Sanders.

~~~

Audrey entered the back room of the Empowered Hearts shop. Bryan followed with a gentle hold on the tips of her fingers. He hadn't allowed Audrey to hang onto him or kiss him the past week, but often, he caught hold of her hand as they walked or talked. The warmth lulled the lonely cord that daily tightened around her heart. When would the pain go away?

A variety of women stood at waist-high tables in the sunny room with pale blue walls. Some cut fabric, others sorted beads. Along a partition, sewing machines whirred, blending with the sound of the praise music playing through speakers and the smell of the flavored coffee that brewed in the attached break room.

Katerina entered carrying two steaming mugs. "Have some gingersnap coffee, free trade, of course." Small lines crinkled around Katerina's brown eyes as she smiled. "Thank you for volunteering again today, Audrey. And for bringing Bryan along. Everyone is looking forward to the little concert you two will perform this evening."

Bryan took one cup and handed it to Audrey, then accepted the other for himself. "I've been looking forward to this all week. Between the 5k and the Art Frolic, you're sure to have a fantastic open house today."

Ever positive and enthusiastic Bryan.

Audrey sighed inside. If only she shared his optimistic spirit. All week, she'd tried to be upbeat. The fake-it-'til-you-make-it routine. But in the wee hours of the night, she lay awake flipping over her wet pillow. Why couldn't she just forget Oxford and all that went with it? The lack of sleep wore on her nerves. She gulped down two large swallows of the aromatic brew.

Katerina pointed toward a storage room. "Bryan, I'd love to get you started pulling out all the boxes labeled 'Fall,' then you could set them near the door to the shop. You know, halfway through the summer, we put everything on sale and bring out the next season. It's past time now." She held onto Audrey's arm when she tried to follow. "I would like your assistance with a computer issue in my business office, Audrey."

"I don't know if I can help with that, but I'll try." In a daze, she shadowed Katerina to the office decorated with pictures of smiling women of all races. Women who'd graduated the program and overcome their pasts. Audrey stood with both hands hugging the warm mug and stared into the liquid.

"Sit." Katerina motioned to an old armchair across from her desk.

"I thought you wanted me to look at a computer issue?"

Lifting her bangs to reveal the scar on her forehead, Katerina's eyes flashed. "The lifelong reminder of my mistake the first time I ran away to the wrong thing. Terrifying. Your mistake, not so terrifying, but still wrong. My issue with the computer?" Her gazed focused harder if that were possible. "After today, I will only allow you to help me, via computer, from Oxford. You should go back. Do not drop out of school and run away from your problems."

Panic welled up in Audrey's chest. "But why? I thought you wanted me to work for you, and I want a new life."

"A new life is different than what you are doing." Katerina's earrings swung like little pendulums as she shook her head. "I've watched you all week. I know your uncle passed away, but I felt there was more. You have changed, so I called Sarah Beth. She told me about the misunderstanding with your boyfriend, and I will not be a party to your escape from reality." Her chin lifted toward the door. "That young man, Bryan, deserves better than second place, too, don't you think?"

Audrey only partly processed Katerina's last couple of sentences. She'd gotten caught on one word. "Misunderstanding? I saw my boyfriend with another girl with my own two eyes."

"Did you talk with him to hear what he had to say?"

Audrey averted her gaze for a moment. "No. But didn't you run away?"

Tapping one finger on the desk, Katerina's smile flattened, and she angled her body toward Audrey. "Not the same, and you know it. Go back and hear him out, then make your decisions. Besides, I want my marketing manager to have a college degree." One corner of her mouth lifted, and her smile returned.

Janet W. Ferguson

Why did Katerina want to force her to endure more sorrow? The words pulled at her heart. Bryan did deserve to be with someone who truly loved him, but couldn't she learn to love him? He was such a good guy—the perfect guy. He would never hurt her. With Bryan, her heart would be safe.

~~~

Outside his door, Cole turned the key to lock his deadbolt. Once he finished, his hand formed a fist, squeezing the key into his flesh. Saturday night. Audrey should be with him, attending the praise gathering at the CSU. His gut simmered at the emptiness that harassed him. All week he'd pushed himself to his physical limits on the field, prayed, and studied the Scriptures and the book Chris had given him. Still, the agonizing gash in his heart never let up. He forced his feet toward his car. No matter what, he'd keep his faith. It might be all he had left inside.

"Hey, Cole. Can I catch you for a second?" Red hair appeared from behind a minivan. Emma's sister, Cassie.

His chest heaved with a sigh. This could be an embarrassing conversation. "Okay."

The petite redhead took slow steps toward him, rubbing the back of her neck. "It's Emma. I'm worried about her. She's not herself. I'm here to try to get her to the CSU. Do you have any idea what's wrong? If she…" Her voice faltered. "I'm worried, and any insight you could provide would be appreciated."

Oh, man. Cole scratched his head. How much should he say? "She and Grant broke up a week ago. There was a party here. Bad scene."

Cassie's hand went to her temple. "A party. Was Emma acting strange? I mean, you know—"

"She said she fell off the wagon. I tried to help her that night."

"And the rest of the week?"

Heat swept up Cole's cheeks. He'd allowed his anger too large a foothold. He'd chosen to ignore the dark windows every night in Emma's condo. "I'm sorry, Cassie. I didn't check on her. I…"

"Not your responsibility." She shook her head. "I'll see about her. Maybe I can get her out tonight. Thanks for your honesty."

Not his responsibility, but a nagging in his soul told him that as a Christian, he could've told Emma he'd forgiven her and encouraged her to get help. Doing the right thing required strength. A man had to be tough to follow through. Funny how the world didn't seem to notice that fact.

~~~

The last note left Audrey's mouth, and her arms fell limp at her side, joining the rest of her drooping spirit. She'd sung her best and pressed on a smile for the crowd, but her heart disconnected from the words of praise. Had anyone noticed how fake she was?

Shoppers clapped and patted her back. The women of Empowered Hearts embraced her and Bryan, some of them openly weeping.

She refused to weep. Theirs were tears of joy at the freedom Christ had brought them, but hers would be tears of heartbreak and confusion. Nothing alike.

Bryan caught her hand. "What do you say to a walk around the Parthenon after we lock up the equipment? The monument's staying open late tonight because of the art festival."

"The Parthenon?"

His eyes lit up. "You've never seen it? It's a full scale replica of the building in Greece. And so cool. Now it's an art gallery."

"Sure. It's probably as close as I'll ever get to Greece." Audrey tugged her small purse over her shoulder and helped Bryan wind up the cords. They carried his guitar and amp to a storage room and locked the door.

His fingers found hers again and laced between them as they walked to the Jeep. He opened her door. "My lady."

"Thank you, kind sir."

The door shut, and she slumped into the seat. Why couldn't she fall for him?

The silence smothered her on the way over, but her

thoughts kept returning to Katerina's words. And how did Sarah Beth know what had happened, anyway?

"You're still sad. When are you going to talk to me?" Bryan eased the Jeep to a stop on the side of the street near the glowing ancient replica. The majestic white columns stood out against the falling darkness.

Her thoughts stifled. No words came.

Bryan turned and exited, then came around to open her door again. His expressive blue eyes searched hers. No smile lifted his lips the way she'd become accustomed to.

He deserved better. "I'm sorry, Bryan."

"If you don't want to talk, we won't. Let's go see some art." His arm encircled her waist as they walked side by side.

That was a first.

Inside the gallery, the massive statue of Athena towered over them. Focusing on the walls and the paintings only proved to intensify her melancholy. Bryan should be sharing this with a girl who could fully give him her heart.

Back outside, the darkness deepened, allowing a few stars to shine through the trees. Bryan stopped and stared at the sky. "Only the bright ones can be seen in the city. Nothing like stargazing in Oxford." He turned his eyes to Audrey. "Do you ever like to sit out and look at the stars?"

The tennis courts, the stars, the gift, Cole's eyes. Audrey's hand went to her neck to touch where Cole's necklace would've been if she hadn't thrown it somewhere in the back of her car. Her heart fluttered. "I like to look at the stars. In Oxford."

Chapter 36

At the CSU, Cole claimed a barstool near the back wall. Maybe no one would notice him. The musicians up front were good but they didn't compare to Audrey. And Bryan. His rib cage sunk into his stomach. He pushed back visions of her and Bryan laughing and singing together somewhere in Nashville.

Let it go. Let her go. Something good had come of Honduras and Audrey. He'd changed. At least he had that. And God was at his side.

Halfway into the service, snaking around the back edge of the crowd, Cassie entered with Emma not far behind. Cole rubbed his eyes as they edged closer. That was Emma, right? Her blond hair was held tight against her head, slicked back in a ponytail. Swollen puffy eyes avoided him, no makeup, and she wore a wrinkled T-shirt over gym shorts. Like she'd just rolled out of bed after a week of crying. Crud. The nagging urge to go speak to her kicked in full force. *Lord, help me have the right words, because I sure don't know what to say.*

Coach McCoy joined his side. "Where are you going?" His chin pointed to Emma. "You're not going to give her any grief are you? She looks pretty sad."

"I was going to try to let her off the hook. You know, forgiveness, all that."

Coach McCoy's lips pressed together, and he gave Cole a slow smile and a nod. "Good job."

"Wanna go with me?" Cole blew out a chuckle. "Serve as a witness for the defense or however that works. She's got her sister the lawyer beside her."

"Sure."

Concern crossed Cassie's face and lifted her eyebrows as they approached. "Is something wrong?"

Cole pointed, indicating the side door. "Can we all step outside for a minute?"

Never lifting her head, Emma trudged toward the exit. Once the door closed, she turned. "I know I don't deserve to be here, but Cassie made me come. We can leave."

"That's not true, Emma." Cole lowered his voice. "You deserve to be here as much as anyone. I wanted to say..." What did he want to say? Blurting out that he forgave her for causing all kinds of trouble seemed heartless. "Um...I wanted to clear the air. So things aren't uncomfortable. No hard feelings—just normal."

Tearful blue eyes met his. "I broke up you and the love of your life. How can you consider forgiving me?"

Cassie and Coach McCoy exchanged anxious glances and waited for him to answer.

Cole swallowed back the fear closing his throat. "With God, all things are possible. Besides, you didn't break us up. If Audrey had been willing to listen...I mean you told Grant the truth. She left and wouldn't answer my calls."

"She wouldn't even answer her phone in all this time?" A frown wrinkled Emma's forehead, and she punched her fists to her hips. "Aren't you gonna drive up to Nashville and explain things? You've got to try."

Hadn't he walked out to his car, keys in hand, at least ten times, thinking the same thing? "If she doesn't trust me, I can't change her mind."

"Humph. I don't know about that." Her face softened. "Thanks, Cole. I am sorry. I...I'm a terrible person."

"You're not any different than I was before Honduras."

"Ain't that the truth?" Coach McCoy laughed and slapped Cole on the back. "Let's go back inside."

The humor melted away the stress as they returned through the heavy wooden door.

~~~

Outside the Parthenon, Bryan hesitated before he turned the key to start the Jeep. "I'm hungry. You up for food and music on the strip? We could listen to someone else sing for a change. Maybe even dance?"

Audrey shrugged. "I could eat, and I'm a better dancer than Grant, but that isn't saying much."

With eyebrows raising and lowering, Bryan laughed. "Should be entertaining. I know just the place. They serve great yucca fries with their garden burger."

"Yucca fries? Garden burger? You are weird, you know that right?"

A smile played on his lips, but he shot her a sarcastic glance. "I'm sure they have a fried bologna sandwich or something more *normal* for you. Maybe some Vienna sausage in a can."

"Hey. That's a low blow. Besides, Vienna sausage are the best when you go hunting and fishing."

He gave an exaggerated shudder. "Maybe if you used them for bait."

Audrey smiled at his revulsion. He was fun to be with.

After circling three blocks, they finally found a parking place near the strip. By now cars occupied all the convenient spaces, and tunes filled the air. A melting pot of music styles blasted from the entrances of the clubs and restaurants they passed along their walk. Neon lights ignited the night sky, some flashing as Bryan and Audrey filtered through the throng of pedestrians. A world of music. Bryan should feel right at home.

A bouncer stood at the door of the popular night spot where Bryan stopped. "This is it. A lot of famous singers got their start here."

Audrey fished her ID from her purse and glanced around at the chipped paint on the well-worn walls. The dive reminded her of an old restaurant in Jasper. Not much to look at, but good food. With any luck, the same held true here. The dim lighting made it harder to avoid bumping into the hordes of people that crowded the place.

The bass and the drum vibrated her eardrums, and Bryan shouted to make himself heard. "Someone's leaving a table over there. Hurry." His fingers clamped around her hand, and he pulled her through the mass of full tables.

Audrey took a seat and pushed away the dirty plates and

half empty glasses of beer in front of her. "I hope they clear this soon. It's a wonder we didn't knock over someone on the way. You're really aggressive on the table-finding front. I'm shocked."

"So much you've yet to find out about me."

They both yelled, but she'd barely picked out his words. Smiling and nodding might be a better course as they listened to the band.

After forty minutes, their table had been cleared and they had their own half-empty plates. Audrey wiped her lips with a napkin. "Greasy, but good. Yours?"

Bryan nodded as he chewed the last of his yucca fries. A new band warmed up and then began an old dance tune. He pushed away from the table and held out a hand. "Come on. Show me your skills, or lack thereof."

Heart accelerating, Audrey followed. This could be really embarrassing. They danced and laughed, and Bryan twirled her and pulled her to his side, blue eyes shimmering. He was really cute and funny.

But he wasn't Cole.

The music ended, and another song began. Patsy Cline's "Crazy." Her grandma's favorite. The song brought back a memory of the old black albums spinning on a record player while she sang along at the top of her lungs.

Bryan's eyes searched hers. "Slow dance?"

"Why not?"

After stepping closer, he placed his hands on her waist.

With ginger movements, she rested her hands on his shoulders, then leaned closer, his warmth comfortable. Safe.

She allowed her eyes to close and rested her head against his shoulder. The words filtered through the warm air and wrenched around her heart. Cole's face filled her mind. Then Emma in that gown. No. She was forgetting all that. Her eyes popped open, and she found Bryan's lips, touched them with her own. He didn't back away this time but returned her kiss.

The motions stirred nothing. The moment fell flat compared to… She pulled away and pressed her lips together.

When the song ended, she turned her back and walked to the table.

The wound in her heart gashed open. Why couldn't she get past this agony? Her eyes caught Bryan's, and she forced a smile. Thank goodness he couldn't read her mind.

~~~

Once the singers left the stage, Cole waved a salute at Coach McCoy and headed out the exit for home. Near his car, a hand caught his bicep. A big hand with a grip like a snapping turtle.

He groaned and turned to face Grant. "I'm not looking for any trouble, man." Where had the guy been at the CSU? Or was he stalking the parking lot, waiting for a good time to attack?

Grant chewed one side of his lower lip then released his arm. "Me, neither." His eyes darted around the parking lot, as if to make sure no one else lurked nearby. "I heard your conversation with Emma tonight. I'd just gotten here and couldn't make myself go in." He swallowed and wrinkled his nose. "You have changed, and you do love my sister." His eyes still darted around, avoiding Cole's. "Unlike Emma, who never gave a hoot for me."

Had to be tough for Grant to say. "I think Emma cared for you, but she's still figuring life out. Give her time." Cole lifted one shoulder. "And I do love Audrey, but now—"

"You want me to talk to her for you?" The big guy's eyebrows lifted.

"She has to decide to trust me on her own."

"But she doesn't know the truth. If I hadn't freaked—"

Cole held up his palm. "I'll wait. She needs to decide about this Nashville opportunity."

"If you change your mind, let me know."

"See ya on the field." Cole returned to his trek toward the car. What a weird night. Emma had encouraged him to drive to Nashville, and now Grant had offered to intercede for him. Should he change his mind and reach out to Audrey?

$$Chapter\ 37$$

Audrey fought to smother another yawn. At least Bryan had agreed to come to the late service of the huge Nashville church. All night she tossed and turned, replaying the kiss in her head. Even now, beside Bryan in a pew waiting for the church service to begin, her thoughts returned to the scene. Which they shouldn't be doing. But the kiss had left her empty. Had Bryan noticed? What was going on behind those blue eyes?

She glanced at him, then fidgeted with her skirt, smoothing the fabric toward her knees. *Lord, help me. Have I made a mistake? Am I really running away from life? I thought I was making the right choice. The best choice. I'm so confused. What should I do?*

At the end of the row, a tall blonde woman attempted to climb over five or six people, her designer purse thudding against the frame of the seat in front of them. Her hair hung down in her face. Why was she forcing her way into an already crowded pew? Should they scoot over? Audrey glanced at Bryan. A huge grin spread across his lips as he gazed at the woman. Did he know her? Audrey studied the shiny hair and the peach-colored lace dress, snug in all the right places. Too familiar.

The woman inched closer with another thud, then flipped her hair back.

Emma? What in the world?

"Surprise. I'm at church and planning to stay for the whole service." Emma shot a sideways glance at Bryan. "If you know what I mean."

No idea. Audrey's muscles tightened as Emma stepped over her and plopped down in the small space separating her from Bryan.

Really? First Cole, now Bryan? Hot anger and humiliation

pelted Audrey like buckshot. So maddening. "What do you think you're doing here?"

Emma's eyes popped open wider, long lashes fluttering. "Number five in the twelve steps. And really number eight, nine, and ten, too. It's an AA thing, but that's not the point. I had to find out where you were from Chris and leave at a really ugly hour of the morning to get here for church, because you need to know the truth."

Honesty coming from Emma? "This isn't the place or time." Audrey fumbled to find her purse. She needed to leave.

Emma's fingers grasped her forearm. "This is the perfect place and time for the truth." With a dramatic wave of her other hand, she motioned. "We're in a church. Truth is I wronged you and Cole. I tried to, um, come between you, but he wouldn't be a part of it. Flat out told me no, because he loves you. What you saw was him trying to keep me from hurting myself. I'd taken some painkillers that I shouldn't have."

The nerve of this girl. "What are you doing in Nashville?"

"I'm here trying to fix something I messed up, thanks to my addiction. Okay, and due to selfishness." One perfectly waxed and lined eyebrow raised to an arc. "The question is what are *you* doing here?"

Emma's message struck Audrey like a slap in the face.

Oh mercy. Had God sent an answer to her prayer in the form of the curvy blond she'd assumed Cole cheated with?

After releasing Audrey's forearm, Emma pointed toward the exit. "Go on. If you leave now you can get home for the evening service in Oxford." She turned toward Bryan. "I'll take care of Mr. Wonderful. He'll survive, and he can show me all of Nashville today after church. I might even find a place we can karaoke."

Bryan nodded as he stood and pulled keys from his pocket. "I know you still love him. Take the Jeep to the house and get your car. Emma will give me a ride back."

Staring at his keys, Audrey reached toward them, then hesitated. On the stage, the worship leader addressed the congregation with a welcome.

The road home. Back to Cole.

If it wasn't too late.

~~~

Heart beating fast, Audrey gripped the wheel as she entered the Oxford city limits. The last three and a half hours had passed at a pace more like fifty years. Why hadn't she stayed that night and heard Cole out? Believed in him and in his love? Hadn't Grant jumped to conclusions and been wrong about him? Now she'd done the same thing—assuming Emma was telling the truth.

Doubts, fears, insecurities may've robbed her of the man she loved and hurt another one she cared for. How many lives would she mess up?

From the west, sunlight shimmered and glowed through the leaves of the oaks lining the road, flickering splashes of light across the dashboard. She pushed on her sunglasses as a shield. Light, heat, and colors of summer loosened a bit of the tension traveling down her arms. Maybe things would work out.

In the parking lot of the condos, Cole's BMW stood in its usual spot near the sidewalk, like a promise that hadn't shifted. Audrey parked as close as she could to his car, as if somehow the proximity mattered.

She grabbed her duffle bag and slung it over her shoulder. Not much to unload when you run away. Her feet took the path straight to Cole's door, and she dropped the bag on the ground. Fingers trembling, she formed a tight fist, gulped in a mouthful of air, and knocked.

Please let him be alone.

What if he wasn't? What if he was with another girl, and it was her fault? Maybe she should call instead.

But her legs held her in place as she watched a crowd of blue jays fuss and caw from a nearby tree at a gray cat stalking in the grass beneath. The sound pecked on her resolve. Then the knob clattered. It twisted, and Cole appeared, wearing a pale yellow polo and khaki shorts. Strands of caramel-colored hair fell across his forehead, and her fingers itched to touch them. Stubble covered his chin and cheeks, as though he hadn't shaved since she left. Audrey's face numbed as she stared into the wide brown eyes probing her face.

"I..." She struggled to release words from her dry mouth. "I'm sorry I didn't stay. Didn't trust you. I should've listened to what you had to say. Answered your calls."

His lips pressed together, and his arms hung at his side. He cocked his head. "But now you want to hear my side? You trust me?"

"Emma said...I was wrong to run away without talking to you."

His gaze fell to the ground. "Emma? She called you?"

"She came to Nashville today. Strolled in church being Emma, you know."

A small smile came, then left his lips. "I know." Bouncing his attention back to her face, he focused on her. "So you'd still be in Nashville if she hadn't convinced you to give me a chance?"

Audrey brought up her index finger and twisted a strand of her hair round and round. "I don't know. I—"

"I think I know. Did he kiss you?"

"What?" The full weight of what she'd done pommeled against every bone in her body. She'd been the cheater. The user.

"You heard me. Did Bryan kiss you?"

Oh mercy. Why had she been so stupid? "Not really."

Lines carved between his brows. "What does that mean?"

Audrey yanked at the strand of hair wrapped around her finger. If she could rip every piece out right now, it would feel better than answering with honesty and witnessing what the truth would do to those soulful eyes. "He didn't kiss me. I kissed him." The atmosphere seemed to jolt with her confession, crowning Cole's forehead with pain.

"You?"

Releasing her hair, she reached toward him, but he stepped back. "Cole, I only did it in an effort to forget you. I was hurting because I thought you'd been with Emma."

Cole shook his head, moisture welling up around his lower lids. "And I'm the one who can't be trusted? When you ran straight to another guy and kissed him?"

"The way it looked with you standing there, no shirt. The negligee she had on... I trust you...now." The words came out too late. A huge mistake. This couldn't be happening. Desperation emptied the air from her lungs and clouded her vision with tears. "I love you, Cole. I'll do better. Please, forgive me." With two quick steps, she closed the distance between them, then latched her arms around him and held on tight.

~~~

Cole squeezed his eyes shut, moisture trickling down his cheeks. Hadn't he hoped for Audrey to come back? To hold her again?

But though Audrey clung to him, bitterness crushed his joy. Anger and betrayal weighted down his chest like iron shoulder pads.

He'd given his full heart to her, done everything he could to get things right, but his best hadn't been good enough.

"Say something, Cole, please. I didn't feel anything for Bryan because I'm in love with you." Her body shook with sobs, and she held on tighter.

Compassion nicked at his heart when she turned her brown eyes up at him, eyelashes drenched and freckled cheeks soaked. His chest wrenched at the pain he found in her eyes. But could he just pretend like nothing happened?

One of Audrey's hands went to his cheek. Her voice quivered as she spoke through weepy breaths. "Don't give up on me. Fight for us. You're strong and smart, and we can figure this out."

His resolve melted. He'd never been a quitter and wouldn't start now. "I just need time. And space to think." He held her upper arms and took a step back. "Maybe we should take a break, hit pause, and get to know each other as friends." Could he be just her friend? His insides shuddered at the thought. He'd love to hold on and never let go. Forget Nashville ever happened. But they needed to clear up whatever baggage cluttered their past before they could move forward.

Her hand covered her eyes, and she wept harder. "Take a break. I know what that means." She turned away and took a step down the sidewalk.

Her bag lay outside his door. "Wait. You forgot this." He couldn't let her go like that. He caught her arm. "Audrey. Stop. I'm not giving up, but we should cool things off, do things together, but with other people around." The statement lingered. His tone softened. "For a while."

She nodded, quivering jaw locked together, gaze downcast.

"You said you trust me now, right?"

Her eyes found his, and she gave him another quick nod.

"How about Saturday, let's get Grant and whoever else we can load up in his big truck and ride over to the CSU together. Okay?" Tipping her chin, he offered the best smile his lips could form. Could he wait until Saturday, knowing she'd be right down the sidewalk, across the yard?

He had to. If they didn't have trust, they had nothing.

Chapter 38

The bag tugging on Audrey's shoulder had to weigh more than it had when she'd left the car. In fact, heaviness draped her whole body, and deep pain spread through her chest. She'd held so much hope coming home. Taking a breath, she swiped at her cheeks. If only she could go back and hold onto the moment at the tennis courts when Cole had given her the necklace—his heart. She'd relive that night and change every stupid mistake since, forget Nashville and stay right by his side.

Too late.

Like living out a nightmare, she stood at her door and unlocked the deadbolt. Alone. How could she get through this? Audrey rested her head against the wood frame. If she went inside now, she'd fall apart. It was as if an invisible battle raged around her, dragging her toward hopelessness and despair.

God, help me. Pain and insecurity drove me to insanely selfish acts. Hurtful acts. I don't know how to fix the mess I've made. Please forgive me.

After setting her bag just inside the door she checked her phone. Still time to make evening worship service. Maybe Grant would go with her. She needed to let him know she'd come home, anyway, and there was no way she could get through this agony without the Lord.

As if on cue, her brother's door opened, and he stepped out, keys in hand. "Audrey? What are you doing here? You should've told me you were coming home." Twin lines wrinkled between his brows.

"I made a mistake running off." A quiver echoed in her chest, and the deluge of tears threatened. "Are you going to church?"

"Yeah, but what happened? Didn't you talk to Cole? Work

things out?" His eyes held concern, but also hollowness. Had he lost weight?

"I did, but he's upset that I didn't trust him. Wants to take a break." A slew of sniffles followed her words.

"I could talk to him, explain why you have trouble trusting guys. If he knew about Harrison, it might change the way he sees everything."

If only the past week had been a bad dream. Regret weighed on her like debris she couldn't dig out from. She exhaled before forcing out the other hard truth. "He's also hurt because I kissed Bryan."

Grant let that sink in and glanced around, chewing his lower lip. "Give him time." He jangled his keys. "Let's go to church. We both have some thinking to do."

In the truck, Audrey wept quietly until they reached the parking lot.

Grant shifted into park and scrounged around until he pulled out an old T-shirt from under the back seat and handed it to her. "Here. I don't have a tissue or anything."

Stains smudged the crumpled wad of fabric, and Audrey scrunched her nose. "Any chance this is clean?"

A slight curve lifted Grant's lips. "It was clean once."

What choice did she have? She pushed down the mirror on the visor, held her breath, and wiped her eyes and nose. "Let's go." After flinging the nasty cloth to the back, she opened the door. She could do this. *Breathe.*

Inside the auditorium, the slim crowd allowed them plenty of benches to choose from. Audrey slumped into one near the middle, on the end, in case she needed to go bawl in the bathroom. Oh, goodness. She should've picked up some tissues in the foyer.

A young man she'd never seen before came forward and led the singing. Her thoughts drifted to Bryan. Was he having a better day than she was? She'd never intended to hurt him. At least Emma was no doubt keeping him occupied.

Capturing her thoughts and returning them to worship, Audrey pushed oxygen through her vocal chords. Her voice quivered and sounded raspy in her own ears. Though it seemed each note ripped out throbbing pieces of her heart, she praised the Lord.

The minister stood and spoke of giving thanks in all circumstances. Was he preaching to her? She glanced around just to make sure the congregation wasn't staring her way. Nope. But God knew exactly what she needed to hear. She'd seek His face and enter into His gates with thanksgiving. God was enough to complete her life. Even though she prayed Cole would be a big part, too.

The evening sun filtered in through a side window, and the light descended across a communion table that stood near the back of the platform, reminding her of Christ's sacrifice. She had to trust the Lord with her life.

Even in the middle of the mess she'd made, calm settled over her.

~~~

Cole's gut whispered one thing, then another. *Forgive her. Forget her.* Opposing forces ramming each other in his heart. He'd been stunned to find her at his door, then sucker-punched to hear her say she'd kissed Bryan. How could she?

God, I don't know the next move. Please guide me.

He paced the floor, and though it was his resting day, his feet itched to run. He laced up his shoes and took off out the door. Once the parking lot ended, gravel crunched under his feet as he jogged along the shoulder of the road. Even in the evening light, the brutal summer humidity assaulted him. Tears mingled with sweat as he ran harder. Nothing would stop him until he buried all these defiant emotions.

Someone tapped a car horn and waved out the window. "Hey, Cole. Looking good."

He pretended not to hear. Why did everyone in town have to recognize him? After a couple more miles, he reached downtown and turned toward South Lamar Boulevard. Where was he going?

His feet stopped in front of Coach McCoy's house. Advice. He needed advice. But he didn't want to bother Coach at home.

A loud bark and a thud sounded from inside. The big dog must've spotted him. Sarah Beth peeked out the window then opened the door and waved. The usual large grin and soft chuckle welcomed him. "Cole, don't just stand there and stare at the door, come on in."

Cole swiped at the sweat running down his brow with the shoulder of his T-shirt and headed to the door. The dog and cat rubbed against him as he approached, the cat shedding chunks of fur that clung to his damp legs. "I'm sweaty."

Sarah Beth shrugged and rolled her eyes. "Like that matters around this house. Go jump in the pool if you want, though. Jess has extra trunks in the laundry." She headed down the hall. "Speaking of stinky men, help yourself to a drink while I go knock on the bathroom door. Jess was in the shower."

"Thanks." He grabbed a bottle of water from the refrigerator then returned to the living room. This was a bad idea. Bothering Coach at home. "Sarah Beth?" He craned his neck the direction she'd disappeared. "I'll call him later."

"Why?" A low voice returned. "I'm not letting my star quarterback jog home after dark and get hit by some knucklehead texting on their phone." Coach McCoy strolled down the hall wearing gym shorts and a T-shirt, rubbing a towel through his wet hair. "Let's go outside on the front porch and talk, then I'll give you a ride."

Cole followed him out and took a seat on the swing that hung on the far end of the porch. The chains creaked as he shifted.

Coach McCoy pulled an old wicker rocking chair across the wooden floorboards and sat. "Want to tell me what's got you running across town on a Sunday night? Not football, I imagine."

Cole raked his fingers through his hair, not quite sure what to say. "Audrey's back. Says she made a mistake."

A rumble of distant thunder reverberated through the air. Leaning forward, Coach McCoy propped his elbows on his knees. "That's a good thing, right?"

"It would be if she came back without Emma driving up there to convince her nothing happened and…" Should he tell Coach about the Bryan thing?

"And?"

Cole shrugged and shook his head. "Just junk with Bryan, but she says she doesn't have feelings for him. Wants to work things out with me." The wind kicked up and rustled the leaves in the large oaks near the house. "I told her we should take a break. Hang out as friends. Like you said."

Coach's back straightened in the chair. "Since when did you start listening to me?"

A chuckle slipped out, despite his foul mood. "I listen to you every day. And you did say something like that." Cole studied the top of his knuckles for a second. What was Coach getting at? "You think I made a mistake?"

"I don't know your motivation. Are you taking a break to get to know her on a different level? Or because your pride's stinging? Or maybe you're afraid of getting hurt?" The man knew how to call 'em. Behind his eyes lay an amused challenge. "Don't let pride or fear cost you the one you love."

Shoot. Why had he wanted the break? Looked like he needed to do some soul-searching. The storm blew closer, pushing the smell of cut grass through the air. A sure sign the rain was near. "Maybe I do need a ride home. Sounds like that shower's headed this way."

Lightning split the air, and thunder boomed beside them. Coach McCoy stood. "Our cue to go inside. How about some leftovers while we wait for a break in the weather?"

Cole fell in step beside him. "You know I like to eat. And there's a Braves game I wanted to watch."

"I'm on it." Coach grinned and clapped Cole's shoulder. "Glad you came by instead of going out and getting trashed. I'm proud of you."

This man's approval meant the world to him. Cole stood taller. "Coach, how do you learn to trust? To love unconditionally?"

Coach stopped and locked his tough gaze on Cole. "Trust

is work. Remember the other part of what I told you? With man it's impossible. With God, all things are possible. I didn't make that one up."

"Right."

"Hey, I've got an idea. Let's take the CSU gang out to the lake again next Saturday. There's something about the water and sun and sky. It soothes out troubles. Washes away the stress."

Cole cringed. "You mean like me, Audrey, Grant, Emma, the works?"

"Yeah. Be brave. Let's shake things up."

"All right. But sometimes when you shake things up, they explode." Pointing a finger, Cole sunk into the chair by the TV. "And it was your idea."

Chapter 39

Audrey's phone chimed. With each text, hope accelerated her pulse. She checked the screen.

Ivy.

On my way.

Not Cole. What did she expect after she'd kissed another guy? A line had been crossed. Maybe they'd never get over her idiotic mistake. She groaned and rolled over in the bed, untangling her legs from the sheets. At least she still had the job at the country club since she'd decided not to become a famous singing star with Bryan. A sad commentary of how most of her decisions in life turned out.

She checked the mirror and ran the brush through her medium brown hair away from her very *average* freckled face. The nap hadn't done much damage. Good thing, since they were meeting at Grant's truck in ten minutes. Not that she ever looked that special anyway. Would Cole show up?

Another chime. Hopeful eyes flew to the screen.

Mom.

Audrey touched the phone.

You are beautifully and wonderfully made. God created you and prepared a purpose for you before you were born. Be amazing.

Audrey's eyelids blinked hard. God must've been bending Mom's ear. And vice versa. She curled her lips into a smile and tilted her head upward. "Banishing all negative self-talk now. I am blessed beyond measure." The children of Honduras flitted through her mind, then the women at Empowered Hearts. *Yes, very blessed. No more whining.* She gathered her purse and headed to the door.

Outside, humidity wrapped her like a blanket of plastic wrap. Not a cloud in the sky, and no breeze. Mississippi needed another shower to break the stifling heat.

Across the sidewalk, Cole's door opened. If only she could ignore the way his tanned muscles pulled at the sleeves of his polo and think of what to say. This was the moment she'd been anticipating. What would tonight be like? As friends? On a break...

He turned and met her gaze, lifting a finger in acknowledgement. Her insides dissolved. Every instinct told her to go back to her apartment, lock the door, and cry. Forget this painful arrangement. He'd never forgive her anyway.

A thud from behind jarred her from her stupor. "Y'all ready?" Grant stepped up. "Come on, Audrey." He attempted a whisper. "You can do it. Remember what Dad always says."

She mumbled under her breath, "I know, Vaughns bend, but they don't break." How many times had she heard that over the years? A trillion. Maybe that was only true of the Vaughn men.

A horn beeped, and Ivy hopped out of her Jeep. "Hey, guys. Thanks for inviting me to ride with you." She shot a look toward Audrey, followed by an inquisitive smile.

At his truck, Grant opened the front door for Ivy. It had been his idea for Audrey to ask another person along to ease the tension. Kind of silly though, since the CSU wasn't that far. Now that he'd put Ivy in the front, that left her and Cole in the back.

Audrey tottered as she climbed up onto the running board. The crazy tires were so tall. A hand steadied her. Cole's hand. The touch jolted her heart, leaving her tongue stumbling to form a word. "Thanks."

His fingers lingered before he let go. "You're welcome."

How she loved his voice. She'd missed his voice. This would be a long night.

~ ~ ~

Tingling spikes of delight crept up from Cole's fingers as he helped Audrey into the truck. Man, he'd missed her. He glanced at her face after he climbed inside, wincing at her puffy eyes. She'd clearly been crying. Maybe this pause thing couldn't work. But how could he tell her what he felt when he didn't even understand himself? The whole situation drove him mad.

At the stop sign, Grant directed his attention to the front seat passenger. "So, Ivy, did I hear you say you changed your major?"

"Yes. But I shouldn't have to take many extra courses, and I can apply for medical school in the fall."

He lifted one husky shoulder. "Oh, smart girl. Looking to make some money?"

Laughing, she shook her head. "More like become poor. Medical missionary is my goal. Honduras opened my eyes to the need."

The thought barbed at Cole. The way Audrey had given him comfort on that trip. "Honduras changed a lot of things."

Grant nodded. "It was good. I'd like to go back."

"You would?" Eyebrows hiked, Ivy gave Grant an admiring look.

"I liked the work, the kids, the worship. Why not?"

"No reason."

Was Grant moving on already after Emma? And would Audrey move on that fast if—

"What about you, Cole?" Ivy swiveled toward the back. "What are your plans after college? That is on the off chance you don't get drafted."

The question smelled like a setup. Maybe Grant and Ivy were in cahoots. "I don't know. I started in broadcast journalism, switched to marketing. But I might have to take winter session and summer school to finish either way. I don't take many hours during football season." He sighed. "Let's hope I can depend on my strength to make some money, not my brain."

"No." Audrey broke her silence and pointed at him. "That's not true. You're smart. You'd be great in broadcasting or marketing. Whenever you're in front of the camera, you shine." She frowned and pinched her lips closed, as if she hadn't meant to say any of it.

"Thanks." Her words hummed in his mind like a cheerful

song. The girl believed in him.

Without reply, she averted her eyes to something fascinating outside her window.

At the parking lot, Audrey scooted out and hurried away from the truck as if it were about to blow up. Cole mashed his fingers into his temples. Kind of hard to be friends without talking to each other.

Chapter 40

Being friends? Too painful. Audrey pushed through the heavy doors of the CSU and headed straight to the coffee bar. With any luck, Sarah Beth needed help organizing supplies or something behind the counter. Away from Cole.

Humming a happy tune, Sarah Beth unloaded sacks of two-liter drinks and bottles of flavored creamers onto the counter. Her baby bump grew larger each week and, with it, a glow of joy. What would it be like, having a child with the man you love?

Audrey stared, lost in the agony of knowing she'd blown her chances with Cole.

Turning around, Sarah Beth spotted her and grinned. "Hey, I didn't see you there." Her smile faltered as she took a step closer. "You don't look so good. Trouble in Eden?"

A sad laugh pressed its way through Audrey's lips. "I think you mean paradise." The question stung her eyes like that time when she'd mistaken swim-ear medicine for eye drops. "Trust issues. Can I please help?" Audrey held out her hands. "I need to stay busy."

After a quick scan of the sacks, Sarah Beth pointed toward the cabinets. "You are welcome to organize supplies however you like. Wipe down the woodwork, whatever floats your boat."

"I've never been so happy to clean." She opened the pantry, then gathered two bottles of soda. "And Sarah Beth, would you take me off the tutoring schedule. I can't do it anymore. Will you let the coordinator's office know?"

"I will." Sarah Beth caught the sleeve of Audrey's T-shirt between her fingertips. "But you should try to work things out with Cole. Don't let the scars of your past determine your future."

The admonition suffocated Audrey like a chokehold. Was that what she was doing? Again? She set the drinks on the shelf, and then faced Sarah Beth. "It seems happiness is like water running through my fingers. I touch joy, but then it's gone."

"And you're left wet. I know exactly what you mean." Her voice held tenderness. "Don't give up. Hold onto God, and keep plugging at it."

"But I'm not sure the relationship between me and Cole can be repaired. I wish I could sublet my condo so I wouldn't have to see him coming and going. It's so hard."

"Here's where you disappeared to." Ivy patted the counter, the three silver rings on her fingers clacking against the laminate. "Did I hear you say you want to move? You could bunk at my place. We have three bedrooms and only two filled. The apartment manager is going to lock that room off if she doesn't find a renter for the fall."

Though it had been her idea, the reality of moving jarred her. "Okay, I'll check into it with my landlord."

Ivy grinned and clapped. "Cool, we might be roomies."

"Now you're moving?" Anger shadowed Cole's face where he stood near the door frame. "Running away again?"

The sarcastic tone struck Audrey's already shattered heart, sending shards of pain through her chest. She stared at Cole, unable to form the right words to explain. If he wanted to only be friends, she couldn't live in such close proximity, and she couldn't tutor him. Too much had changed.

~~~

The silent moment crept along in slow motion as Cole waited for Audrey to answer. Her intentions hit him like fisted knuckles. How could she just move off and give up on him? Again? Ugly words settled on the tip of his tongue. His jaw clamped shut. He didn't talk like that anymore.

His gut twisted into a knot as he gazed into her puffy eyes. She'd defended his intelligence in the truck, and she'd come back to him from Nashville. Eventually. But a piece of the Audrey puzzle still escaped him.

"You want a drink, Cole?" Sarah Beth offered him a cup of soda. "As my husband likes to say, let's stay in positive town."

"Yes, ma'am. Thank you." He took the cup.

From the stage, the student minister, Chris, called for the group's attention. "Gather around. I have a couple of announcements."

With reluctant steps, Cole moved to the front of the large room. He caught a glimpse of Audrey and Ivy trailing a few feet behind him.

"People, next Saturday Coach McCoy and others will bring their watercrafts out to Sardis for a few hours in the sun. Sunday afternoon, we'll serve the elderly in the Sunnyside Nursing Home by assisting during recreation hour for the dementia unit. Please sign up on the sheets provided here at the front to give us an idea of attendance. I know many of your schedules get packed once school and football take over the town, so let's end our summer of service on a high note. Really get out and contribute to the community."

Coach McCoy stood near the front and shot Cole the look he knew so well. He could hear the words in his head. *Cole, you're a leader, and leaders lead.*

Cole's feet made a path to the front table, where he signed his name on the top of all the lists. He would be there no matter how he felt, no matter what went on in his life. Coach McCoy and football had taught him that much.

Behind him, Grant held out his hand for the pen. "You and I need to talk about Audrey when no one's around."

When would the guy ever let go? Cole sighed and rolled his eyes.

"It's not what you think." Grant shook his head then leaned closer, his voice low. "I want you to understand the full picture of why Audrey is the way she is."

Now that sounded helpful. Grant had his attention. "When?"

"After practice this week. We'll go somewhere and talk privately." The big guy signed his name on the next line, then glanced both ways and took his leave to another part of the room, as if on some covert mission.

Another bizarre night with the Vaughn family.

A young man took the stage and invited the group to join him in song. Around him, voices combined in worship. Cole inclined his ear toward the corner of the large room where Audrey stood motionless. Nothing. He sidestepped at an angle towards her. Was she even singing anymore? Had he destroyed her spirit that much? He should leave.

Finding Grant, Cole tapped the massive shoulder. "I'm gonna catch a taxi. I'm beat."

Chapter 41

Audrey hauled her mammoth suitcase up another flight of stairs to her new temporary living quarters. Maybe temporary. Bringing groceries to the third floor would be such a hassle, but she couldn't live so close to Cole anymore. It was just too painful. She tapped her knuckles against the green door and waited.

Ivy slung it open and grinned. "Hey, this is so exciting. I know it might not be for long, but still, we're gonna have fun hanging out."

With a nod, Audrey entered and pasted on a smile. "My parents were okay with me subleasing. They said since it's Grant's last year, they'd keep my condo for game weekends."

Grabbing the other end of the suitcase handle, Ivy pulled her to the unused bedroom. "Our rental office shampooed the carpet after the last girl moved out. There's a standard bed, a chest of drawers, and a desk. All you need is sheets, clothes, and towels. Oh, I put your key in the desk."

Forcing her feet to carry her forward, Audrey surveyed the small room and bathroom. At least the décor was up-to-date, and the carpet was much newer than what lay in her other condo. Bigger closet. "I have everything I need for a while in the suitcase, and the manager said she'd let me sign month-to-month, since they hadn't found anyone."

"I know this isn't what you really want. Maybe we'll just have a lot of fun girl talks and late night snacks for a few months."

Months? Audrey fought the urge to throw herself on the bed and cry. "You're a good friend. I haven't been close to many girls over the years. Mostly hung out with Grant and his buddies."

"That's changing now." Ivy's cheeks spread into that bright smile. "After we unload this monstrosity you call a suitcase, we'll pop popcorn and put in a chick flick, maybe throw cookie dough in the oven."

Cookie dough. Her stomach squeezed. Why did even her favorite foods remind her of Cole?

~~~

Sweat dripped from Cole's forehead into his eyes as he hung up his pads, then tossed his practice uniform into the hamper in the locker room. He wiped his hair and face with a hand towel. With the first game so close, practice had amped to full speed. Not much time to think about the fact that he and Audrey had barely spoken. But what few moments he had when he wasn't running the field or sleeping, her face haunted him. He missed her like a part of him had been severed.

"Dude, let's go mud riding before it gets dark." Grant's deep voice bellowed, followed by a look with raised eyebrows and an exaggerated head bob, waving him toward the door. "You can leave your prissy car here, and I'll bring you back to pick it up later."

This must be the big conversation. "BMWs are not prissy. They're the best-made car in the world." Cole threw on a T-shirt and shorts from his gym bag. "Guess I don't need to shower since I'll probably have to help you push your big truck out of the mud."

"Don't worry about my truck." Grant shook his keys in front of him. "Let's go."

In the lot, Cole climbed into the shotgun seat. He'd been in Grant's truck more this summer than the past four years combined. Before that, Audrey's brother took care of business on the field but hung out with a select few of the other players. Only the by-the-book sort of guys.

"So, you wanted to clear up something." Cole eyed him as they sped down the road. "Like why Audrey is the way she is."

Grant squeezed the wheel with both hands. The guy's knuckles whitened. "When we were in high school…" He paused, and his forehead creased down the middle. "Actually the night of graduation. My best friend offered to take Audrey home from a bonfire at the Warrior River. He was the quarterback. Mr. Everything at school." He glanced at Cole. "I'd been friends with him my whole life." Grant's lower jaw punched forward. "I trusted him."

A sinking feeling crept through Cole. He forced out words, his voice gravelly. "What happened?"

"There was a field along a back road that led to our house. People went parking there." Grant cleared his throat. "Audrey called me screaming. My mind went straight to that field. I took off in my truck."

Acres of land planted with cotton lined the old highway. Cole pictured those fields, dark and empty, Audrey alone with this guy. A guy not much different than himself on the outside.

Grant turned onto the gravel path leading to the lake and came to a stop. "I was too late. He hurt her. Took her innocence." The air leaving Grant's mouth shook. "I should've known." He shook his head. "I tried to kill Harrison. Beat him to a pulp. If the girl riding with me hadn't called the sheriff along the way, he'd be dead."

"Harrison. The name she screamed when…" It all made sense. The way Audrey had to force herself to hug him after the little boy's death in Honduras. The fear of kissing him at first. Freaking out about the notes on her car. The attack from that weirdo after the summit. She'd been through so much. His shoulders dropped as he leaned forward and let his face fall into his hands. "If I'd known, I could've handled things differently. I—"

"But you didn't. I see you've changed, and you're not now and never were Harrison."

"Where is the guy? I'd like to whale on him myself."

"Ran off." Grant shook his head. "Heard he stays drunk. I've always stayed close to Audrey in case he ever showed up again."

"He's not in jail? He raped her." The words left a bitter taste.

"His skunk of a father is my daddy's boss at the coal mine,

and he said if she pressed charges, they'd press charges against me for attempted murder." Grant slammed his palm against the wheel. "I told them to go ahead and put me in jail. I'd finish Harrison off there. Audrey wouldn't do it."

Out the windshield, the sandy banks along the water met a brilliant blue sky. Too cheerful a sight for the way Cole felt inside. Nausea swarmed his throat like angry hornets. Grief for Audrey's lost security and innocence swallowed Cole. "I don't think I can mud ride. I feel sick. Can you take me back now? I need to talk to Audrey. Make things right."

Grant turned the key and the truck rumbled on again. "Wait and pray before you talk to her. Be *sure* you can handle the burden she carries." A weighty stare nailed Cole. "Please."

Chapter 42

In the mirror of her little bedroom, Audrey examined the makeup Ivy had applied for her. Gray shadow, black eyeliner, and mascara, then powder and blush. More than she was used to, but Ivy had convinced her this event required something extra. Friday night at eight seemed like an odd time for a wedding, but this wasn't just any wedding. The marriage of one of Hollywood's hottest actors had captured the interest of the media for weeks. Dylan and Cassie hoped to keep the time and place a secret, but looking extra nice seemed to be a good plan in case the press's cameras found them.

Would Cole show up tonight?

She'd splurged on a new dress, shopping with her roomie. It was fun having a girl as a buddy for a change. Ivy was a better shopping companion than Grant.

The pale pink silk-chiffon material fitted close at the waist and draped down not quite to her knees. Audrey pushed dangly pearl earrings through her earlobes and then reached for the matching necklace. Her fingertips brushed the chain of the one Cole had given her. She'd unpacked it last week and kept it near as a reminder to pray for Cole to keep his faith in the Lord. After spending time away from him in her new place, she'd read the Bible and done some soul-searching. If nothing else came of their time together, the transformation she'd seen in him over this summer made the pain bearable. Most of the time.

"Whoa. Look at you." Ivy stood in her doorway, wearing her own new dress. A yellow one with delicate lace and billowing pleats. Bright. Like Ivy's smile. "A certain quarterback's going to fall in love with you all over."

Audrey stifled the moan rippling through her. "He can't get

past the Bryan incident."

"That's not true." Ivy waved a playful shake of her finger. "From what Grant tells me, he needed a bit of time. That's all."

"Grant?" Around the edges of her heart, hope sprinkled and grew. "Since when do Grant and Cole talk?"

With rapid, innocent blinks, Ivy shrugged, then pivoted toward the hall. "Let's go. We need to catch our ride on the double-decker bus before it's too late."

~~~

Where was Audrey? Cole fished the paper from his pocket and followed the others onto the red two-story bus. All the students who'd gone on the Honduras mission trip held invitations to the mystery location for Cassie Brooks and Dylan Conner's wedding. Surely Audrey had been invited, despite the Emma drama. Cassie didn't strike him as the type of person who'd leave anyone out. Of course, the invites and instructions arrived last minute to keep the press off the trail. Maybe Audrey had other plans already. He hadn't called her but had spent time praying and thinking about the implications of what Grant had shared. What would her past mean for their future, their intimacy?

After showing his invite and his ID to security, Cole ducked his head for the low ceiling and took a seat downstairs. Alone. Amid the chatter, his heart raced as he glanced around. The motor rumbled and chugged. The last students from the parking lot entered. A few football players climbed the stairs to the top level. The driver spoke to someone outside the window, checked his phone, and then announced their departure over the intercom.

No Audrey. Cole released a pent up breath. Probably just as well, except with this pounding headache, he might've stayed home if he'd known she wasn't going. He sat back and closed his eyes.

The bus maneuvered forward then stopped with a jerk. Cole raised his lids and pivoted toward the back door. A second later, it opened. Ivy Patterson entered, then Grant, and finally Audrey. All at once, his breathing halted, his mouth fell open, and he stood. Like a dream, dressed in pink, Audrey filled his vision and smiled. A little shaky, but a genuine kind of smile. And so beautiful.

Ivy sat two rows ahead, and Grant joined her. With what had to be a goofy look on his face, Cole grinned back and motioned for her to take the seat beside him. He continued staring shamelessly. "You look so pretty, Audrey."

She hesitated, then sat. "Are you going to sit down?"

Yep. He was still hopelessly in love with this girl. He plopped down on the vinyl bench. Her nearness warmed him more than the August heat. A sweet fragrance tickled his nose. Something like vanilla mixed with oranges.

"I've missed you." Cole held in a groan. What a conversation opener. "And you smell nice." Another cool line.

"Ivy spruced me up a bit." Audrey stared at her hands.

He'd practiced asking this question over and over since he and Grant talked last week, but still the words jumbled in his mind. "Have you ever done a Bible study? I mean, like, with another person? Together? Just you and that person?" Good grief.

Wrinkles formed between her eyebrows. "I'm not sure what you're asking."

Cole massaged his forehead. "I'm trying, not very well, to ask you if you'd meet me at the student union steps or a coffee shop in town every night after practice and do a Bible study with me. Chris gave me a workbook." If they talked through the topics, maybe they could work through the issues holding them back.

Eyes hopeful, she nodded. "Okay." Her teeth dug into her bottom lip.

"Can we start tomorrow night?"

"I don't have any plans after dinner."

As the bus wound around the outskirts of town, he studied her face, taking in every detail, every sweet freckle. Her cheeks flushed with a light pink, but she kept her gaze down. They rode up a hill and around a curve to stop in front of an antebellum-style home that had been converted into an inn.

With steps slow and even, they exited the bus and crossed the lawn together. They were silent, and he couldn't think what to say, couldn't stop gawking at her.

Security guarded the inn, took the name of each guest entering, and verified that they were on a list. Cassie and Dylan weren't taking any chances of some crazy fan or reporter ruining their wedding.

Inside the mansion, Cole rested his hand on Audrey's back as they made their way to a row of white folding chairs. "Are these seats okay?"

She nodded and fiddled with her small purse.

For the next fifteen minutes, guests entered with hushed conversations, but he and Audrey sat in silence. Seemed like he could come up with some small talk. Why was his mind such a blank?

At last, an acoustic guitar broke through the voices. Cole's stomach plummeted as Bryan's voice lulled the chatter to an end.

Audrey's eyes widened as she turned to him. "I didn't know, or I would've... Sorry."

Her fearful expression left no doubt that she was telling the truth. Cole touched her hand with his fingers. "It's okay." His abs loosened. They'd get through this. He let his fingers stay on top of hers. She didn't pull her hand away, but she didn't clasp his either.

After two songs, Dylan and his groomsman took their places at the front, and the tune changed to a wedding march. Sarah Beth entered as the first bridesmaid, her smile huge. Behind her the other redheaded sister. Not quite a smile on her face.

Then Emma. His headache worsened.

Cole resisted the urge to sigh and let his chin fall forward. Why had he thought coming to this wedding was a good idea? His touch became a grip on Audrey's fingers. With a sideways glance, her lips pinched together, and she returned the grasp.

The guests stood as Cassie entered, red hair flowing down her shoulders. Beside her giant father, Cassie almost looked like a little girl.

Cole turned his attention to Dylan. Tears evident in an adoring gaze, emotion caused the man to touch his fingers to his lips.

What would it be like to commit the rest of his life to one person? Cole's eyes found Audrey's. Could they spend their lives together? His heartbeat quickened, and his mind fuzzed a bit. Thank goodness they got to sit.

Words from the minister followed. Words about Christ and His bride the Church. Words about love and promise. Words that had always seemed stupid in the past but now made sense. There was beauty in commitment. Holiness.

~~~

A lump formed in Audrey's throat. She'd always cried at weddings, even before the rape. Now add in the fact that Cole sat next to her, being so kind, despite Bryan and Emma being right in front of them. Had Cole forgiven her? She battled not to blubber like a baby.

Looking at the faces of Cassie and Dylan gave her hope. The way they looked at each other, both so overcome with joy. Audrey swallowed back the emotion and took a deep breath. Could she ever have intimacy with a man? A husband? Would she always feel tainted?

Lord, my life's in Your hands. I'm going to follow You, no matter what.

At last, the minister pronounced the couple man and wife, and the guests cheered as Dylan kissed his bride. Audrey's eyes and nose stung as she fumbled at the latch of her small purse. She needed a tissue.

Once the reception began in the next room, Cole led Audrey through the food line and to a table. Grant and Ivy joined them. Another band played for the newlyweds' first dance. While they ate, Cole smiled and stared, barely speaking.

Audrey sighed. The whole situation left her speechless, too. At least Grant kept up a conversation about the food. This appetizer was good. Another dessert was even better. No lack for culinary commentary.

After the cake had been cut, Dylan toasted his bride and took the stage. "Ladies and gentlemen, thank you for being a part of our special day. You are welcome to continue the festivities as long as you like. The double-decker bus will shuttle guests back to Oxford about every fifteen minutes." He grinned, his gaze turning to Cassie. "But I'm whisking my wife away to a private island. God bless you all."

The couple hustled out the back door and into a waiting helicopter. A satisfied warmth swept through Audrey. What a sweet wedding. At least someone had a happy ending.

Cole tapped her shoulder. "Hey, I'm thinking of cutting out. I have a headache. I think it's the heat. You came with Ivy and Grant, right?"

The warmth from a second before dissipated. "See you for Bible study?"

"I was hoping to see you at the CSU lake party tomorrow. Do you ski?"

"I never got the hang of it. I love to ride the inner tube, though."

His gaze fell to her lips. "What's not to love?"

She nodded, heat creeping across her cheeks.

"So, you'll come?"

"Yes." How could she refuse?

Chapter 43

The water sparkled in the sunlight. Renewed rays of hope rushed through Audrey as she stepped onto the boat, Cole at her side.

Grant and Ivy took turns on the ski equipment first. It had been nice to have them along at the picnic table to keep the conversation flowing. Especially when Emma and Bryan arrived with the Jet Skis. So odd. Neither couple seemed more than friends at this point, judging from their body language, but it was still weird to see.

Watching Cole, another story. Audrey took in the view of him. His muscular arms, his caramel-colored hair sticking out from under his baseball cap. Too bad she couldn't see those eyes behind the sunglasses. But his lips. He hadn't stopped smiling. Something had changed. Being with Cole last night and again today blossomed hope within her heart. Awkward at first, yes, but still, it felt like she'd come home.

The boat stopped, and Coach McCoy cut the engine. "You ready to ride the tube?"

Cole stood. "I'm ready. You?" He held his hand out to her.

Audrey took it and stood. "Ready."

~ ~ ~

The wind kicked up, ruffling the water that had been smooth ten minutes before. Additional boaters churned up waves, as well. Cole gripped the handles on his side of the double tube. Should be a fun ride. "You ready for this, Audrey? Gonna be a bumpy one."

She smiled and nodded, her freckles darkening in the sun. The girl had been quiet, but she'd probably been wondering what he was thinking. During the Bible study, maybe they could get deep and really talk about their issues. At least, that was his hope. "Hit it, Coach."

After Cole's signal, the rope surged forward, wind whipping and bouncing the tube over the waves. Audrey giggled as they rocked and swayed.

Boy, he loved the sound of that rare laugh. As the boat accelerated, so did Cole's adrenaline. "You want to cross the wake?"

"Sure." Audrey's voice was barely audible over the spray.

The air smashed their hair against their faces as they skimmed the surface, bouncing higher as they swung out from behind the craft. Too bad Coach McCoy wouldn't go faster, though. Cole chuckled. He'd love to catch some air.

After a while, Audrey teetered from side to side, holding on with white knuckles. Her smile flashed satisfaction with the ride and the speed.

The boat made a sharp turn as a larger yacht charged by full speed. The waves heightened, and Cole swung out in the opposite direction. A large swell loomed ahead. No time to change course.

They hit hard, catching air. The tube flipped forward, and water slapped Cole's face. The blow propelled water into his nose, mouth, and eyes. Though he wore a vest, his mind buzzed as he fought to find the surface.

At last, hands pulled him up into the light. He coughed the dirty liquid from his throat.

"Cole?" Audrey's voice. "Can you hear me?"

His eyelids fluttered open. "Yeah." He coughed. "Water in nose. Fine." That was all, right?

She stayed near as the boat circled.

Coach McCoy cut the motor and leaned out. "You guys okay?"

Cole gave a thumbs-up.

"I tried to steer around the drunk in the yacht going way too fast." Coach shook his head and held out a hand.

"You first, Audrey." Cole motioned.

"No. You spilled hard. I fell off the back somehow."

With a sputtering sigh, Cole accepted the help. When he

stood, the boat blurred and spun. He dropped into the closest seat and closed his eyes.

"You sure you're okay?" Audrey's voice echoed in his ears.

"Fine. You?" He opened his eyes, smiled, and shot her a pleading look.

Her lips pushed together when she nodded. No fooling her, but maybe she'd give him time to recover without mentioning it to Coach. All he needed was a few minutes, and the dizziness would disappear. It had to.

By the time they reached the dock, a slight headache troubled him, but not as much as the nausea clawing his stomach. He gathered strength to balance himself while he exited the rocking vessel.

Audrey stayed near until they reached the picnic table again. "Let me drive you home now. I can tell you're not feeling well." She touched his cheek. "Like the night when that terrible man attacked us."

"It's not that bad." A wave of drowsiness settled over him, like a morning fog. "But you can drive me home if you want." He handed her the keys.

"I'll start the car and get the AC going. You get in, then I'll run tell Grant I'm leaving."

He followed her to the BMW and got in. Once she'd cranked it, she turned the air to high.

"I'll be right back."

It took a minute to cool, but the air blew against Cole's face, relieving a bit of the queasiness. Sleep would be good. He let his eyelids close.

The driver's door opened, but he let his mind drift. A voice yanked him awake.

Someone shook his shoulder. "I'm telling Coach if you don't open your eyes right now so I'll know you're okay."

He forced his eyes open. "I'm fine. Just resting."

Audrey grabbed his chin and tipped it toward her. "Are you sure?"

"Yes." He smiled at her concern. And cute sunburned nose. "But you can stay with me a while when we get home, just in case."

~~~

With Cole settled into his recliner, Audrey dropped onto the couch and studied the information she'd pulled up on her phone. She'd closed the blinds and cut off the television. From what she'd read about concussions so far, Cole needed quiet and rest. And a concussion had to be what happened. Again. Or maybe he never recovered from the last one. Had he endured concussions before? The damage could compound.

A soft tap at the door sent her to her feet.

Grant stood there, clean and showered, but the August heat pressed in the door along with him. "I got your text. Let me look at him." He stepped past Audrey. "Cole, you hit your head again?"

Cole's eyes fluttered open. "Just on water. Nothing like the other whacks."

"Other whacks?" Bracing her arms against the back of the recliner, Audrey eyed her brother. "I only know about one." Grant averted his gaze to the floor and fidgeted with his keys. Something reeked about this secret. She folded her arms across her chest. "Truth time."

Cole sat up. "I took a bit of a fall at practice and hit my head on the ground the same day Berkley Long attacked you."

"You fell?" Audrey asked. She looked between her brother, who still wouldn't look at her, and Cole. "What happened before your *bit of a fall?*"

"It was my fault." Grant squared off with her, his eyes pleading. "I need help with my anger, and I'm getting it. Audrey, I promise I'll cover him in next week's game. No one will get past me." He kneeled to take a look at Cole. "Not to say he shouldn't see Dr. Marlow if he's hurt. Concussions can be dangerous, but your pupils are the same size. Not enlarged. Is your vision blurry like that time last year during the Arkansas game? Or what about the year before against Georgia?"

"I sucked in some water." Cole waved him off. "Chill. I'll get plenty of rest." He glanced up at Audrey. "Do you mind if we start our Bible study here tonight?"

"Bible study?"

One look at Grant's face told Audrey her brother was fixing to say something stupid. With a hard shove, Audrey pushed him. "What about it?"

"Shoot, girl. You didn't have to shove me. I might want to do the study. Where's the book?"

The recliner squeaked as Cole struggled to get to his feet. "I don't think you'd like this one."

"Why? Where is it?"

Cole didn't answer, but Grant followed his gaze to the end table.

They both rushed to pick up the book turned facedown.

Grant won. He flipped the paperback over. "Questions to Discuss Before Marriage." His head shot around so fast, he'd probably need to see a doctor, too.

An inferno of emotions blazed through Audrey. No doubt her face was three shades of red as she pushed her brother toward the door. "You were here to check on Cole. You're done."

With a smirk, Grant threw the book to Cole and took slow steps to the door. He hesitated with his hand on the knob. "Good idea to talk about things. I should've done that with Emma." Then he snorted. "Maybe not with that book, though."

"Shut up." Cole's forehead wrinkled in the middle. "Chris gave me this. He said there's good stuff—"

"Leave now, Grant." Audrey shooed her brother through the door and closed it with a vengeance. She whirled to face Cole. "And you, hand me that book, then sit back in the recliner."

The room held a quiet buzz of tension. Should she be thrilled or insulted by Cole's assumptions? She stared at him. A small ray of sun filtered through a bent blind slat and touched the top of Cole's head. His hair shimmered golden in the light. With his eyes closed, she dared gawk longer at his strong jaw, notched with the single dimple. He'd been sweet last night and earlier today. She smiled, warmth filling her. She was thrilled. Definitely not insulted.

But questions plagued her. What happened at the Arkansas game? How many concussions had Cole suffered? Not only that, could she handle marriage like a normal person? Be a good wife to him in every way? One thing was certain. No more putting it off. She'd have to tell him the truth.

Chapter 44

Three hours later, Audrey stirred on Cole's couch. Between the fatigue from water and sun, and the quiet in Cole's condo, she must've dozed off. Her last memory was rehearsing the way she'd tell Cole about the rape. How she hated that word. The profanity of it. The sound of the letters twisted her stomach. Someone should rip it from the human vocabulary. Rip it from the human consciousness. Rip it from her memory and push it under a gravestone. How different her life might've been.

Thoughts of saying the word to Cole formed a chokehold around her neck, shame and fear crushing off her breath.

He tilted his head toward her with a sleepy smile. "Have a good nap?"

"I shouldn't have slept. I'm supposed to be watching you." She pulled to her feet and shuffled over to the recliner to look into his eyes. His gaze did funny things to her brain. Why was she so close?

"Are my pupils messed up? I think it's bad if one is bigger than the other." His breath warmed her chin.

That's it. Checking his pupils. "There's nothing wrong that I can tell, but I'm not a doctor. You should go see one." She forced herself away from him and gathered her phone. "I can call for you."

"Don't. I'm fine."

"What about the other hits? I want details."

The footrest of the recliner shut with a snap. He sat up and took a deep breath. "Bible study first. You promised to do one after supper. And I'm hungry." He patted his abs as he stood. "We could call for takeout and get started. With a little something to eat and rest, I'll be good as new." He held the book toward her. "You want to read the questions after I call for food?"

Shackles of fear tightened around her heart. The time had come. She had to do it now. "I need to tell you something first." Her hands accepted the book. She hugged it to her chest like a shield and took a deep breath. "Something that happened to me. Changed me."

With one step, Cole reached her, then caressed her shoulders. "I know. About graduation night. The field."

His eyes filled with tears and became like liquid globes reflecting pain back at her. A mirror of her shame covered in pity. Exactly what she didn't want.

Hot anger and humiliation pushed her back a step. "Grant or Emma?"

"What?" Confusion pinched his brows.

"Which one told you?"

"Grant. But, Audrey—"

"No buts. It wasn't his place to tell you or Emma. When?"

He closed the distance between them. "Audrey." His voice was soft. Comforting. "Don't let the past come between us anymore. We've wasted so much time."

"When?"

A quiet sigh passed through his lips. "A little more than a week ago."

The heat ebbed to a warmth. "So not yesterday. You've had time to think about it?"

"Yes. Yes." He nodded and smiled. "I've prayed about us. About how to deal with our issues."

"Our issues?"

Cole took her into his arms and kissed the top of her head. "I love you, Audrey. We both have problems to tackle. Everyone does, really. Some are just bigger and tougher than others."

His strength and warmth enveloped her. Saturated her with hope. "I love you, too."

"You were so brave to try to explain. I guess you've never told anyone before?"

Audrey's stomach twisted. Could she just stay quiet?

His hands stilled. "What? You tensed up again."

No more holding back. "I told one person besides my counselor." She licked her dry lips and squeezed her arms around Cole. "Bryan. Not long ago. I was going to tell you, too, but we had that fight."

A heavy groan came while Cole pulled away. "I don't understand." He shook his head. "That's so personal..."

"He asked what happened in my past because of the words of my songs. And I thought I could practice the words with him before I told you."

Silence surrounded her, stealing the warmth from a moment before. "I'm sorry." Why did her mistakes have to overshadow her chances at happiness every stinking time? She was like a broken jar where the joy seeped in, then spilled immediately back out to spoil. "I can leave and hang out at Grant's. Call us if you don't feel well."

His chin lifted, his gaze touching her then dropping to the floor. "Okay."

Her feet trudged across the room, carrying her out the door. Why? Why couldn't she pry away the fingers of ruin the rape kept squeezing around her life? *God, help him understand.*

~~~

The pounding at the door couldn't be anyone but Grant. No one banged that hard. Cole moved to answer.

Grant held up his phone. "Past time to go to the nursing home. You wearing that?"

The same shirt and shorts he'd thrown on after boating the day before hung from his frame, wrinkled. "I was thinking about skipping."

"Nope. You signed up. We're leaders." Grant's massive arms crossed his chest. "I'll wait."

Of course, he'd wait. Probably to give him another knock on the head. Cole left the door ajar while he changed.

Moments later, he and Grant traveled toward the other side of town in silence. When was the big guy gonna let him have it?

In the parking lot of the one-story flat building, Grant eased to a stop. "I have one thing to say before we go in."

"Finally. I was waiting for it."

The look on Grant's face shook the sarcasm from Cole. Grant's features contorted as if in great pain. "If you'd been there, seen what happened, you wouldn't let your stupid pride tear a good thing apart. I've accepted my sister loves you. I've accepted you're different than you used to be. Now be different."

Grant pivoted and left the vehicle. Cole sat there, unmoving. Pride? Was that ruining his chance at love? Hadn't Coach McCoy said pretty much the same thing? *Lord, show me the truth.*

Inside, a scent smacked Cole's nose. Antiseptic mixed with something sour. *Don't go there.* Students sat next to their bingo partner. Grant had already taken the last open chair.

Chris waved Cole to the front of the room. "Great, our master of ceremonies has arrived. Our star quarterback." He handed Cole a microphone and pulled him toward the wire basket holding the letters. "You, sir, are the bingo caller and emcee extraordinaire."

"Nice, Chris."

With a smug smile, Chris chuckled. "Your prize for being late. I've already gone over the rules."

Cole gathered his game face and held the microphone near his lips. "Welcome, ladies and gentlemen. What an honor to be here today. It's my great pleasure to begin the games."

An elderly woman near the back raised her hand. Audrey sat beside her as partner, her eyes shining.

Cole acknowledged her. "Ma'am, did you have a question?"

"Are you ready to swallow your pride and fight to save your marriage?"

The other students smiled. Chris leaned close and whispered, "She's asked everyone else already. Used to be a family therapist."

Warmth covered Cole. God worked in the funniest ways sometimes. "Yes, ma'am. I am." His eyes met Audrey's, and he gave her his best smile. "God's straightening me out."

An hour later, the patients all held small prizes. A few tired out or lost patience and left early. The remainder saddened when he announced a number-letter combination, and someone yelled "Bingo."

Cole returned the microphone to Chris, then joined Audrey at her table. He smiled at Audrey and the elderly woman beside her. "Hi. I see y'all won a brush and comb set."

"She did. You want me to open it for you, Mrs. Jordan?" Audrey held out a hand.

The elderly woman nodded. "Mighty kind of you to offer, Belinda. I'd love for you to brush my hair. I haven't been able to make it down to your shop in a couple of weeks."

Eyes wide, Audrey removed the comb and brush from the packaging, then stood behind Mrs. Jordan. "Are you tender-headed?"

"Not any more than the last hundred times you styled me."

Cole's stomach tightened. Should he laugh? Take over? He wondered how Audrey would handle this.

With slow strokes, Audrey brushed the thin gray hair. So gentle. The Audrey he'd fallen for in Honduras.

Walls of pride crashed down from around his heart. God put this girl in his life for a reason. Even Grant could see it.

And he wouldn't miss out on love. "Audrey?"

Still brushing, she tilted her head toward him with a wary gaze. "Yes?"

"Can we meet later? I have the pre-game press conference then film to watch and stuff for a few hours, but after that?"

Her small nod was enough. More than he deserved, actually.

Chapter 45

Reporters camped around Cole, at least ten microphones pointed toward him at the table. More in the audience. Cameras beeped, snapped, and a few flashed as he began. "Thanks for coming out. We're looking forward to a great season. Strong recruits joined the team. A lot of chemistry and cohesion. Good tempo." He looked toward a few of the larger network cameras and smiled. "I'll take questions now."

"Cole, you've always enjoyed a great passing game. How's the arm?"

"My arm's better than ever. I've been blessed never to have any shoulder injuries in all my years of football."

"A couple of big defenders graduated. Is the team strong enough to go to a bowl game again this year?"

Cole nodded with a wink. "It's a tough league, but the championship is always our goal. Each game is its own battle, though."

More questions followed, and he fielded each one with humble confidence the way Coach McCoy had taught him. "One more before we close out."

"Cole, how did the summer of service that some of you participated in benefit the team?"

Unexpected question. How to describe the way his life had changed over the summer? "Serving others grew me as a human being, as a man, as a leader. The various components worked together to bring about enormous change in me and others. A change that I will take, not just to the field, but throughout the rest of my life."

After hours of film and team meetings, Cole walked out of the practice facility. A light headache buzzed his forehead. Long day. But he'd gladly meet Audrey at the Union.

"Cole, wait." Coach McCoy jogged up. "I meant to catch you earlier. You did a great job at the press conference. Have you ever considered a career as a sportscaster?"

The question both honored him and nagged at him. The pro scouts were expected next week. Did Coach know something he didn't? Cole lifted one shoulder and shook his head. "Why? You heard I wouldn't be chosen in the draft?"

"Not at all. It's just that sometimes what you dream of doesn't turn out to be all you'd hoped." They took steps toward the parking lot. "I thought I wanted pro, but one injury was all it took to end that dream. What I ended up doing is what I was meant to do. I love it. You might love coaching or broadcasting or sports marketing. Think it through. Professional football is brutal work. And it seems like you're pretty serious about Audrey. Maybe even considering settling down."

Grant must've told him about the book. "I'll think it through. I know you waited until you were a good bit older to marry. Do you think I'm too young at twenty-three?"

One side of his mouth cocked up. "Um, thirty-three isn't over the hill, but I waited for a lot of reasons, the biggest one was I hadn't met the right woman."

"Right. But plenty of guys in the league are married. If I still want to give it a shot, what will they look for?"

"The scouts evaluate game video, practice, and live games for all positions. They'll do some body-typing. How you carry your pads, your muscular structure. Even arm length and hand size. They gather character info like family stability, work ethic, accountability, mental aptitude."

Cole groaned. "Mental aptitude? Doesn't sound too promising for me."

With a tight grip, Coach McCoy seized Cole's shoulder. "You've convinced yourself, or someone else has along the way, that you're not smart. It simply isn't true. You know the plays as well as I do, you analyze the other teams, give it your all at practice, and still maintain your GPA."

"Not without tutors."

His grip loosened. "I think the tutors have become a crutch. A crutch you could've thrown away two years ago. You're holding onto insecurity you need to bury and move on."

Was Coach right? The stigma of needing extra help and comparing himself to his brother had always caused him self-doubt. "Thanks. I'll give your advice some thought."

~~~

The evening heat of Mississippi August still pressed in, but at least the rows of magnolias and oaks shaded the last of the sun's rays. Audrey leaned against an oak wider than three men. Or two Grants.

Cole sat beside her. The size of his hands never ceased to amaze her. Warmth filled her as they covered her own. She bowed her head. Never in a million years did she imagine this picture of them praying together in the Grove.

"Lord, guide us in your will. Bind us in your love. Lead us in your wisdom. We love you, God. Amen."

Cole's voice, reverent and beautiful, left her with moist eyes.

"Amen." Audrey sniffed.

He released her hands and lifted the cover to the first page of the book lying across his lap. "Before we start. I need to apologize for how I reacted. About Bryan and…well, you know. My pride got the better of me, and I'm sorry. Can you forgive me?" His lashes lowered as his gaze went from her eyes to her lips.

"I can." Audrey pushed back the urge to kiss him. "Where do we start?"

"I'd like to start like this." With a chuckle, he pecked her on the cheek, his lips warm and soft.

Could he read her mind?

"Questions. Lots of questions. That's how we really start."

They discussed having children, religion, love languages, solving conflict. All in agreement so far.

Cole read the next line. "What type of career do you want? Whose career will take priority if the need arises?"

Good one. Audrey twirled a finger around a strand of her hair. "You know I'd like a career with a non-profit, preferably like the one Katerina runs. One that helps women. But I'd follow…my husband wherever he went."

"That's good, because some husbands have to move around. Especially in sports." He nudged her with his elbow.

"You're still hoping to be drafted?" The thought of Cole being tackled and slammed to the ground every week for years punched her in the stomach.

"Coach McCoy suggested a few other options."

Thank God for Coach McCoy. "Like what?"

Audrey's mind raced as he ran through the ideas. A weight seemed to lift from her shoulders.

"I love those options. Especially sportscasting. It still means the possibility of travel or moving around, but not so much getting sacked and injured."

But would Cole choose one of those careers if he had the chance to stay on the field as a player?

The last bit of sun faded, and mosquitoes nibbled on Audrey's ankles. She swatted at one particularly ambitious bug.

Cole laughed. "I'd forgotten how sweet you are. You attract all us pesky varmints." He closed the book with a slap. "We can go. I'll walk you to your car."

Her hands caught his cheeks and pulled his face close. "Don't ever stop buzzing around me. I love you, Cole Sanders." She captured his lips with her own, his scent and the night air mingling in her senses. His sweetness and the taste of him weakened her and strengthened her all at once. Such delight.

Cole pulled away with a soft groan. "I love you, too, Audrey."

Chapter 46

"My parents will be at the restaurant in thirty minutes or so. We've got one last question to answer." Cole opened to the final page of the workbook. The smell of the coffee shop overwhelmed his senses, sending a wave of nausea through his stomach. He fought against another round of dizziness. When would this finally go away?

A slow smile spread across Audrey's face. "I'm not sure whether to cheer or be sad."

"Yeah." His eyes found hers. "Some of the topics were tough, but I can see the value of talking things out. Tackling the big issues."

Her gaze fell to the coffee in her cup. She stirred the swirls of melted whipped cream.

She'd straightened her hair and worn a dress to meet his parents. Cole touched her hand. "You look great, by the way. Don't worry. My parents will love you."

"Thanks." The skin around her freckles grew pink as her eyes found his. "What's the last question?"

He scanned the page. "What causes you the most anxiety about your future together?"

Audrey's smile faded. Moisture pooled in her eyes. "Intimacy. Because of what happened."

He squeezed her hand. "It'll be okay. We'll work through it." If he'd brought the ring with him, he'd get on one knee here and now. But he'd wanted to wait until he could officially meet her parents first.

She sniffled and brushed at her eyes. "What about you?"

A lot of the reason he hesitated to ask her. "Making a good living to take care of a family. If I don't go pro, how will I cut it in the real world? Football's been a part of me as long as I can remember. The guys, the locker room, the strategy, the battle on the field. It's in my blood, a part of me. What am I without it?" There. He sank forward after he'd spit out the whole truth. All his fears.

Audrey left her side of the booth and slid in beside him. "Oh, Cole. There's so much more to you. I know how you love the game, the comradery. I've lived and breathed football with my brothers as long as I remember, too. But you are more than what you do on the field." Her arms encircled him. "If you don't play, you can coach or commentate or find a new career you'll love. Please. If you think you have a concussion, get checked out. I want you alive and well to teach our kids to throw a ball. Or kick a ball. Or fly a kite. Whatever they want to do with their dad."

Tension he'd not realized he held in his chest released. It faded and ebbed away like a bad dream long forgotten. "I want that, too." His lips brushed hers. "I love you." The phone in his pocket chirped, and he pulled it out to check the screen. "My parents are parking down the street at the restaurant."

"Sorry my parents couldn't make it before the team leaves to stay at the hotel. My little brother can't miss too many days his senior year, but they'll be around Saturday night after the game and Sunday." She rubbed his nose with hers. "Actually, they'll be staying in my place, right across the sidewalk from you."

Cole chuckled. "Now that does cause me a bit of anxiety. Grant, your other brother, *and* your dad."

Chapter 47

A sea of red filled the stadium. Cole stood shoulder pad to shoulder pad with Grant, waiting to run out of the tunnel. The roar of the fans and rumble of drums escalated Cole's heart rate and sent adrenaline coursing through his body. The first game of the season. Always his favorite.

At the head coach's signal, artificial smoke bellowed at the exit. Cole turned back to face the team. "We're ready for this! All in!"

The team shouted back. "All in!"

Grant fist bumped him. Hard. The black marks smudged under the big guy's eyes made him even more intimidating. "I've got your back. Let's do this."

"Glad you're on my side. Let's do this."

The team shouted and ran behind the coaches as they took the field. Cheerleaders waved huge red and blue flags. The crowd surged to their feet, their chants echoing in Cole's helmet, ramping up the buzz in his forehead. If only he could shake this headache.

~ ~ ~

A cannon blasted after the home team scored. The pom-pom waving in front of Audrey's line of sight only served to annoy her and up her apprehension about this game. The team was up by seven now, but was Cole really well enough to be playing? Even though he hadn't been sacked so far, there was no way Grant could guarantee Cole's safety.

The guys had to be burning up under those helmets and pads. Sandwiched between her parents, sweat dripped down her back. The ninety-degree temperatures melted what little makeup she'd applied. Too bad they didn't have a sky booth with some shade like Cole's parents. Their lunch meeting on

Thursday came to mind. It had gone well, but doubts trickled in. His parents were so sophisticated. Would they really accept her?

Her daddy tugged her ponytail. "Your boy sick today? His passes are hanging a little at the top. Never happened in the past."

The question caught her off guard. "I don't know. Maybe."

"Could be this heat. Speaking of, I'll grill some steaks tonight, then give him a little grilling, too." He chuckled and elbowed her.

Audrey twisted to face him. "I think Grant's grilled him plenty."

"I'm teasing you, sweetie." His warm smile erased her concern.

They turned their attention back toward the field.

~~~

The trainer squirted water into Cole's mouth, quenching a tiny bit of the heat that smothered him.

Coach McCoy leaned close to his ear. "You're as talented as any quarterback I've seen. Find your rhythm." Coach turned to Grant. "Low center of gravity. There's a lot of game left. Be hungry out there."

"Right. I've got some hurt stored up for those guys." Grant's forehead wrinkled into angry crevices.

The big guy had been true to his word. No sacks so far. Cole sighed. Between the heat, the headache, and dizziness, his passes hadn't been up to par. Maybe he should tell Dr. Marlow. Or just drink more water.

Grant slapped his back. "Fumble recovery. Here we go."

Cole ran back onto the field.

~~~

One small breeze swept through the stands, a foretaste of fall. All the fans were on their feet as the offense drove the ball down the field. Audrey clenched her fists watching Cole let the ball fly. The pass lofted and held in the air a second too long. The opponent's cornerback picked the pass and took off the other way.

"Interception! Crud. Stop 'em, Grant." Her father's voice boomed.

Grant scrambled and cut toward the player carrying the ball with unbelievable speed and force. They clashed with a sickening crack. The fans quieted after a collective gasp. Both players still lay on the ground.

Audrey's stomach dipped. "Did you see how Grant's ankle and leg twisted back? Do you think he broke it?"

Medical personnel ran onto the field. Grant rolled over, holding his ankle. Then he stood and shook his foot in front of him. The other player still lay motionless. Grant jumped twice, then shooed off the medics and took a knee in respect of the other injured player.

"You know what I always say. Vaughn's bend, but they don't break."

"Daddy, I'm starting to believe you."

~~~

Swept with a wave of nausea, Cole bent over on the sidelines, clenching his stomach. The guy from the other team took a hard lick and was being wheeled off the field. Not a place anyone wanted to end up. Audrey's words came back to him. *I want you alive and well to teach our kids to throw a ball.*

"You okay, Sanders?" Coach McCoy's hand touched Cole's shoulder.

Cole couldn't answer.

"It's hot out here, and everyone throws an interception now and then. There's still plenty of time on the clock."

Cole lifted his head, but his vision blurred, and he swayed forward, grasping at the air. "My head. Tried to ignore it." His stomach lurched and heaved, emptying.

Coach McCoy clapped his hands three times, hard. "Dr. Marlow. Cole needs help!" He held a towel out for Cole. "Your life is more than what happens out here. Get yourself taken care of."

~~~

"I need to go. Something's wrong with Cole." Audrey grabbed her purse and stumbled around her mother, her heart pounding in her ears.

"Wait." Her father's voice stopped her. "You can't get in the locker room."

"I have to go down. They may take him to the hospital. He hit his head a while back."

Her mother's forehead pinched. "You want one of us to go with you?"

"No. Stay. Grant may need you, but I have to leave now." She pivoted and climbed up the stairs to the nearest exit. Her hands shook as she pulled out her keys. The hospital wasn't far. Unless it was really bad, and they airlifted him to a bigger one. *God, please let Cole be okay.*

Chapter 48

Minutes passed like hours. When would they hear back from a doctor? Between the air conditioner vents blasting in the hospital waiting room and the fear coursing through her, Audrey's whole body trembled. She wrapped her arms around herself and glanced at Cole's parents beside her. What did they think about her being here?

His father rested his elbows on his knees. A designer watch wrapped around his wrist. His size and body shape reminded her of Cole's, but his skin tone and hair were dark. His mother sat erect in the chair, holding a stoic pose, but her eyes stared at the floor. Her caramel-colored hair and eyes matched Cole's. Other than a quick greeting, neither had spoken. Was it worry, or did they resent her being here?

A nurse entered. "Family of Cole Sanders?"

His father stood. "That's us."

"We've got Cole in a room. You can come see him now. The doctor will be in shortly."

Thank goodness. Finally, they'd find out what was wrong. She straightened as Cole's mother stood.

What should she do? Audrey's stomach twisted. She wasn't family. They may not want her back there yet.

Mrs. Sanders touched Audrey's shoulder. "You come, too. I know he'll want to see you."

"If you're sure." Her knees wobbled as she stood.

Cole's father took her elbow, steadying her. "He's crazy about you. It'll cheer him up to see you, whatever the news."

Doubts about Mr. and Mrs. Sanders accepting her slipped away. She braced herself to see Cole and followed them down the sterile halls.

The nurse swung the door open, revealing the small room. Cole semi-reclined in the hospital bed, holding a cup of ice chips. His weak gaze found her, and he smiled. "Audrey." His voice was soft. "You came. Thanks."

The sight of him awake and alert overwhelmed her, and she ran to his bedside stopping short. "Thank the Lord. Of course I came. I ran out of the stadium, picturing you in a coma or something. It's your head, isn't it?"

His parents moved to stand on the other side of the bed.

"You hurt your head?" His father removed his glasses and studied Cole's eyes.

Cole gave the tiniest of nods.

~~~

Seeing Audrey eased some of his disappointment, but not all of it. Cole's throat still constricted, and tears stung his eyes. No reading on the CT yet, but the likelihood of him playing next week dimmed. When would he get back to normal and back to the game he loved?

"Sit on the bed, Audrey. You're not gonna hurt me." Cole patted the mattress near his legs.

"I didn't want to shake your head." She gave him a pitiful look.

He smiled and pretended he wasn't nauseated and sleepy. "As long as you don't jump up and down on the mattress, I think I'll be fine."

She chewed her lip and moved in slow motion to sit beside him.

His father fidgeted with his watch. "I don't remember seeing you take any hard licks to the head today. Did I miss something?"

He needed to tell his parents, but they'd be so disappointed. Cole blinked and held his eyes shut. "Not today, but—"

A knock signaled the entry of another medical person, and Cole opened his eyes.

"I'm Dr. White. Cole, we've got results back on a couple of your tests." He turned his attention to the others in the room. "Can y'all give us the room for a minute so we can go over his test results?"

"They can stay. These are my parents and my girlfriend, Audrey."

The doctor made eye contact with each of them. "Nice to meet you." He studied a chart in his hand. "Cole's CT scan revealed a brain contusion. Now, we're lucky here, since he hasn't been having seizures, and there's no sign of a hematoma." His head lifted and his brows joined above his nose. "But—and here's the big but. This is very serious, Cole. I know you football players want to play through the pain, but not with this type of brain injury. You need weeks, if not months, to heal. If you go back on the field, and let's say you take a hit, or maybe even a hard fall, you could end up with a permanent seizure disorder. Or much worse. We're talking coma, permanent brain damage, death."

Cole's stomach dropped. His throat squeezed closed. He fought the urge to sob. His last season. His dream. Gone.

His father took his hand. "Son."

Cole had to look at his father, had to face the disappointment there. He blinked away the tears and looked up.

His Dad squeezed his hand. "You've had a great run, and we're so proud of you."

Proud of him? His father was proud? Cole's addled brain tried to deny what he was hearing, but his heart knew. The pride shining in his father's eyes—there was no denying that.

Dad continued. "But now, you've got to let the game go. For your health. For all of us." With a nod, he pointed at Audrey. "For the future."

His mother caressed his cheek. "We don't want to lose you."

Tears blinded Cole. Words choked out. He looked at his dad. "What will I do? I'm not smart like Mason."

His father chuckled. "Who is? Look, we never wanted you to feel that kind of pressure. You've got things he doesn't. Charisma. A way with words. Street smarts. You don't need to worry. You've got everything it takes to be successful. You always have."

The pain strangling him eased a bit. "You really think so?"

"Of course."

Audrey let out a loud sigh. "Mercy, boy. What have I been telling you?"

"Thanks." Warmth settled over him. Maybe they were right about his future, but the game, the season? How could he lose his senior year? "But I'll miss the brotherhood. The locker room. The battle."

Dr. White shuffled his feet. "No doubt a tough emotional letdown, but you sound like a smart guy to me. Got a good support system. You'll get through this." He tapped the chart. "I'm going to keep you overnight to monitor you. If you do well, I'll release you tomorrow with instructions. You could always go to a larger hospital for a second opinion. More tests. But my instructions for the next six weeks are to keep things quiet. Nothing but walking from the parking lot to your classes. Don't run, don't ride a boat, a bike. Nothing."

Cole nodded.

"One of you can stay with him overnight if you want, as long as you keep him quiet."

"I will." Audrey and his parents all spoke at once.

His parents exchanged glances, then his mother smiled. "Audrey can stay with him. She'll do a great job taking care of our son."

~~~

Light peeked through a crack where the thick curtains didn't quite meet. Audrey stretched and shifted her weight. All night she'd kept watch on Cole. His diaphragm rising and falling with each breath. *Thank You, Lord.*

What if Cole had been hurt worse? She knew he'd been struggling. She should've begged him not to play or told Coach McCoy. From now on, she'd keep him safe no matter what. He was fixing to see a different side of her. A protective side that already stirred a fierceness deep within her for this man she loved.

The door opened, and light flooded the room from the

fluorescent-lit hall. "Knock, knock, I need to check our patient." A short nurse came in carrying supplies.

Cole's eyes fluttered open. He smiled at Audrey, then the nurse. "They don't let you get much rest here."

"Nope. We wake you up at all hours, poking and prodding. Makes you want to go home sooner." She moved to his bedside. "My shift's ending, and I wanted to see how our star player is doing. How are you feeling?"

"All right. Not much like a star player, though." His smile faded.

"Oh, now." She took his hand and patted. "My son named his puppy after you. Fans won't be forgetting you led us to the bowl game last year. Your name will be a legend in these parts for years to come."

The smile crept back across his lips. "A puppy named after me? That's something. Maybe I'll come see your son and the puppy."

Her eyes widened. "You would make his day. You just don't know how much."

Audrey stood and tapped her foot. "When you're well, you can visit. I'll give her my number, but you're not doing anything but school for a while. And studying with your tutor."

Cole shoved a thumb toward her. "You'll have to set it up with my manager-tutor. She's a strict one."

"Getting stricter all the time, mister."

The nurse released his hand. "Sounds like you have a good one. Listen to her." She smiled. "The doctor will be by after a while."

Audrey scribbled her number on a scrap of paper she found in her purse. "Here you go. Give us a couple of weeks."

Two hours later, Dr. White came through. He checked Cole's pupils and reflexes and then read the notes from overnight. "If you promise to chill, you're good to go home."

"I will." The smile didn't cover the emotional pain behind Cole's eyes.

With soft strokes, Audrey ran her fingers through Cole's hair. "He will."

Chapter 49

After a long day lying around his condo with his parents hovering, Cole showered just for the privacy. It was nice they'd stayed all day, but he'd appreciate the space once they left after dinner. He took a heavy breath. *Dinner.* Audrey insisted he couldn't get out in the heat where her parents were grilling across the parking lot. All he needed was a few minutes alone with her father so he could ask his permission. Scary thought.

The steam from the shower brought back a wave of dizziness, so he cut the water and dressed. Audrey would be back from the other apartment soon. At least she'd decided to move across the sidewalk again to keep an eye on him. How good that sounded, having her so near. And how soon could they live under one roof? *If* she said yes.

"Cole, you okay?" His mother's voice drifted under the bedroom door.

"Yes, ma'am."

"Audrey's back from her other apartment with Grant and her stuff. She said the food's ready. We'll be back in a few minutes."

He opened the door. "Y'all don't rush. Eat your dinner and relax. I'm fine."

"If you're sure." She studied him with wary eyes.

"Go." He waved her off.

As they walked out, he hurried to the open door. "Dad, wait a sec."

His father paused and turned. "I won't forget to send Mr. Vaughn over."

"Thanks."

As they walked away, Emma stepped out of her condo wearing yoga pants and a long T-shirt. She pushed her sunglasses onto the top of her head. "Hey. How are you? It's all over the Internet about your injury."

"I'll live."

"But it's got to be a hard pill to swallow. I went through something similar when I broke my back during the fall of my senior year of high school. The end of a cheerleading career may not sound like much to you boys, but for me, the squad was my life. Left a huge void. Between the physical pain and emotions, I got hooked on the pain pills."

For once, Emma made sense. He even sympathized with her. "I can see how that could happen. Is that why you left college? Where was it? Alabama?"

"Yeah, plus I ran my car into a fraternity house. Daddy smoothed things over, then made me come home for intensive treatment. After that, I had to get a job to pay back part of the money."

A laugh he'd tried to stifle escaped. "That was *you* who hit the fraternity house? Talk about all over the Internet."

Her pink lips pooched. "Shut up."

"Sorry."

Emma chuckled. "It's okay. Not something I'm proud of. One of the many things I'm not proud of." Her head snapped toward the sidewalk leading from the pool. "Speaking of. He seems to have moved on pretty fast."

Cole followed her gaze to where Grant and Ivy walked side by side. "I think they're just friends. So far. What about you and Bryan?"

"Just friends." She closed her eyes for a second. "So far. Bryan's like the nicest guy in the world."

"You may be right about that one." Not going there, though. Cole rubbed the back of his neck.

"Well, I'm on my way to the gym. I'm praying about your injury."

And another surprise. "Thanks. See ya."

Now to wait for the next weird conversation. He shut the door and returned to his recliner. Audrey insisted he shouldn't watch TV or use the computer. Just rest his brain. How was that even possible without the tube on? He let his eyes close.

Minutes later, the rattling door woke him from a light snooze. "Dad, is that you?"

"Not your dad yet, but I have a feeling that's what we're fixing to talk about." Mr. Vaughn appeared by his chair.

Cole's stomach flipped. "Oh, sorry." He let the footrest of the chair down.

Hands up, Mr. Vaughn shook his head. "Stay seated. I'll sit on the couch, and we'll talk."

The smoky scent of the grill followed the man. He'd seen Grant's father before and after games. A tall man, but not as big as Grant. He exuded strength but had warm brown eyes and freckles a lot like Audrey's. Maybe this talk would go all right.

Cole swallowed hard. Better to get straight to it. "I wanted to ask your permission to propose to Audrey."

Leaning forward, Mr. Vaughn nodded. "I figured. I have a couple questions for you." His mouth twitched before he spoke again. "You gonna be faithful? Will you put God first, then Audrey, then yourself?"

"Yes, sir, to both questions." A couple meant two, right? Was that it?

"Do you mind if I pray with you?"

Cole's ribs squeezed as he shut his eyes. Was he supposed to pray or just Mr. Vaughn? "I'd like that."

"Lord, first, I ask your healing touch for Cole. Then, Father, I thank you for my sweet daughter and this young man who wants to become a husband to her. Bless them with love and faith and wisdom to do Your will. Oh, and a few athletic grandchildren would be okay with us, too. We love you, Father. In Jesus's blessed name we pray. Amen."

Cole couldn't stop a small chuckle.

Mr. Vaughn grinned, smile lines almost reaching his salt and pepper hair. "Can't hurt to ask."

"I've never heard anyone joke with God."

"Me and God have a good relationship. He's a holy God *and* a friend, you know?"

"Not exactly, but I'm learning."

Mr. Vaughn rose to his feet. "Good. That's what I like to hear." He raised his eyebrows up and down. "I'll send Audrey over with your steak now."

One down. One to go.

~ ~ ~

Plates balanced in each hand with silverware on top, Audrey made her way over to Cole's. She hoped he had drinks. If not, water would do.

The door was ajar. When she entered, he stood holding something in his hand.

She set the plates on the table. "What are you doing up?"

Tender brown eyes captured her gaze. "Waiting for you."

"Sorry. Were you getting hungry?"

He knelt and took her hand. "Nope."

Her heart skipped, and she blinked hard. "Why are you down there? Are you dizzy?"

"Nope."

"You shouldn't—"

"Audrey."

The intensity in his voice hitched her breath.

"Audrey Vaughn. This is for you, if you'll have it. If you'll have me." He offered a small red velvet box.

She released his hand and took the gift. Hands shaking, she lifted the hinged top. A ring, platinum with an emerald cut solitaire, sparkled up at her. "Is this a—?"

"I'm not sure how I'll make a living off the field, or where we'll end up, but will you marry me?"

"Oh, Cole." Audrey fell to her knees, tears filling her vision. She wrapped her arms around his neck. "I'm not sure how I'll be a good wife because of my past, or how I'll make you happy, but if you really love me, I'll marry you in a heartbeat, Cole Sanders."

"I really love you." He pulled her into the circle of his arms. "And we'll tackle our fields together."

Don't miss the next book in the series.
Southern Hearts travel to
Mobile & Fort Morgan, Alabama!
Be the first to know about the release by signing up at
http://www.janetfergusonauthor.com/under-the-southern-
sun

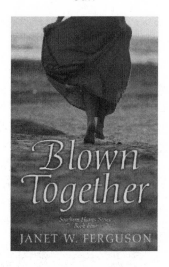

Blown Together

When love storms in...

Wealth manager Sam Conrad is accustomed to his domineering father ordering him around, especially at the bank where they both work. But when his father demands that Sam manage the inheritance of his bossy ex-fiancée, Sam has finally had enough. He leaves in search of a new life, and attorney Big Roy Bosarge from

Mobile, Alabama agrees to mentor Sam on his quest for direction. Sam didn't expect to be thrown together with Big Roy's eccentric and opinionated daughter.

Storm damage forces lonely romance writer Elinor Bosarge and her hairless cat, Mr. Darcy, out of her Fort Morgan Beach cottage. She plans to take refuge in the boathouse on her parents' estate, but finds the place already occupied by one of her father's "projects." She's shocked her father would allow another young man onto the property after his last mentee robbed her family and broke her heart. And from the moment she meets Sam Conrad, they disagree about everything from her cat to how to best renovate a local nursing home.

Between her mother's health issues and the hurricane brewing in the Gulf, Elinor feels like her life is being ripped apart. It doesn't help that she's falling for the man she's determined not to trust. Sam finds himself drawn to Elinor, wanting to help her and this new family he's grown to love. But can he overcome the barrier she's built to keep him out? When the storm rages and the two of them are blown together, can Elinor find the faith to open her heart again?

Dear Reader,

Thank you for trusting me with your time and resources. This is a story I didn't want to write, but felt called to tackle. The loss of the dream, the loss of innocence, and life's other unfair struggles can challenge our faith—can make us captive to fear and disappointment. God is able to set free the captives, set you free from the bonds that hold you. My prayer is that you find comfort in that truth.

Blessings in Him who is able!

Did you enjoy this book? I hope so! **Would you take a quick minute to leave a review online?** It doesn't have to be long. Just a sentence or two telling what you liked about the book.

Would you like to be the first to know about new books by Janet W. Ferguson?
Sign up at <u>www.janetfergusonauthor.com.</u>